KU-531-452

THE ILLEGITIMATE MONTAGUE

Sarah Mallory

MILLS & BOON

In memory of the incomparable Penny Jordan.
A friend and an inspiration.

All the characters in this book have no existence outside the imagination of the author, and have no relation whatsoever to anyone bearing the same name or names. They are not even distantly inspired by any individual known or unknown to the author, and all the incidents are pure invention.

All Rights Reserved including the right of reproduction in whole or in part in any form. This edition is published by arrangement with Harlequin Enterprises II BV/S.à.r.l. The text of this publication or any part thereof may not be reproduced or transmitted in any form or by any means, electronic or mechanical, including photocopying, recording, storage in an information retrieval system, or otherwise, without the written permission of the publisher.

® and TM are trademarks owned and used by the trademark owner and/or its licensee. Trademarks marked with ® are registered with the United Kingdom Patent Office and/or the Office for Harmonisation in the Internal Market and in other countries.

First published in Great Britain 2012
by Mills & Boon, an imprint of Harlequin (UK) Limited,
Large Print edition 2013
Harlequin (UK) Limited,
Eton House, 18-24 Paradise Road, Richmond, Surrey TW9 1SR

© Sarah Mallory 2012

ISBN: 978 0 263 24414 4

2023361 4

MORAY COUNCIL
LIBRARIES &
INFORMATION SERVICES
F

Harlequin (UK) policy is to use papers that are natural, renewable and recyclable products and made from wood grown in sustainable forests. The logging and manufacturing process conform to the legal environmental regulations of the country of origin.

Printed and bound in Great Britain
by CPI Antony Rowe, Chippenham, Wiltshire

Chapter One

'Whoa, Bosun.' Adam ran his hand over the horse's lathered neck. It was still early spring, but the day had been a warm one. On the evening air he could smell the hedge blossom and wild garlic as he descended to the valley. It was ten years since he had travelled this road and nothing looked different—the high peaks behind him, the stone-walled fields and the uplands were just as he remembered them—but Adam knew that *he* had changed. He was no longer the angry young man who had ridden away from Castonbury full of rage and hurt pride. He could smile now at the arrogant boy he had once been—if only it was not too late to make amends.

He gazed at the westering sun, gauging how many more hours of daylight were left. 'We could make Castonbury Park by nightfall,' he mused, rubbing his chin. 'But we've no guarantee of a warm reception, Bosun, and in truth I don't deserve one. Safer then to drop anchor in the village, and go on to the Park in the morning.' He gathered up the reins again. 'And if my memory serves, there is a ford around the next bend, old fellow. You can cool your heels in the river.'

At that moment the peaceful calm was shattered by a pistol shot. This was followed by shouts and a woman's voice raised in alarm. He urged Bosun into a canter and rounded the bend to a scene of confusion and mayhem.

A wagon stood this side of the shallow ford and a young woman in an olive-green redingote was trying to prevent two men from throwing the contents into the river, while on the far bank a third man was sitting on the ground, nursing his bloody arm.

With a shout Adam jumped down to join the fray, heading for the man who was grappling with the young woman. Adam grabbed his collar and delivered a well-aimed punch as the fellow turned to face him. He dropped like a stone. A second man was hurling bolts of cloth from the wagon into the water and the woman was already running towards him. With a shriek of fury she hurled herself at his back and he dropped the roll of fabric he was carrying onto the path as he tried to shake her off. Adam shouted.

'Stand aside!'

The woman jumped clear and Adam launched himself at the man, doubling him with a heavy blow to the body. His assailant grunted, weaved and ducked to avoid the next punch and threw himself at Adam. They wrestled fiercely, toppling into the water. It was only knee-deep and Adam was the first to recover, which gave him the advantage. As his opponent rose up, coughing and spluttering, an uppercut sent him sprawling back into the river, from where he scrabbled away to join his injured companion on the far bank.

Breathing heavily, Adam looked around. His first victim was struggling to get to his feet, hands over his head to protect himself from the woman, who was raining blows upon him with the handle of her horsewhip.

'Aye, go on, run away!' she cried, cracking her whip with an expert flick of the wrist as the ruffian splashed across the river to safety. 'And tell your master that I am not to be frightened away by the likes of you!'

She stood, hands on hips, her chest rising and

falling, watching the men until they disappeared from sight.

Adam raked his wet hair back from his face.

'I had not expected to refresh myself quite so thoroughly,' he began, a laugh in his voice. 'I trust you are not hurt?'

'Not at all.' She scooped his hat from the ground and held it out to him. 'You are lucky this was knocked off before you took a ducking. My bonnet was not so fortunate—it is probably at Castonbury bridge by this time.'

Her words were accompanied by a dazzling smile and Adam's mind went blank as he took his first good look at the young woman he had just rescued. The sudden jolt of attraction threatened to tumble him back into the river. He forgot about his soaking clothes and bruised knuckles as he gazed at the vision before him. Her deep brown eyes positively gleamed with excitement.

'I only wish I had been able to shoot more than one of the villains!'

Adam scarcely heard her. Quite what it was about her that stirred him he did not know. There was nothing exceptional about her plain olive-green riding habit, although the tight-fitting jacket showed off her generous figure. His preference had always been for fair, blue-eyed beauties, but the woman before him had deeply golden skin and an abundance of thick, dark brown hair. It had come loose from its pins and hung in a dusky, rippling cloud around her shoulders.

Her triumphant look softened into amusement as she said in her laughing, musical voice, 'I am greatly indebted to you for your help, sir, and would be even more grateful if you could help me to recover my cloth?'

He did not reply and with a tiny shrug and no less good humour she turned away. Completely unaware of the effect she was having upon him, she hitched her skirts high, revealing not only a pair of exceedingly pretty ankles, but also affording Adam a glimpse of the ribbon garters at her knees.

Amber tucked up her skirts. She had seen the washerwomen do it dozens of times and never thought that she, too, would need to wade into the river. But this was an emergency. She had invested a great deal of money in those rolls of cloth and she was not prepared to lose them. She was a little disappointed that the man should not help her now, but perhaps pulling sodden bolts of material from the water was too mundane for so chivalrous a knight.

And that was how she saw him, for he had ridden so gallantly to her rescue. She had not looked at him properly until her attackers had taken flight, but then, when she had turned to him, exultant at their success in driving them away, she had found herself looking at the embodiment of a dream. A tall, broad-shouldered, handsome crusader gazing at her with blue, blue eyes that seemed to pierce her very soul. The water had turned his hair to near black, but the glints of red-gold told her it would be a dark, golden blond when dry. He was everything she had ever envisaged a hero to be. Far too good to be true. So let him go on his way now, she thought, for she was afraid if he did not he would trouble her dreams for a long, long time. Swallowing a sigh she turned towards the ford.

As she stepped into the water Adam came to his senses.

'No, let me, I am already wet through.'

He strode onto the ford and began to pull the bolts of cloth from the water. The exercise helped him to regain control of himself. He was shocked to realise that for a few moments he had been speechless, more like a callow schoolboy than a thirty-two-year-old man with more than a little experience of the fair sex. She was standing at the edge of the river, waiting to help him, and he kept his mind firmly fixed upon the rolls of cloth as they lifted them out of the water.

'Damned villains,' she muttered as they struggled with the last roll, a dripping bundle of blue linen. 'Thank heaven they didn't get the superfine though. That is worth five-and-twenty shillings a yard!'

She shook out her skirts and dropped to the ground, putting her hand to her hair.

'Good heavens, I must look like a virago, with my hair about my shoulders! What must you think of me?'

Adam dared not tell her and merely shrugged, with what he hoped she would interpret as unconcern. It seemed to work, because she gave him another of her blinding smiles.

'Again I have to thank you, sir. I could not have recovered my cloth without your help.'

Adam stripped off his sodden coat and sat down beside her.

'But the rolls are as wet as my jacket—will they be ruined?'

She shrugged. 'Once they are dried out I have

no doubt there will be some value in them. The problem is, I can't put them on top of the dry ones, and the oilcloth that I use for protection from the weather is already lost downstream. Besides, the wet cloth is so much heavier that I doubt my poor horse would be able to cope with the extra weight.' She looked up at the sky. 'And it is growing late. I should go now if I am to reach Castonbury before dark.' Her buoyant mood dipped. 'I suppose I will have to come back in the morning with an empty wagon and pray that no one comes along in the meantime.'

'There is another solution.' She turned to look at him, disconcerting him again. He gestured to the trees. 'Where I come from in Lancashire the cloth is stretched and pegged out to dry in the tenterfields. We can't do that here, but it is a warm night, we could hang the wet cloth over the branches.'

She was silent for a few minutes, then the smile returned.

'That might work. I can spend the night here and gather everything up in the morning. Only…' She looked up at him under her lashes. 'I might need a little help to reach the branches….'

Adam laughed.

'I will put myself at your disposal, madam.' He jumped to his feet and held out his hand.

Her fingers wrapped themselves around his and as he pulled her to her feet he felt again that spark of attraction. Despite his wet clothes his body was on fire and they stood for a moment, hand-in-hand, regarding each other.

She was a tall woman. Adam stood six-foot-two in his stockinged feet and it was rare for any woman to approach that, but the one now standing before him was tall and shapely, her eyes level with his mouth so that she only had to look up a little to meet his glance. She did so now, candid, unafraid, her brown eyes fringed with long black lashes. With her dark hair and tanned skin she looked faintly exotic, reminding him of the luscious foreign beauties he had seen during his years at sea.

Even as he gazed at her, the candid look disappeared and she seemed a little troubled.

'Perhaps, sir, I should know to whom I am so indebted?' Her voice was low, husky, as if she, too, was having difficulty breathing.

He cleared his throat and gave a little bow.

'Adam Stratton, ma'am. At your service.'

She inclined her head.

'Amber Hall.' He was still holding her hand, the left one. Instinctively his fingers shifted to the plain gold band on her finger. She said quietly, 'I am a widow.'

The devil she was! Adam was surprised at his feeling of relief. Why did she feel it necessary to explain? Was she warning him off, or appealing to his chivalrous nature to respect her predicament? The defensive look in her eyes suggested the latter.

With an effort he released her. Dear heaven, it would be so easy to forget his manners. He hoped his nod was sufficiently sympathetic, then he turned his attention to their present situation.

He said lightly, 'Well, Mrs Hall, shall we unroll your cloth?'

'What about you? Your shirt and breeches are wet through.'

'Would you like me to remove them and hang them up to dry?' Immediately his mind rioted at the thought of undressing before her. He continued hastily, 'I beg your pardon, a tasteless jest. Do not concern yourself with my wellbeing, the exertion will keep me warm.'

'We must at least hang up your coat.' She picked it up and shook it out. 'Oh, dear, how sad it looks now—I think I owe you a new one, sir. And you are missing a couple of buttons. I fear they have gone the same way as my bonnet, and are lost in the water.'

'No matter, they are a small loss. Throw the coat over a bush for now.' He picked up the smallest roll of linen and looked around him. 'Now, where to begin...'

They worked together, unrolling the bolts of wet cloth and draping them over the tree branches around a small clearing at the edge of the road. He left Amber straightening out the hanging cloth while he gathered dry sticks and bracken to light a fire.

'Leave that,' she ordered him. 'You have done more than enough for me already. If you go now you can still reach the village while there is light enough to see your way.'

'I am staying here.'

'Thank you, Mr Stratton, but that is not necessary. I do not think those villains will be back tonight, and besides, I have my pistol. I shall reload it and be ready for them if they return. You need not stay on my account.'

'If you think I intend to ride to the Rothermere Arms in wet clothes, then you are mistaken, madam. Nothing could be more uncomfortable. I shall dry them in front of the fire.' He smiled at the look of alarm that flashed across her face. It was a relief to know that he was not the only one aware of their situation. 'I do not intend to undress, they will dry just as well if I wear them.' He added mischievously, 'In fact, it is a common practice for gentlemen of fashion to damp their buckskins and let them shrink to fit.'

She laughed, blushed and shook her head.

'Never let it be said that I stood in the way of fashion. But, seriously, sir, if you are determined to stay I cannot stop you.' She paused, taking her full bottom lip between her white, even teeth. 'I admit I shall be glad of your company.'

It was another hour before they could enjoy the fire, by which time the darkness was almost complete. The wagon had been moved off the road and the two horses tethered to the wheels, where they could be heard quietly snuffling and cropping at the short, sweet grass. Amber pulled a pair of shears from the cart and a roll of heavy woollen cloth, which she spread on the ground and proceeded to cut into lengths.

'We can use this for bedding,' she explained. 'I have plenty more frieze at the warehouse so this can be easily replaced. It is such a balmy night that if we didn't have wet cloth to dry I would not bother with a fire at all.'

Adam eased off his boots and stockings, placing them close to the fire to dry. Amber did the same, again displaying her shapely ankles. Adam did his best not to ogle. She touched his sleeve.

'Your shirt is still damp, sir. Should you not remove that too?' He hesitated and she said with a hint of impatience, 'I have seen a man's body, before, and I would rather you took it off than died of an inflammation of the lungs.'

He laughed.

'Very well, madam, but you will not object if I spare my own blushes and keep my breeches!'

The shirt soon joined his jacket on a convenient bush. Adam threw a length of the frieze cloth around his shoulders and sat down by the fire. After a moment's hesitation Amber came to sit beside him. She held up a leather bag.

'I have wine, sir, and bread and cheese, if you would like some?'

'Gladly, Mrs Hall, if you can spare a little.'

'Of course. I packed it for my journey but have used none of it.'

She pulled packets, napkins and a flask from

the bag and spread it all before them. She offered him the wine but he shook his head.

'After you, madam.'

She uncorked the flask and lifted it to her lips. The firelight was playing on her face, accentuating the fine cheekbones, the short, straight little nose and those beautiful almond-shaped eyes. The smooth skin of her neck gleamed golden as she tilted back her head and drank. Adam watched, fascinated. He wanted to reach out to her, to place his lips on the elegant line of her throat and trail kisses down to the dip where the breastbone started, and then onwards—

'Your turn.'

She was holding the flask out to him and he was staring at her like some besotted mooncalf. Adam cleared his throat awkwardly and reached for the flask, trying to ignore his mounting desire and the way it spiked through his blood as their fingers touched. He picked up a piece of bread. Perhaps he should eat something. Beside him, Amber seemed completely at ease. They shared the bread and cheese, washing it down with draughts of wine.

'So who are you, Mrs Amber Hall?' he asked her, breaking a chunk of bread into two and handing her a piece.

'I am a clothier, a seller of cloth.'

'An unusual trade for a woman.'

'I inherited the business from my father, John Ripley.'

'Ah, yes, I remember he owned a warehouse in Castonbury.'

'Yes.' She added, a touch of pride in her voice, 'We have been selling cloth in Castonbury for twenty-seven years.'

'That is very precise.'

'It is easy to remember, my father established the business in the same year as I was born.'

Adam handed her the wine again.

'And your husband?'

'Bernard Hall, his business partner. He joined my father twelve years ago, and married me three years later. We had been married barely eighteen months when he died.'

'I am sorry,' he said softly. 'You must have been distraught.'

He could not interpret the look she gave him. She took another sip of wine and after a brief pause she continued her story.

'I convinced Papa not to look for another partner but to let me help him. I found I had a talent for the business. When my father died three years ago he left everything to me.' He watched her, trying to understand her pensive look, the slight downward turn to her mouth that gave her a rather kittenish look. At last she gave herself a mental shake and turned to him again. 'Enough of me. Tell me about you, now.' She shot him another of those sideways glances. 'You said your name was Stratton. Are you the housekeeper's son, from Castonbury Park?'

'I am.'

'Then I know you, Adam Stratton.' Her dark eyes gleamed. 'We played together before you went off to become a hero at Trafalgar.'

'Surely not, I would remember.'

'My father used to take me to the house, sometimes, when he was delivering cloth. I remember Mrs Stratton asked you to take me away and amuse me.' He shook his head and she laughed. 'Do not look so uncomfortable, I would not expect you to remember. You were, what…ten, eleven years old? You probably found a seven-year-old girl a blasted nuisance.'

'I *do* remember now. You were a scrawny little thing, but useful for fetching and carrying. As I recall I treated you as my very own servant! Outrageous. Did you not mind?'

She shook her head. 'Not at all, I enjoyed fetching and carrying for you. Besides, you looked after me. One occasion in particular I remember, when the Montague children came out and began to tease me. You drove them away.'

He grinned. 'Well, it is all very well for *me* to mistreat you, but I was not going to let anyone else do so!'

A slight frown creased her brow, as if she was looking into the past. 'Did they ever tease you, the Montagues? Because your mama...'

She broke off and he took pity on her confusion, saying quickly, 'Because I had no father? No. Lord James was a year or two younger than I. I suppose I should be thankful that both he and Lord Giles saw me as a playmate rather than the housekeeper's son, but perhaps that was because... well, never mind that. Suffice to say we thought well enough of one another.'

'I am glad,' she said warmly. 'And I thought you were quite...wonderful.' A faint colour tinged her cheek and for a moment she looked a little self-conscious. 'You were very kind to me, you see. And now you have saved me once more.'

Her very own hero.

Amber drew up her knees and clasped her arms

around them, as if hugging her memories. That explained the attraction she had felt for him as soon as he had appeared. It was not merely that he had come to her aid, but a half-acknowledged memory. He was the hero she had dreamed of since she was seven years old. Looking back, she supposed that the children at Castonbury Park had not intended to be cruel, but their teasing had frightened her, until Adam had arrived and sent them away. He had seemed to her the embodiment of those princes she read about in fairy tales, tall, strong and oh-so-handsome, protecting the maiden in distress. She had carried that early memory of him with her throughout her childhood and hoped, prayed, he would return one day.

He never had, of course. Once he went to naval college she never saw him again and when she was eighteen she put aside her childish dreams and gave in to her father's demands that she should marry his partner, Bernard Hall. It was a business decision. It did not matter to her father that Bernard was twenty years older, that she found his bad breath and wandering hands repulsive, a marriage would secure the future of Ripley and Hall.

Bernard Hall had never awoken in her any spark. Unlike the man sitting beside her now. When she had looked into Adam's eyes for the first time that day it was as if someone had applied bellows to a smouldering fire. She had burned, really *burned*, with a desire so strong she had almost thrown herself upon him.

Thankfully he had not noticed, merely staring at her, clearly shocked at her dishevelled appearance. She had brazened it out, of course, and she was thankful that he had stayed to help her. She was grateful, too, that he showed no sign of wanting to ravish her. Wasn't she? Amber had to admit that his patent lack of interest piqued her. He was once again her hero, her knight in shining armour, but he clearly did not see her as his princess.

They sat in silence, consuming their simple meal. The cloth hanging around them was billowing gently in the breeze, washed in the golden glow of the fire.

'What will you do with the damaged cloth?' he asked.

'I will rescue what I can. The linens and cottons can be laundered and should be almost as good as new. The rest I hope to sell off cheaply to the villagers. What is left I will take to the vicarage to give to the poor. I am sure Reverend Seagrove will find a good home for any cloth I cannot sell.

I will have to order replacements for some things. I have to fulfil an order for Castonbury Park, you see. New curtains and bed-hangings, as well as livery for the servants. They will need the fabrics as soon as may be for the wedding—but you will know that, of course.'

'Er, no.'

'Surely your mother will have told you in her letters that Lord Giles is to be married?'

'We have not been in touch.' He could not meet her eyes and it was a struggle to explain. 'When I was last here we argued. No.' He had to be honest with her. 'My mother never said a harsh word to me. It was all my doing.'

She touched his arm.

'Will you tell me?' she asked gently.

Adam hesitated. There was nothing but kindness in her manner, and suddenly he wanted to talk about it.

'It was ten years ago. I came to tell her that I had quit the navy, that I was going to try my hand at business. She was shocked. Disappointed, I suppose, that I was giving up a promising career and uncertain that I would make a go of it.' He sighed. 'I was young, impatient. I had been given my own ship to command at twenty and that went to my head, I thought I could do anything. My mother was less certain.'

'I am sure she only wanted what was best for you.'

'I know you are right, but at the time I saw it as a slur, a lack of confidence in my abilities.'

He looked up at the sky, his jaw tightening. It had also brought back his own lack of confidence in his birth. Away from Castonbury Park he was Captain Adam Stratton, hero of Trafalgar, a clever and courageous sailor. Here, he would always be known as the duke's bastard. Oh, no one said as much to his face, but he had heard the whispers, the gossip. His mother never spoke of her husband, there were no portraits of "Mr Stratton" in the housekeeper's quarters at Castonbury Park. As a very young boy his questions had been met with evasion, and when he grew older Adam stopped asking about his father, afraid of what the answer might be. Then, when he had quit the navy and come back to Castonbury Park, full of plans for the future, he had asked the question one more time. He gave himself a mental shake. No need to go into that now. Taking a breath he continued.

'I stormed out, vowing that I would not return,

would not contact her, until I had made my way in the world.'

'And is that why you are back, because you have now…"made your way in the world"? You are perhaps a wealthy man,' she added after a slight hesitation, 'with a wife and family…?'

He shook his head. 'No, no wife. No family.'

He thought of the fair-haired beauties he had met on his travels. Many of them were ladies of noble birth, eager to know more of him. After all, a captain in the king's navy was a romantic, heroic figure. Several of them had thrown out lures, making it quite plain that they would welcome his addresses, but he had resisted them all. He might tell himself that he was his own man, but at that stage the question of his birth still rankled, and he was determined to make a name for himself before taking a wife. And he had done so. He was now a mill owner, a captain of industry, but he had soon discovered that those well-bred families wanted nothing to do with trade. Only his fortune made him acceptable to them, and perversely, he did not want anyone to marry him for his fortune. He wanted to find a woman who would marry him for himself alone.

Amber's thoughtful brown eyes were fixed on

him, waiting for him to continue. He kept his tone matter-of-fact.

'I promised I would not return until I could provide her with a house of her own. Looking back, it seems so petty, so very arrogant and foolish, but I held to my vow while I toiled to achieve my goals. I was determined to be successful, no debts and money in the bank, before I contacted my mother again. It was hard work, but I achieved it. I owe no man anything. But at what cost?' He sighed. 'I am ashamed to say I have not written, have had no news of my mother, for ten years. It is no fault of hers,' he added quickly. 'I left no forwarding address. I severed all links with her. In fact, until you told me last night, I did not even know if she was still at Castonbury Park.'

'And, is that why you are back now? Do you have a house for her?'

'Yes, I have a house now. In Lancashire.'

'And what is this…business that you are engaged in, Mr Adam Stratton?'

'Oh, this and that.' He waved one dismissive hand. 'I have several ventures ongoing, they are all of them more or less successful.'

'Then your mother will be very proud of you.'

'That is not what I deserve. She should berate

me for the fool that I have been. A damned stub-
born-headed fool! I only hope that she will re-
ceive me.'

Adam tried to keep the uncertainty from his
voice but he was sure she heard it, for she has-
tened to reassure him.

'From what I know of Mrs Stratton I am sure
she will be overjoyed to see you. Any mother
would be.' A smile tugged at the corners of her
mouth. 'But perhaps you should tidy yourself up
a little before you see her.'

Adam glanced across at his damaged coat.

'I fear you are right. I shall be turned away as
a common beggar if I arrive on the doorstep like
this!' He ran his hand over his chin. 'And without
a looking glass I dare not shave in the morning.'

She laughed.

'Come to my shop with me and we will see what
we can do for you!'

Amber gave her attention to her food again,
surprised by how readily she had issued the invitation. He was little more than a stranger, after
all, even if he had come to her rescue in the most
dramatic way. Perhaps it was the knowledge that
they had known each other as children. She felt
at ease, comfortable to be sitting beside him. If

she were fanciful, she could believe they were in some different world, one where the constraints and dangers of real life did not exist.

'You are very pensive,' he said at last. 'What are you thinking?'

'I feel like I am in a fairy tale,' she said, smiling. 'We might be in an Oriental pavilion with sumptuous fabrics decorating its walls.' She chuckled. 'Not that there is anything very sumptuous about block-printed cotton!'

'This is no fairy tale, madam.' His voice was stern. 'Far from it. I cannot think what possessed you to be moving such a valuable cargo on your own.'

'Normally I would not do so, but I had no driver and I needed to fetch in these supplies urgently.'

'You could have hired a carrier.'

She shook her head.

'Not in time. There is no one in Castonbury who would take the risk.'

'Risk?'

She crumbled a piece of cheese between her fingers, searching for words.

'Things have been…happening recently. The carrier was attacked on his last run and decided he dare not take out another wagon for me. He has a family, you see—'

'Wait.' Adam stopped her. 'Do you mean to say someone threatened him?'

She nodded.

'It cannot be proved, of course, but…' She hesitated, wondering if she dare tell him her suspicions. She said in a rush, 'I think it is Matthew Parwich. He is a rival cloth merchant from Hatherton and he would be glad to take over my business. I am sure it was Parwich who sent those ruffians to waylay me. They did not want to harm me, only to ruin my stock.'

'You knew this might happen and still you set out alone?'

His angry tone flayed her. She had been afraid he would laugh at her suspicions, think her fanciful. Instead he thought her foolish. She spread her hands.

'Frederick had to stay at the warehouse. And I didn't really think I would be attacked.' The excitement was still bubbling through her veins, making her reckless. She put up her chin, giving him a challenging look. 'Besides, I had my pistol and I *did* wing one of them.'

Adam's blood chilled at the thought of what

might have happened. He rammed the stopper back into the wine flask with unwonted force.

'That's as may be, but if I hadn't come along—'

'I know, I am so very glad that you did.' Her glowing look acted like a fever, turning his blood from ice to molten lava in an instant. 'Together we sent them to the right-about, did we not?' She leaned closer until he thought he might drown in her dark eyes. 'I am so grateful to you. How can I ever thank you?'

He held her look, knowing what he would like from her, knowing equally well it was impossible, yet there was something in her eyes, some spark of recognition, as if she could read his thoughts. She put her hand on his shoulder and raised herself until she could touch his mouth with her lips. They were soft and warm and it took all his willpower not to respond.

'Not in that way.' His voice was gruff, barely audible even to himself, but perhaps that was because she was so close, her face only inches away, and his breathing was so constricted. 'Madam— Amber, I…do not want…to…dishonour you, but…I am no…saint.'

Amber's pulse was racing. She still felt exultant, powerful, after successfully repelling the attack and saving her precious cargo. She remembered something Bernard used to say about his friends, when they were hunting—'there was no stopping them when their blood is up.' That was how she felt now, unable to stop. And she did not care.

'I would not have you be one.'

The low words were no more than a whisper against Adam's skin. She put her hand to his cheek and he responded to the pressure of her fingers to close the small distance between them. He slid his mouth across hers and as his kiss deepened she responded. His tongue touched her lips and they parted eagerly. She pushed the blanket from his shoulders and ran her hands over his bare back. Gently he eased her down to the ground, the blood pounding through him as her hands snaked around his neck and pulled him down with her. The buttons of her mannish jacket gave way easily to his fingers and soon he had pulled away the neck cloth and opened her shirt. When he placed his mouth on her throat it was every bit as soft and smooth as he had imagined. She trembled beneath him, sending his passion soaring out of control. His hand moved over the swell of her breast and she moaned softly, pushing against his fingers. She struggled to sit up and he released her immediately, trying to quell his disappointment, but she was not repulsing him. She dragged off her linen shirt and twisted round.

'Unlace me.'

His fingers trembled on the laces. He bent to kiss her bare shoulder and her head fell back. She sighed, eyes closed, dark lashes fanned against her golden cheek. Hastily he dragged the laces free and the restricting corset fell away. He pulled her against him, cupping her breasts. They tensed beneath the thin cotton of her chemise. The next moment she was throwing off this last hindrance and turning back to face him.

A sudden stillness enveloped the little clearing, only the faint crackling of the fire disturbed the silence. Amber knelt before him, head bowed and that glorious hair cascading down over her shoulders. In the golden firelight she took his breath away. Gently, slowly, he reached out and pushed the hair back, his fingers caressing her neck, cupping her face, pulling her closer. Their kiss began tenderly enough, but he felt its latent power, like the rolling breakers he had seen on so many beautiful, dangerous shores, from Cornwall to Corunna. An inexorable force that carried all before it.

Amber gave him back kiss for kiss, dragging him down again onto their makeshift bed, her hands scrabbling to unfasten and remove his breeches. His skin was chill and slightly damp from the buckskin and she pressed herself against him. His reaction to her warm, shapely body was immediate, as was his gasp when her fingers closed about his erection. He had to force himself to ignore the havoc she was creating within him. The blood was pounding in his ears; he fought down the urge to satisfy his own need and concentrated on pleasuring her. He placed his mouth over one taut breast, his tongue circling, teasing, while she groaned beneath him. His hand swept over her hip, caressed the hinge of her thigh and moved on to where she was opening for him, inviting his touch. She writhed beneath his fingers. She was nearing the crest of her passion. He shifted his body and eased himself into her, stroking, caressing, containing his own excitement while she began to move wildly against him, her nails digging into his back.

'Adam!'

The anguished cry broke from her. She quivered; he could feel her tensing around him, possessing him. There was nothing he wanted more than to remain inside her and complete their union, but that would be reckless, irresponsible. It took all his iron will to withdraw and make his own shattering ending against the soft skin of her belly.

A languid peace settled over them and they lay, sated and content, until the dying fire could no longer keep them warm. Amber wiped a napkin across her stomach, then tossed it aside and pulled the frieze blanket over them.

'My dear—'

'Shh.' She pulled him into her arms. 'Enough. Sleep now.'

Chapter Two

Amber drifted back to wakefulness, amazingly content and at peace, like a feather drifting gently back to earth after a great storm. It was almost dawn, a grey twilight hung over the clearing. She was lying in a man's arms, their naked limbs fitting snugly together in the most natural way and she felt relaxed. More than that, she felt cherished. Loved. She had been an innocent maid when she had married Bernard, and he had been a selfish lover, their coupling had left her feeling lost and dissatisfied. At the time she had not known why but now, lying here with Adam, she understood.

Adam. She moved slightly, tentatively touching the lean body stretched beside her. They had not met since they were children, yet she had felt an immediate affinity with him. Perhaps it was because he had come to her rescue once again.

She smiled in the darkness. It was more likely his magnificent physique. She recalled how she had reacted to the sight of his naked chest, when he had removed his wet shirt, the firelight glinting on his wide shoulders, the rippling muscles of his chest. Just the thought of it sent shafts of aching lust running through her again.

Reluctantly she moved away from his warmth and curled herself into a ball. How wanton he would think her. How shocked she was that she had thrown herself at him! Amber had no idea what had come over her. Could she blame it on the wine, perhaps, or on their situation, surrounded by the gently billowing fabrics, as if they were in some exotic pavilion? No, nothing could excuse her behaviour. She had thrown caution to the winds and given herself to Adam. Something within had taken over, compelled her to kiss him, and after that, she was lost.

Amber sat up, fear chilling her heart. She had never been so completely out of control before. Adam had withdrawn early, so there could be no baby, no lasting evidence of her weakness, but what if it happened again? She must make sure it did not, or she would risk losing everything she had worked so hard to achieve.

She had been a widow for more than seven years, in charge of her own life, and this sudden vulnerability was terrifying. She had known nothing like it before. Amber had been fifteen when her mother died and she had stepped into her shoes, taking over the accounts and running the shop. It had not been difficult; she loved the business and as a child she had spent all her spare time in the warehouse, learning about the different fabrics, talking to the customers and accompanying her father on his business trips. She had soon realised that while her father was an excellent salesman, it was her mother who knew which fabrics to buy and how much to spend to keep the finances in order.

Amber had inherited her mother's natural flair for business and she had hoped that her father would listen to her advice, that with a little economy they could make the savings and investments needed to expand. Instead, without his wife's moderating influence, he had spent his money foolishly and within the year it was clear that the business would need substantial investment if it was to continue. Bernard Hall had been a gentleman by birth and knew nothing about trade, but he had had a little money which he was willing to invest. Amber knew now that she had been the bargaining tool her father had used to entice Bernard into partnership. She had resisted his advances for three years, but at eighteen she had given in to the pressure from Bernard and her father and become Mrs Hall.

It had not been a happy time. They had needed Bernard's added investment to continue, but his strong, bullying personality had dominated her father and Amber had been obliged to watch the business she loved sinking further into decline. She had thought that by marrying Bernard she might have more influence, instead she had merely become his chattel, to be used or ignored, and any remonstrance had been met with a swift and violent rebuttal. He had constantly belittled her; she had been reduced to the role of a servant. Amber could admit now her relief when Bernard had died less than two years after their marriage. By then her father was a broken man and she had taken up the reins of the business, dragged it back from the brink of disaster and with steady perseverance she had built it up.

It had taken her years to recover from Bernard's constant bullying and at the same time she had struggled against prejudice, customers and sup-pliers who thought that because she was a woman alone they could cheat her—or seduce her. They did not succeed and over the years she had grown stronger, more confident. Independent. She would not allow anything or anyone to prejudice her position.

So what was she doing here, lying with a man she hardly knew?

Adam sighed and rolled over, slipping one hand around her hips. Immediately her body responded, relishing the contact, the way he moulded himself against her. Amber tensed, trying to ignore the siren call of her own desire.

She felt his breath on her thigh.

'Is anything wrong?'

Something close to panic engulfed her. She must not give in. She must not allow these new and terrifying feelings to possess her, to swallow her up. This man was a danger to everything she had lived and worked for. If she allowed him to take her in his arms again she would be lost. He must be set at a distance. Like a drowning man she clutched at the only lifeline she could see.

Summoning every ounce of resolution, she gave a careless laugh.

'Wrong? No, of course not. But I have to get on. There is a lot to do here.'

Immediately he released her and she could not ignore the little stab of disappointment that he did not argue. She said brightly, 'I have my business to think of, and you will be returning to Lancashire very soon, will you not?'

'Tomorrow, if matters work out well for me.'

Amber nodded. How right she was to distance herself from him! Adam threw back the covers and got up.

'Where are you going?'

He turned back to look down at her, a rueful smile quirking his mouth and setting loose a net full of butterflies in her stomach.

'To get dressed. I cannot lie with you naked beside me and *not* make love to you. I think that would be beyond any man.'

She blushed. 'No, of course.'

She watched him walk away to gather up his clothes and pick up his saddlebag. He moved gracefully; his naked body was lean and lithe in the morning light, like any hero should be. She was grateful he had been hers, if only for one night.

'I will take myself over there,' he said, pointing to a clump of bushes, 'and allow you to dress here undisturbed.'

He disappeared into the green undergrowth and Amber hunted for her own garments. The sight of them scattered around reminded her of the passion that had made it necessary to divest herself of them so haphazardly last night. Her blood heated at the very thought of what they had done, but almost immediately she shivered.

Such wanton, abandoned behaviour was quite shocking. If anyone learned of it her reputation would be lost and her business would almost certainly be ruined. She did not think Adam would speak of it to anyone. She trusted him, even more than she trusted herself. Hurriedly she picked up her chemise and scrambled into it.

Adam shook out his clothes and sighed. They were dry, but sadly crumpled and muddy from their time in the river. He had a clean shirt and neck cloth in his saddlebag, but had not thought to pack anything else.

A rueful smile touched his lips. He had not expected to rescue a damsel in distress and get a soaking for his troubles! However, the night that had followed had been more than ample reward. His mind drifted to lying beneath the stars with

Amber in his arms. His lack of control troubled him. It could only be the consequence of the fight: he knew from experience how one's senses were heightened by a battle. The exhilaration of victory made men reckless. That would account for the immediate, overwhelming attraction he had felt for her. It was completely foreign to him, but then all his other battles had taken place at sea and by the time they had reached port his euphoria had died and the harlots on the quay had held no appeal for him. He told himself it would be no different with Mrs Amber Hall, in the light of a new day. They could go their separate ways and think no more of each other. Thank goodness he had withdrawn in time, and there could be no risk of an unwanted child to complicate matters.

He shrugged on his jacket and raked his fingers through his hair one final time. No, she would be dressed by now, that luscious dark hair scraped back into some semblance of order, and they would be able to treat each other as polite, distant acquaintances.

Unfortunately fate had one more joke to play on him. When Adam stepped back into the clearing he found Amber dressed only in her chemise and stockings, a frieze blanket pulled around her shoulders. She had pinned up her hair, but she looked so fragile, so forlorn, that it was as much as he could do not to run to her and fold her again in his arms. His voice was sharper than he anticipated when he asked her what was amiss.

She jumped. The forlorn look was replaced by a bright smile as she held up a complicated tangle of pink ribbons and webbing.

'I think I will need you to lace up my stays again.'

His lips twitched.

'That is not something I have ever done before.'

'Then consider it part of your education, sir!'

Amber placed the corset around her and presented her back to him. She bit her lip as she felt his hands against her spine, so close, so personal, but she must act as if this was nothing out of the ordinary, as if she was a woman of the world, used to a man's touch.

'There.' He finished tying the laces and his hands moved to her shoulders, waking that traitorous demon of desire again.

With a light laugh she slipped away from him.

'Enjoyable as it would be to dally here with you all day, Mr Stratton, I have work to do.'

She gave him an arch look and saw his frown,

a quick contraction of his brow before he joined her in packing away the bolts of now dry cloth.

Amber found it easier to be working, avoiding awkward questions, but she had to force herself not to flinch when their hands met accidentally, and she was careful to restrict any conversation to their current task.

At last the final roll was packed and they set off, Adam riding beside the wagon. When they passed a field gate she lifted her whip and pointed.

'You could reach Castonbury Park in half the time if you cut across country.'

'Are you tired of me already, Mrs Hall?'

His quizzing tone made her heart lurch, and it was a struggle to smile and respond airily.

'I am, of course, grateful to you, but I have my business to attend to, and I have no wish to keep you from yours.'

'I should like to see you again, before I leave Castonbury.'

'Oh, that is quite unnecessary, Mr Stratton.'

He shot a frowning look at her.

'Have I offended you in some way?'

Heavens, how difficult it was to do this.

'My dear sir, of course not. You have been a perfect gentleman.'

'Then why are you acting like this, as if...last night never happened?'

'Last night was quite delightful, of course, but we both know it cannot be repeated. There is a naval term for it, I think...ships that pass in the night.' She achieved a giggle. 'Although we did not quite *pass* each other, did we?'

His face took on a stony look.

'Do you really think our meeting quite so insignificant?'

Open your eyes at him, Amber. Give him that guileless expression of surprise.

'*Of course* it was significant. Without you I would have lost a great deal of stock. I am very grateful to you.'

He made her an elegant bow over Bosun's neck, his voice and his manner thick with sarcasm.

'I am glad to have been of service to you!'

Inwardly she flinched, but she had wanted to put him at a distance, and seemed to have achieved her aims. Surprising, then, that she should feel like bursting into tears.

She waited for him to turn his horse and gallop away, instead he continued to ride alongside her.

'Much as I am eager to reach the Park,' he said coolly, answering her unspoken question, 'you pointed out to me last night that my coat is in need of a little attention. I shall stop off at the Rothermere Arms to see what can be done to repair the damage.'

Amber's conscience stabbed her.

'You have lost two buttons. I do not think the inn will be able to help you there.'

'Yesterday you said I deserved a new jacket,' he reminded her.

Those blue eyes threatened her defences again and she kept her gaze fixed on the road ahead.

'Goodness, you do not suppose I remember every little word I say?' she quipped. 'You may come to the warehouse and I will mend your coat for you there, if you like. Or I could direct you to one of the seamstresses I know, although none of them live on this side of Castonbury.'

'Thank you, madam. I have lost enough time already and have no wish to go chasing around the countryside! I will come to your warehouse. And if you could allow me the use of a mirror and some water, too, I would be obliged to you.'

His clipped tones told her he was keeping his temper in check. Good. She did not want him to be kind to her, just as she was beginning to regain control over herself.

It took them an hour to reach Castonbury. They saw no one on the road but all the same Amber was glad to have Adam's company, the memory of yesterday's assault still fresh in her mind. They said very little, but as they entered the village she pointed to a tall, stone building at the far end of the street.

'There, that is my warehouse, with the shop built on the side. Ripley and Hall, cloth merchants.'

Adam heard the note of pride in her voice as she read out the words on the sign. She followed it with a soft laugh.

'Oh, dear. I do hope poor Fred isn't laid low with worry about me!'

Another surprise. From the moment he had first seen Amber Hall she had taken the wind out of his sails. When they had seen off those ruffians he had expected to find her shocked, tearful, even faint. Instead she had positively beamed at him, full of energy. The immediate and mutual attraction was undeniable, but he had tried to fight it, whereas Amber… He remembered that first, tentative kiss. Had she intended to seduce him? Looking back it seemed quite possible, especially when he thought of her behaviour this morning. He would not have been surprised to find her

regretting their actions, afraid of what had occurred, but she had acted like a worldly-wise mistress, eager to move on. And now, just when he
was beginning to think that she was nothing but
a heartless strumpet, she knocked him off course
with such warmth and concern in her voice as she
spoke of 'poor Fred.'

He dropped back and followed as she guided
the wagon through the double gates into the yard.
Even before she pulled up a lanky youth and an
old man came hurrying out.

'Thank goodness you are here!' The youth put
up his hand to help her down.

'Aye, we bin that worrit about thee,' growled
the old man, going to the horse's head. 'We was
gonna get up a search party if you 'adn't shown
up soon.'

'Well, I am here now, and safe, as you see. And
we have Mr Stratton to thank for that.' She jumped
down and turned to him, her smile lighting up
the yard. 'This is Frederick Aston, my clerk, and
holding the horse is Jacob, who helps out in the
warehouse.'

Adam looked from the pale, thin youth to the
gnarled old man holding on to the dray horse and

realised why Amber had thought it necessary to fetch the cloth herself.

'But what's happened?' cried Fred, looking in horror at the damaged bolts of cloth.

'A few ruffians thought it would be a good joke to cast my load into the river,' she replied. 'If Mr Stratton had not come along, then it might all have been ruined. As it is, only those bolts on the top were soaked. They have dried out somewhat, but you had best put them to one side for laundering.'

Frederick turned to her, his rather colourless eyes filled with anguish.

'Oh, Mrs Hall, if only you had let me come with you—'

'What, and leave old Jacob to look after my shop and warehouse all alone? I needed you here, Frederick.' She glanced up at Adam, and some of the certainty seemed to leave her. 'Now, if you and Jacob would look after Mr Stratton's horse, and kindly unload the wagon, I shall take our guest indoors.'

She led the way in through the warehouse. It was stacked high on all sides with rolls of fabric—gaily patterned cottons, creamy muslins, shiny silks in a rainbow of colours, woollen cloth in every shade from black and deepest blue through autumn browns to greens the colour of spring leaves.

'So Frederick and the old man are the only help you have?' he asked her.

'Yes, but they are very loyal, and we manage very well.'

There was something defiant about the way she spoke but Adam did not question it. Silently he followed her between the racks to a door leading into a small corridor with a narrow staircase.

'Ah,' he said, following her up the stairs. 'You live above the shop.'

'Of course. I grew up here.' She led him to a bedroom with a washstand and a mirror in one corner. 'This was my father's room. I think his shaving box is here somewhere....'

Adam held up his saddlebag. 'I have my own razor, ma'am, and a brush and comb, thank you.'

He eased himself out of his coat, his grazed knuckles and a certain stiffness in his shoulders reminding him of yesterday's confrontation at the river.

'Good.' She reached out and took his coat, making sure she did not touch his hand. 'I will find Maizie and send her up with some water.'

She picked up the jug and Adam watched her

hurry away. She was nervous, but that was only to be expected: she was a woman alone, and he was in her house. It occurred to him that she had not been so nervous when they had been alone together under the stars, but now she was acting as if that had never happened. The woman was an enigma, but if she wished to forget their encounter, so be it. He had enough worries of his own. With a sigh he sat down on the edge of the bed and waited for the maid to return with the hot water.

When he had washed and shaved, Adam went downstairs in search of his coat. The shop was empty and he took the opportunity to look around.

A bow window looked out onto the street and allowed the morning sun to flood in, making the polished mahogany counter gleam with the lustrous sheen of a dark ruby. Lengths of ribbon hung in a profusion of colour at one side of the window, while behind the counter rows of drawers lined the walls, topped with shelves where rolls of fabric were neatly stacked. Returning to the rear of the shop he now noticed that a fire was burning merrily in the hearth, for although the spring sun streamed in through the window, its warmth did not extend to this nether region. He sat down on one of the two armchairs placed on either side of the fire and waited for his hostess to return.

He did not have to wait long. The door at the back of the shop burst open and she hurried in, his jacket over her arm. She checked when she saw him, then came forward, shaking out his coat and holding it up for inspection.

'There. I have brushed it clean as much as I can, and sewn new buttons on for you. I am afraid they are not a perfect match, and the coat looks a little shabby too. I am sorry for that—if you were staying longer I would have a new one made for you.'

He took the coat and shrugged himself into it.

'Then perhaps I will stay.'

He noted the look of alarm in her dark eyes before she turned away, busying herself with straightening the candlesticks on the mantelpiece. She said haltingly, 'About last night…Fred and Jacob will not mention to anyone that we were alone together. I trust I may count on your discretion too?'

'You have my word upon it.' He paused, watching her back. She was tense, ill at ease. He wanted to know why, but doubted she would confide in him. He said quietly, 'You sent breakfast up for me. I thank you for that.'

'After your kindness yesterday it was the least I could do.'

'Kindness! Amber, I—'

'Yes.' She interrupted him. 'Your arrival was fortuitous, Mr Stratton, and our time together was a pleasant interlude, but I am sure you wish to get on now.'

'A pleasant interlude?' His brows snapped together. 'Is that all it was to you?'

'Of course, it would be foolish to think anything else.' She raised her head and put back her shoulders before turning to face him, saying brightly, 'You are looking much more the thing now, Mr Stratton. Jacob has saddled your horse, and is waiting in the yard for you.'

She was dismissing him. She stood, eyes downcast, waiting for him to leave. Her manner was cool, an ice maiden compared to the passionate woman he had held in his arms last night. Should he mention that? Did he want to stir up such memories when he would be leaving Castonbury again shortly?

The answer had to be no.

With the slightest of nods he left her, closing the door carefully behind him.

Amber heard the quiet click as he shut the door.

Only then did she look up. He had gone. And that was what she wanted, was it not? He had no intention of staying in Castonbury—the fact that he was travelling with only one spare shirt told her as much—so it was best that they end it now, before she lost her reputation.

And her heart.

Amber strained her ears, listening to his footsteps fading into nothing. He would walk out through the warehouse to the yard, leap on his horse and ride away. She ran to the window. After a moment she heard the ring of metal on the cobbles. As he passed the window he drew rein and looked in. Amber jumped back, letting the coloured waterfall of ribbons hide her from view. Was it disappointment she saw on his face? She could not be sure. It was gone in a moment, as he settled his hat more firmly on his head and trotted off.

Chapter Three

Adam rode hard to Castonbury Park, determined to forget Amber Hall. It should be easy—after all, he had known her for less than a day—but the manner of their meeting and the passionate night they had spent together were not so easily dismissed. He knew many men who were only too willing to bed a pretty woman as soon as look at her, but he was not one of them. What had happened with Amber had taken him by surprise and he was intrigued by her, wanting to understand just why he was so drawn to her. Unfortunately it appeared he held no such attraction for the lady, since she had been so eager to send him away. Adam's hand tugged angrily at the reins and Bosun threw up his head, sidling nervously. Immediately he released his grip.

'Easy, old boy,' he murmured, running his free

hand along the horse's glossy neck. 'I'm a fool. She wounded my pride, nothing more. I'll be giving Amber Hall a wide berth in future.' He dug his heels into the horse's flanks. 'Come up, now. We've more important matters to deal with!'

The great house looked very much as he remembered it, the sweeping drive and soaring pillars of the portico imposing, designed to impress the most august visitor.

But Adam was not here to visit the family. He turned away from the main entrance and made his way round to the stables. He gave his horse into the care of a waiting groom, tossed him a silver coin for his trouble and strode back to the house, entering by a side door that led through a maze of small passages to the servants' quarters. The corridors were deserted and Adam arrived at the door to the housekeeper's sitting room without meeting anyone. He lifted his hand, hesitated and lowered it again. Then, squaring his shoulders, he raised his hand and knocked softly.

There was no reply. Trying the handle, the door opened easily and Adam stepped inside. Suddenly he was ten years old again, coming to find his mama. There were the cushions and footstool that made the armchair by the fire such a comfort, the large dining table where his mother would entertain the upper servants occasionally, the long table under the window where she would sit when mending or doing the accounts. Even the clock ticking away on the mantelpiece was the same one his mother had used to teach him the time.

The kettle was singing on the fire, a sure sign that his mother would be returning soon. Suddenly his neck cloth was a little too tight and he ran a finger around his collar. What if she was still angry with him? What if she turned him out? Their last meeting was still clear in his mind.

He had been full of hope for the future, but he had not anticipated the shock and anxiety in her face when he told her he had quit the navy.

'I want only what is best for you, my son.'

Her concern flayed his spirit and he turned on her.

'If that was true you would have provided me with a father!' He might as well have struck her, but the angry words kept coming. 'Tell me the truth for once. Was there ever a Mr Stratton?'

'No.' Her lip had trembled as she confessed.

Thinking back, Adam wished he had cut out his tongue rather than continue, but then, with the red mist in his brain, he had ploughed on.

'So who is my father? *Who am I?*'

The shock and pain in her eyes still sliced into him like a knife.

'I cannot tell you. I gave a solemn vow on the Bible that I would never say.'

Even now the memory of her anguished whisper was etched in his memory. At the time he had been determined that it should not touch him, but it had. It had splintered his heart.

He heard the familiar firm step in the corridor, the jingle of keys. The door opened and Hannah Stratton entered the room.

Adam stood very still, gazing at his mother. She looked only a little older than when he had last seen her, a little more silver amongst the dark blond hair, so like his own, and a few more lines around the blue eyes that were now fixed on him. At first they widened, registering surprise. He held his breath. She might reject him. What right had he to expect anything more, after a decade of silence?

Only the soft ticking of the clock told him that time was passing as he waited in an agony of apprehension for her response. Eventually, after a lifetime, she raised her hands and clasped them against her breast.

'Adam.'

It was uttered so softly that he thought perhaps he had imagined it. He ran his tongue over his dry lips.

'Yes, it is I, Mother.' His voice sounded strained, even to his own ears. 'If you will own me after all this time.'

Tears darkened her eyes to the colour of a summer sea. She gave a tremulous smile.

'Adam, oh, Adam, my boy!' She opened her arms to him. In two strides he crossed the room and hugged her, relief flooding his soul.

'Oh, let me look at you!' Between tears and laughter she held him away. 'My, how you have grown!'

His laughing response was a little unsteady.

'Devil a bit, madam, I was two-and-twenty when I last saw you. I haven't grown any taller since then.'

'No, but you have grown *out*,' she told him, her hands squeezing the muscle beneath the sleeves of his coat. 'But ten years, Adam, Ten years! And never a word.'

'I know, Mother. It was so very wrong of me. Can you ever forgive me?'

She shook her head.

'No, nor myself. Those lost years can never be regained. But we both spoke hard words, and I regretted mine almost as soon as they were uttered.'

'Yours were no more than the truth, Mother. I have so much more to regret. I was such a damned proud fool that I could not turn back.'

'If only you had written to me, told me where you were. That has been the hardest part, not knowing.'

'And I can only beg your pardon for that—it was thoughtless of me and I regret it now, most bitterly. I was determined to prove myself, to show you what a success I had made of my life before we met again. What an arrogant fool I was.'

Hannah reached up to push back a lock of hair from his brow.

'There is a trace of red in that blond thatch of yours, Adam. It is in mine too. When the temper is up we are both too hot to be reasonable.'

'When I told you I had quit the navy you were so…upset. I felt I had let you down.'

'No, no.' She fell silent for a moment. 'I was… shocked. The navy was your life, and had been since you were twelve years old. And you were doing so well. A captain at twenty—'

'I know, ma'am, but my advancement was due

to the death of other, better officers. Comrades, friends—all perished. After Trafalgar I had had enough of war, of death. I wanted to be building something, not destroying it.'

'And is that what you have been doing?'

She sat down, beckoning to him to pull up a chair beside her.

'Of course, and very successfully.' He saw her eyes stray to his coat. 'Ah, I do not look like a successful gentleman, is that it? I'm afraid I ran into a spot of trouble on the way here. Nothing serious,' he added quickly, seeing her anxious look. 'Trust me, Mother, I have coats more fitting to a man of means, which I am now.'

'Then I am sorry that I doubted you.'

'No, no, your doubts were perfectly justified. It was wrong of me to storm off in a rage.'

'You were a young man, fresh from the triumph of Trafalgar and full of plans for the future. Of course you were impatient of an old woman's caution.' She hesitated. 'And never knowing your father—'

He flinched away, as if the words burned him.

'Let us not go there, Mother. The circumstances of my birth were not important to the navy, and they mean nothing at all to me now.'

'Truly?'

He saw the shadow of doubt in her eyes and was determined to reassure her. He had inflicted enough pain already and had no wish to reopen the old wounds. So he smiled, saying earnestly, 'Truly. The people I deal with are only interested in how much cotton I can produce for them.'

'Adam, I—'

'No.' He put his fingers to her lips. 'Let us say no more of it. We have not discussed it these thirty years, it is an irrelevance. Instead let me apologise to you again for my long silence. I was headstrong, angry that you doubted me and I wanted to prove I could make something of my life. At first I did not write to you because I was not sure I would succeed. Then, it seemed I had left it too long, I did not know how to explain....' He gave her a rueful smile. 'So I thought I should come in person to tell you how successful I have become. And I *am* successful, Mother, more so than I ever dared to imagine.' He glanced down at his coat and gave a rueful laugh. 'More than this shabby garb suggests.' He leaned forward and took her hands. 'And now I want you to share in my success. I want you to come back to Rossendale with me. I have bought a property there, a small gentleman's residence, quite snug and comfortable.' He read the hesitation in her face and stopped. 'That is, if you can ever forgive me for running away from you like a petulant child.'

'You were hurt that I doubted you,' she said, smiling.

'Your doubts were well founded. How was either of us to know that manufacturing would suit me so well? I was full of arrogant confidence, but it could all have gone so wrong.'

'And instead it has gone right?'

'It has, Mother, it has! And that is why I am here now.' He grinned, pushing out his chest. 'I said I would return, Mother, once I had a house worthy of you.'

'Foolish boy, you know I never asked that of you.'

'No, but I demanded it on your behalf. Look around you. Your quarters here are far superior to many a gentleman's house. It has taken me ten years, Mother. I have worked hard and made shrewd investments, and I have a house now that I think you will like. And I have bought land, too, where I plan to build my own house one day, something bigger, suitable for a wife and children—'

'And do you have anyone in mind?'

Amber's dark beauty flashed into his mind but he banished it instantly. She was not the yielding, compliant partner he envisaged sharing his life with him. He wanted a wife who knew nothing of the rumours surrounding his birth.

'No one yet, but there is time for that. For now I want you to keep me company. Tell me you will come, Mother.'

She put her hands to her cheeks.

'My dear, you must understand—this is all so unexpected. You return after so many years, I must have time to think.'

'I know it is very sudden, but surely there is nothing to consider. I want you to come and live with me, to spend your days in comfort and ease. You will be your own mistress. Is that not what you want?'

'Oh, my love, of course, but…I cannot come with you immediately. His Grace is very sick, and Lord Giles is to be married this summer— the family is all at sixes and sevens! There are so many arrangements to make….'

'Can the family not make their own arrangements?' Adam replied impatiently. 'Surely they

have servants enough to deal with a dozen weddings!'

'Of course they do, but—' she lifted her hand,
indicating the room and saying gently '—this has
been my home, Adam, for thirty years. I cannot,
will not, pack a bag and walk out and leave the
family.'

'I understand that, Mother, but surely, a few
days, a week at the most to arrange everything—'

'Oh, Adam, if only I could.'

'You can, Mother! You have served the family well. They have no right to expect more from
you.' He looked at her closely. 'But that isn't all,
is it? What is worrying you?'

She clasped her hands.

'It is not just the wedding, Adam. There is some
doubt about the inheritance—'

'What, is not James—'

'Master James is dead.'

'Good heavens, when was this?'

Hannah hunted for her handkerchief.

'Some two years since, I do not know the details—it was France, or Spain—something to do
with the horrid war.'

Adam ran a hand through his hair. 'I read

that Lord Edward had perished at Waterloo, but Jamie—that makes Giles the heir!'

'Not quite yet. The family had word that Jamie might be alive, and Lord Harry is gone to look for him.'

'But that is good news, surely.'

'Yes, it is, only not long after he went a woman arrived here, with a baby, saying she is Lady— that she is Master Jamie's widow. The duke is overjoyed to have his grandson here, only—'

'Only you think she is an imposter?'

'I do not know, my son. It is all so confused. She seems true enough, but there are little things— and if she should prove to be a fraud, His Grace would be distraught. And he is so very ill, Adam, a mere shadow of the man he once was. His mind is going, you see, and there are so few of us left that he remembers. I do not think I can leave him while there is so much turmoil here, so much to distress him.'

'I have not seen His Grace since I was twelve,' said Adam pensively. 'I was about to depart for the naval college in Portsmouth and he summoned me, to bid me farewell, do you remember? He told me to make everyone proud of me.'

'And we were, my son. When we read in the

dispatches about your bravery at Trafalgar, His Grace sent down a bottle of his best wine for us to toast your health!'

As if I was his own son. The words rose unbidden to Adam's mind. It was an effort not to speak them, but if his mother had sworn an oath of silence he would not ask her to break it. He had caused her enough pain. He watched his mother turn to put another log on the fire. The plain gold band on her wedding finger was real enough, and there was the emerald ring she wore on the little finger of her right hand on high days and holidays—she had told him once that had been a betrothal gift from his father.

Two substantial rings, tokens from a man of means, such as the duke. As a child, the idea that the Duke of Rothermere was his parent had seemed preferable to not having a father at all but once Adam joined the navy it had ceased to be important. The question was still there, at the back of his mind. It always would be, but he would not let it come between him and his mother again. He was his own man, and proud of it.

Hannah shook off her reverie and looked up, smiling.

'I am eating in the servants' hall today. Will you join me, Adam? I would like to show you off.'

Adam grinned.

'I should be delighted to take lunch with you.' He held the door open for his mother and followed her out into the corridor, where she addressed the maid who was scurrying by.

'Becca, we will be having a guest join us for luncheon in the servants' hall. See to it that another place is laid, if you please.' She looked at the watch dangling from her waist. 'It is not nearly so late as I thought—' Hannah broke off as she saw that the little maid was still standing there, wringing her hands nervously before her. 'Well, Becca?'

'Please, m'm, Cook asked me to go and fetch another pot of cream. If I goes back without it...'

'You may tell Cook that I have sent you back with a message,' said Hannah, patiently repeating herself. 'Make sure there is another place laid at the table, Becca, and I will fetch the cream.' She threw an amused glance towards Adam as the maid hurried away. 'I was going to suggest we might take a stroll, but it seems I now have an errand.'

'Then I shall come with you,' said Adam. He

added mischievously, trying to maintain the lighter mood, 'Who knows, I might catch a glimpse of a pretty dairymaid....'

They turned to make their way outside, but as they traversed the passage a lanky young footman came in and stopped at the sight of them. Hannah smiled.

'Ah, Coyle, here is my son, Adam, come home to visit me. You won't know Joe Coyle, Adam. He joined the family but five years ago.'

Adam nodded affably. The footman nodded back.

'Ah, now, so it's Captain Stratton returned, is it? I heard tell you was at Trafalgar, with Lord Nelson, God rest his soul.'

'I was, but I am no longer a captain. I have sold out.'

Joe cast a critical look over Adam's shabby coat.

'Not doing so well, eh?'

Adam felt his mother stiffen beside him, but he merely shrugged, his amiability unimpaired. 'I'm doing well enough.'

With a nod he took his mother's arm and moved off, leaving the footman to go on his way. Hannah put her hand on his sleeve.

'Adam, you should not let them think your pockets are to let—'

He grinned. 'Better that than they should be dunning me for a loan. But I am sorry that the little fracas on the way here has ruined my coat. I did not pack another, thinking to carry you off within the day.'

'Oh, my dear—!'

'It is no matter, Mother. You have explained to me why you cannot pack your things and fly with me immediately.'

'But I do not want you to disappear immediately either.'

'I promise you I shall not do that. It was truly arrogant of me to think you would drop everything to come with me. I have left my business in good order, so I can stay in Castonbury for a while.' The image of Amber Hall rose in his mind, but he dismissed it quickly. He placed his hand under his mother's elbow. 'Now, let us make haste to the dairy, before Cook is driven to a rage by a lack of cream.'

Hannah led the way outside and they followed the path that ran around the kitchen wing. The sash windows of the servants' hall had been thrown up to make the most of the warm spring day, and as they passed, Joe Coyle's voice came floating out to them, saying with painful clarity, 'So Cap'n Stratton's back, His Grace's by-blow…'

Hannah stopped, her face pale, but before Adam could speak he heard the butler say sharply, 'You'd best keep such thoughts to yourself, lad, if you don't want to be turned off.'

'But 'tis common knowledge, Mr Lumsden—'

'Common nonsense, that's what it is,' retorted the butler. 'You'll get short shrift if you repeat such gossip in this house, Coyle.'

Adam put his hand beneath Hannah's arm and gently moved her away.

'Adam—'

'You need say nothing, Mother. There has always been gossip, even when I was a boy.'

'Ah, my son, I thought to shield you from that!'

He shrugged.

'It was never important.'

'Is that really true? Perhaps it was wrong of me, not to tell you the truth.'

The faded blue eyes were fixed upon him. Adam knew that one word from him and she would break her vow of silence. He paused to consider the matter. He had always looked up to the duke, who had been carelessly kind to him and had paid for him to go to sea. Adam had never felt any bit-terness about his upbringing—after all, it was not unusual for peers to have children on the wrong side of the blanket. What *was* unusual was the care the duke had taken of Adam's mother, per-suading his father the late duke to employ her at Castonbury and allowing her to rise to a position of respect, responsibility and independence. If silence was the price she had had to pay for that, then he was not going to make her break her vows.

'Growing up without a father has only increased my determination to make something of myself,' he told her, smiling a little. 'I have no interest in the past, only in what I am now...which is exceed-ingly hungry. Let us fetch the cream and return for our luncheon with all speed.'

Adam saw the relief in his mother's face and knew he had made the right decision.

'So, Captain—'

'I am merely Mr Stratton now, sir,' Adam cor-rected the butler with a smile, and the old man nodded, his look saying that Adam would always be a captain in his eyes. 'What are you about now?'

'I am a manufacturer.'

Adam glanced around the servants gathered together for luncheon and smiled to himself.

They were all looking at him politely, but he read a touch of disdain in their glances. They were wedded to the past, where a title and land was paramount. A man's status was determined by his birth—and given what Adam had overheard earlier they considered his origins to be highly suspect! Little did they realise that only a few miles away men like himself were making fortunes that would allow them to buy up estates like Castonbury on a whim.

'And you've come back to visit your mother,' Lumsden continued, bending a fatherly eye upon Adam. 'Very commendable.'

'Not just to visit,' said Adam. 'I want to take her to live with me in Rossendale.'

This brought a murmur of surprise around the table and Hannah was quick to respond.

'I shall not go immediately, of course. I would like to remain until after Lord Giles's wedding.'

'And so I should think.' Lumsden nodded. 'We couldn't do without you, not at this late stage.'

Adam smiled at his mother.

'I am afraid you will have to do so eventually.'

She put her hand over his.

'Even though I will not go back with you immediately, I hope you do not mean to leave me just yet.'

'No, no, have I not said I shall stay a little while?'

'How long?' she pressed him. 'More than a couple of weeks, I hope.'

Adam hesitated. To remain in Castonbury, where he was clearly thought of as the illegitimate Montague, would not be easy, but he did not wish to leave his mother again so soon. Before he could reply William Everett, the estate manager, cleared his throat.

'And where might you be thinking of staying?'

'I am sure the Rothermere Arms will have a room....'

'There is the old keeper's lodge, by the south gate.'

Joe Coyle snorted at Mr Everett's suggestion.

'No one's lived there for many a day.'

'True, but the building's sound,' said William. 'I've been in the village this morning, and I think it might be a good thing to have someone living near the south gate again.'

One of the housemaids gasped, her bright eyes lighting up at the hint of gossip.

'Oh, why's that, Mr Everett? Has there been some trouble?'

'It may be nothing, Daisy,' he said cautiously, 'but I heard that Mrs Hall was accosted on her way to Castonbury yesterday. Damaged some of the stock she was bringing back with her.'

'Dear me, never say she was travelling alone?' said Hannah. 'Why did she not use a carrier?'

'No one'll work for her,' replied Joe Coyle, pouring himself another glass of small beer. 'The last carrier she used was set upon. Had his nose broken. She can't keep any staff either.' He wiped his lips and leaned forward, warming to his theme. 'Bad things happen to 'em. They get warned off.'

'Oooh, who by?' breathed Daisy, hands clasped to her breast.

Coyle shook his head.

'Nobody really knows, but I think it's the clothier over at Hatherton. Stands to reason, she's competition.'

'But surely she should go to the magistrate,' said Adam, keeping his tone impartial.

'No proof,' replied Coyle shortly. 'No one will say anything, but I had it from Mrs Crutchley, the butcher's wife, that the new man's been trying to drum up business in Castonbury. She says his prices are very good.'

'Well, I don't care how good he is,' retorted Hannah stoutly. 'We have always used Ripley and Hall to supply our needs and we will continue to do so.'

Adam was heartened his mother's response, but the conversation worried him. He had been inclined to dismiss Amber's assertions about her competitor, but if Parwich really did mean her harm, Adam did not think the boy or the old man he had seen at the warehouse would be much help to her. If he stayed at the lodge he could be near his mother and perhaps keep an eye on Amber as well.

William Everett pushed back his chair and rose from the table, saying as he did so, 'Well, the offer is there if you want it. 'Twould do the place good to have a few fires lit and I'd be glad to have it known that there is someone living there, especially while we have the lady on her own at the Dower House—'

Coyle snorted contemptuously.

'The lady!'

William Everett frowned.

'You'll watch your tone, young man. If the lady's case is proved, she'll be your new mistress!'

'Lord Jamie's widow,' explained Hannah, observing Adam's raised brows. 'She and her child have been installed at the Dower House, which is within sight of the old lodge. I confess I am a little worried for her, living there with only a few servants.'

Adam rubbed his chin. He could afford to pay for the best rooms at the inn, but the lodge was conveniently close to the great house.

'Very well, Mr Everett, I will take up your kind offer and move into the keeper's lodge for a while.'

'Very good. The place was adequately furnished, the last time I went in, but of course there is no mattress.'

'I will send one over directly,' put in Hannah quickly. 'I will look out some spare bedlinen too. Daisy will come over and clean the rooms for you. Perhaps Cook will allow Becca to help her. The place will be inches thick in dust.'

'That is very good of you, Mrs Stratton,' said Mr Everett. He turned to Adam. 'I am going that way now if you would care to come and look?'

'I will,' said Adam. He drained his tankard and set it back on the table.

'P'raps Mr Everett can find you some work on the estate.' Coyle grinned. 'By the looks of you, a few extra pennies wouldn't go amiss.'

Adam smiled. If only they knew!

'Don't worry,' he said mildly, 'I'll manage.'

Hannah's chair scraped back. She said brusquely, 'It is time we were all back at work. Daisy, clear away, will you?'

Thus dismissed, the servants quickly went about their business.

Hannah put her hand on her son's arm.

'Will you come back later, for dinner?'

'Of course. First I am going to see my temporary quarters.' He grinned. 'And then I think I will ride into Castonbury and find myself a new coat!'

Chapter Four

'And there's another two customers have closed their accounts.'

Frederick's tone was as dismal as the gloom at the back of the shop. Amber rubbed a hand across her eyes.

'They live near Hatherton, Fred. I am not surprised that they prefer to buy their cloth from Matthew Parwich.'

'And what about Mrs Finch, when you tell her the block-printed cotton she ordered is ruined?'

Amber drew a breath, fighting back her anger.

'It is *not* ruined, Fred, it has a few watermarks where it was dumped in the river. I will see how it looks once the washerwoman has done with it, and offer it to Mrs Finch at a reduced rate.'

It would wipe out any profit she had hoped to

make, but if her customer was satisfied, then that was all she could hope for.

'And then there's the cloth for Castonbury Park—'

'Most of that was undamaged.' Her hold on her temper was slipping and she waved her hand at her clerk. 'I will finish going through the order book, Fred. Please go and fetch a taper to light the lamps, or our customers will not be able to find their way in.'

She waited until he had left the room, then dropped her head in her hands.

Poor Fred, he was worried about the business, but he had a propensity to gloom and it would do no good to let him see her own anxiety. The attack yesterday must have shaken her more than she thought, for she was not usually so low. The tinkle of the shop doorbell brought her to her feet in an instant, the order book laid aside. Two young men entered. Their clothing was rough, and there was a certain swagger about them that immediately made her wary, especially with the daylight fading. She greeted them as she would any other potential customer, but remained behind the counter.

'We wants some ribbons,' said the taller one,

looking about him with an insolence that made her want to order him from the premises.

'Aye,' sniggered the second, a spotty youth with ginger hair, 'for our lady-loves.'

'They are all there, by the window.' She pointed to the display, the colours glowing in the last rays of the setting sun.

The young men walked across to the window.

'Just these?' The ginger-haired youth sniffed. 'We came all the way from Hatherton and this is all you got? That ain't good enough.'

'Then I suggest you go back to Hatherton and buy your ribbons there,' she retorted. She wished Fred would hurry up and return.

The taller of the two approached her.

'Now that ain't very good business talk, is it? What about this piece here?' He picked up a length of scarlet ribbon from the counter and held it up. He pointed behind her. 'And we'll take a look in those drawers back there—'

He broke off as the bell tinkled again and Amber looked past him. She could not prevent the smile of relief at the sight of Adam Stratton in the door-way.

His quick gaze summed up the situation instantly and he stepped up, eyeing the two youths as he drew off his gloves.

'Good day, Mrs Hall. You have customers, I see. Pray do not fret over me. I shall amuse myself while you deal with them.'

'We was just going, wasn't we, Tom?' The ginger-haired youth began to sidle towards the door.

'Aye, we are—'

'Just a moment!'

The authority in Adam's voice brought both men to a halt. Adam pointed to the ribbon on the counter. 'You were going to buy that, I think?'

Amber held her breath. The lanky youth looked as if he wanted to deny it, but the silky menace in Adam's tone was unmistakable. She saw the young man swallow and look at his companion, but there was no support there.

'Um, well, I—'

'That particular ribbon is one of the most popular,' said Amber. 'It would delight any young lady.' She added kindly, 'Since it is the last of the roll you can have it for tuppence.'

'A bargain,' agreed Adam, his eyes like steel, despite his smile. 'Well, sir?'

The lad swallowed again, dug into his pocket and pulled out two coins.

'A-all right,' he stammered. 'There you are.'

He slammed the coins down on the counter, picked up the ribbon and lounged out of the shop, his companion hot on his heels. Adam followed them to the door and watched them hurry away before turning back to face Amber.

'I hope those two are not typical of your customers.'

'Thankfully, no.' She tried to speak normally.

'I arrived just in time, I think.'

She raised her chin.

'I am grateful, naturally, but I was never in any danger.' His sceptical look told her he thought differently. She reached beneath the counter and pulled out an elegant pistol. 'I am prepared for these occasions.'

He raised his brows.

'Of course, I had forgotten. Having seen you in action, madam, I can believe it! However, I think it could prove, ah, vastly inconvenient to have dead bodies littering your premises.'

She laughed at that, saying as she carefully stowed the pistol away again, 'It would indeed.'

'But, to be serious, madam, who were those young ruffians? Are they local men?'

'No, I have not seen them before. They said they had come from Hatherton.'

'A long way to come for a length of ribbon.'

She shrugged. 'Mayhap they are visiting some-one here.'

'How long have you felt it necessary to keep a loaded pistol in your shop? No, don't tell me,' he continued, noting her hesitation. 'Only since your competitor began making…overtures, am I right?'

She eyed him frostily.

'How I protect myself and my property is not your concern, sir!'

Oh, but how I wish it could be!

Amber was shaken by the thought. Immediately she stifled it. This was dangerous territory and she must draw back. She summoned up a smile.

'Pray, let us not argue, Mr Stratton.' She clasped her hands together and directed a polite look of enquiry up at him. 'What can I do for you, sir?'

'I thought you could tell me where I might buy a coat.'

'Oh.'

'Yes. I am staying in Castonbury for a while and I really think this one a little too shabby, don't you?'

The amusement in his voice, the slight, upward

curve of his lips, set the butterflies loose in her stomach again. She forgot all about her unwelcome visitors and for a moment she could only gaze up at him, marvelling at how blue his eyes were, how they glinted when he smiled at her.

'I heard the bell—' Frederick came hurrying back into the room, a lighted taper clasped in one hand. He stopped when he saw Adam and gave him a nod of recognition.

The spell was broken and Amber was quite put out.

'Yes, well, you are a little late, Fred,' she retorted acidly. She closed her lips, composed herself and said quietly, 'Since you have the taper, perhaps you will light the lamps now?' She turned back to Adam, trying to think rationally. He was only another customer, after all.

'I require a coat,' he prompted her.

She cleared her throat.

'Well, fashionable gentlemen such as Sir Nathan Samuelson would go to Buxton, but there is Mr Leitman, who is a perfectly good tailor and lives here in Castonbury.'

'Your local tailor will suit me very well.'

He placed his hands on the counter. She gazed

down at those long, tapering fingers, remembering the pleasure they had given her.

'Then…' She struggled to bring her disordered
thoughts under control—and her voice, too, which
had suddenly become very husky. 'Then I would
be happy to furnish you with the cloth you need.'

'Excellent. What fabric do you have?'

Amber hesitated. Over the years she had become adept at assessing her customers, but she
could not be sure about Adam Stratton. Thinking
back to their discussions, he had told her he had
been a sailor, and he had a house for his mother,
but that did not necessarily mean he was a wealthy
man. His coat was well-cut but tailored for comfort rather than fashion. His shirt and neck cloth
were of the finest linen; she remembered the feel
of them when she had hung them over the bush
to dry. The thought of their time together in the
woods brought the heat flaming to her cheeks
again. It weakened her knees and she was obliged
to clutch at the counter for support.

'If it is a workaday coat you require, sir, I have
a selection of wools and worsted, then there is a
silk and wool mixture, or the superfine, if you
wish for something better….'

'An everyday coat is all I require.'

'Very well. Frederick, perhaps you will fetch down the—'

'No.' He held up his hand as Frederick ran to bring the steps to the front shelves. 'It is too dark now to see the colours clearly. I will come back in the morning. Perhaps you will have a selection ready for me to see in the daylight?'

He lifted his hat, turned on his heel and departed. Amber watched him go. She felt very odd, as if she had been buffeted by a wild and unexpected storm.

'Hmph.' Frederick replaced the steps in the corner of the shop. 'It seems to me he could have saved himself a journey and just called upon you tomorrow.'

'Perhaps he just wanted to make sure we could supply him.'

She stared out through the window, watching as he hoisted himself into the saddle, turned the large grey horse and rode off. Perhaps he wanted her to know he was not leaving.

A sleepless night followed. Amber had spent all day trying to forget Adam Stratton. She convinced herself that the attack upon her wagon had made her restless, had disordered her senses and she had played the damsel in distress to Adam's gallant knight. Then he had come into her shop, sent those rough youths away and sent *her* into another dizzy spin!

In vain did she argue that the entry of any gentleman would have resolved the situation and persuaded the boys to leave, but she knew that no one else would have caused such a bolt of pleasure to shoot through her. She had been overjoyed to see him, and now she was appalled by her reaction.

Never before had a man affected her in this way. Many had tried to woo her—after all, she owned a lucrative business—but she had no desire to share her hard-won wealth or her bed with any of them. Now, at seven-and-twenty, she considered herself to be beyond the age of love. What she felt for Adam must be infatuation. She had observed it in others, including her own father. He had become besotted by a beautiful young woman and had made a complete fool of himself, installing her in a house in Hatherton, showering her with gifts and neglecting both Amber and his business while he followed the young beauty around like a lovesick puppy. At last, when the young woman had left the area, taking with her a good portion of John Ripley's fortune, he had begged Amber's forgiveness, telling her how very lonely he had been since her mother's death.

Amber had forgiven him, but she could never forget how close they had come to losing every-thing—only her timely marriage to Bernard Hall had secured the extra funding the business needed to continue, but at what a cost. It had taken all her strength to survive her marriage, and Bernard's early death had been a relief. She had then been able to advise her father on the best way to prog-ress, rebuilding Ripley and Hall into a thriving business. Since his death she had controlled her own fortune, made her own decisions, and that was the way she wanted it to remain. She would never allow anyone to have power over her again.

Adam returned from Castonbury to find the lodge swept out and the bed made up. A search of the outhouses uncovered a good supply of logs and a little coal, so he was able to build up a cheer-ful fire, which he left burning while he rode off to dine with his mother. He reached the Caston-bury stables just as another rider was dismount-ing from a huge black horse. Adam recognised the tall, dark-haired figure immediately as Giles Montague and touched his hat.

'Your servant, my lord.'

Giles scowled up at him.

'Mighty formal all of a sudden, Stratton. That's not the form of address I expect from a man I've known all my life!'

Adam grinned, reassured by the other's curt greeting. He slid easily to the ground and handed Bosun's reins to a waiting stable boy.

'I was not certain of my reception.'

'Quite right,' said Giles, the gleam in his grey eyes belying his scowl. 'Ten years without a word to anyone. You should be flogged!'

'I agree with you, and I beg your pardon,' said Adam, as they walked out of the yard together. 'I should have kept in touch.'

'That is nothing to me, I have never been one for letter-writing either, but I know your mother felt your loss deeply. Are you here to visit her?'

'Yes, I am joining her for dinner.'

'Hah! The prodigal returns so the fatted calf must be slaughtered, am I right?'

'No, no, it is merely mutton stew, I believe,' returned Adam mildly.

Giles laughed.

'Much more fitting! And I am late for my own dinner, so I must go—come and drink a glass of

port with me, later, Adam. After you have dined.
I shall be in the study.'

'I will, and gladly.'

Giles nodded.

'Good. Until later, then!'

Hannah paced up and down in her sitting room,
clasping and unclasping her hands. The table was
set, Mr Lumsden had found her an excellent bottle of wine, so all she had to do now was wait for
Adam to join her for dinner.

When he came in she went to him, hands out,
gazing up at him and trying to note every change
that had taken place in the past ten years. His dark
blond hair was short, the side whiskers longer,
framing a face that was leaner and more handsome than she remembered. There were fine lines
around his eyes and his mouth. They were ac-
centuated when he smiled, as he was doing now.
He was still lean and athletic, but a little broader
across the chest, and he carried himself well. Upright, confident, a man in charge of his destiny.

'What is this, Mother, tears in your eyes?' He
pulled her to him and embraced her.

'I am so very pleased that you are here, Adam.'

'Did you think I did not mean to return?'

'I was very much afraid I might never see you again.'

He hugged her tighter.

'I hope we shall see a great deal more of each other from now on.'

'I hope that too.' She pushed away from him, and wiped her eyes on the edge of her apron. 'Come, now, sit you down and Daisy shall wait upon us.'

Hannah ate very little, too busy watching her son, taking in every detail and encouraging him to talk about himself. Away from the other servants he was happy to describe his life in Lancashire. He glossed over the early years, but she guessed more from what was left out than what he said that they had been a struggle as he bought his first woollen mill, toiled for long hours learning the business. He made mistakes, invested badly, then picked himself up and started again. Knowing his proud spirit, she could understand why he had not written to her in those early years, when the spectre of failure was still close.

Hannah waited until the end of the meal, when Daisy had removed the last of the dishes and they were alone again, before she voiced the question that she had wanted to ask all evening.

'And are you happy now, my son?'

'Very happy, Mother. My decision to build a new mill for spinning cotton has proved very successful. I have been careful with my profits, invested well and now I owe no man any money.'

'And you have a house.'

'I do indeed. And it needs a mistress.' He held up his glass to her. 'I want you there with me, Mother, just as I promised.'

Hannah smiled and shook her head.

'You should be looking for a wife.'

She felt, rather than saw, the brief hesitation before he said lightly, 'I have never met anyone to compare with you. When I find your equal, Mother, then you may be sure I shall marry her.'

'Me!' Hannah found herself laughing and blushing at the same time. 'I am not so very special.'

'But you are. You raised me single-handed whilst earning the respect of everyone at Castonbury.' His eyes rested upon her for a moment. 'Not an easy task, given the rumours.' He smiled and shook his head. 'I will not press you any more on that head.'

'Perhaps I should not have come here.' Hannah looked away, twisting her hands together. 'But I had nowhere else to go, and you were a baby...'

He reached across to take her hands.

'You did what was necessary, Mother, no one could blame you for that.'

'And in return I promised never to reveal—'

'Hush now.' He squeezed her fingers. 'Let us be done with the subject. I insist we talk of something else! Tell me about the lady at the Dower House. I saw the lights as I rode over here.'

'I know very little. If she is truly Lord Jamie's wife, then she is Lady Hatherton.'

'There is some doubt?'

Hannah nodded.

'Apparently the marriage was a rushed affair and took place abroad, just before Lord Jamie died. Many of the staff are inclined to think she is an impostor.'

'But not you?'

Hannah spread her hands.

'Who am I to judge? I feel so sorry for her, to be alone with a young child is difficult for any woman.'

'But if her case is proved her son will be heir to the dukedom.'

'But if it goes against her—' Hannah shivered. 'The world is a cruel place for a woman alone.'

'And Castonbury seems to have more than its

fair share of single women.' He looked down at the tablecloth, concentrating on picking off the crumbs. 'There is a widow in the village. A cloth merchant.'

'Amber Hall. A delightful girl.' Hannah smiled as a happy memory came to her. 'She came here with her father upon occasion, and took a shine to you.'

He frowned. 'Why do I not remember more about that?'

'We are going back twenty years, Adam. She has done very well for herself though.'

'Yes. A very independent young woman, who does not think herself in need of anyone's protection.'

Hannah looked at him. He was gazing thoughtfully at the wine in his glass. As if aware of her glance he met her eyes briefly before shaking himself out of his pensive mood and exerting himself to be cheerful for the remainder of his time. At length he glanced at the clock.

'It is growing late, and you are tired, Mother.'

Hannah tried to protest, but she could not prevent a yawn escaping. Adam rose, smiling.

'You have to be up betimes, so I shall leave you now.'

Hannah stood up and gave him her hands.

'You will come back again tomorrow? I am busy during the day, but we could dine again.'

'Of course, as often as you wish. You will have to forgive me appearing in the same clothes. I have written to Cardew and asked him to send some here, but that will take a few days.'

'Cardew?'

'My valet.' He grinned at her. 'Yes, Mother, I told you I was a man of substance now. I have a valet. Not that he will join me here. He would think a mere keeper's lodge far beneath his dignity.'

'And you do not?'

'Not at all. I am very satisfied with my berth, for the moment, especially since it means I can walk across to see you each evening.' He kissed her cheek. 'We have many years to catch up, Mother.'

Hannah kissed him, saw him to the door, then returned to her chair by the fire, gazing into the dying embers.

Adam, her son. So much heartache, but she laid none of it as his door. When he had left her ten years ago, declaring he would not return until he could make her proud of him, she'd known he meant it, because he had inherited her temper as well as his father's stubborn pride. Adam maintained he did not want to know about his father. Hannah thought that perhaps he believed the rumours, that he was Rothermere's son. She wished she could tell him about his father, but she had given her word. Her life at Castonbury, the secure home she had been able to give Adam, it had all been bought by her silence.

If Lumsden was surprised when Adam told him he was going to see Lord Giles he did not show it. Although Adam knew his way perfectly well, Lumsden insisted upon escorting him to the study, where he announced him in the same sonorous tones he used for all visitors to Castonbury Park. Giles was sitting in one of the two wing chairs beside the fireplace but he jumped up when Adam came in and went over to the side table, which held several decanters and a range of glasses.

'I know I offered you port, but there's brandy too.' He held up his own glass. 'That's my own preference.'

'Then pour me a brandy, if you please.'

Realising his presence was no longer required, Lumsden quietly closed the door and Giles lounged back to his easy chair, gesturing to Adam to take the other one.

'So.' Giles eyed him over the top of his glass. 'You are looking very well, Adam. No regrets about quitting the sea?'

'No, none.' Adam warmed his glass between his hands, smiling a little.

'And you are doing very well.' It was Giles's turn to smile. 'Don't bother denying it. You gave a silver sixpence to the groom when you arrived, so the servants already have their suspicions that you are not so poor as your coat would indicate. And that piece of horseflesh you ride cost a pretty penny, I'll be bound!'

'Perhaps I waylaid a wealthy man on my way here,' murmured Adam.

Giles laughed.

'Not you. Honest Adam, that's what Jamie called you, when we were playmates together. How long ago that seems, now.' Giles sighed and was silent for a few moments, distracted. At last he shook off his reverie to say sharply, 'No, you can come clean with me, sir. I have acquaintances in Lancashire who have told me about a certain Mr Stratton, a gentleman who is making a name for himself in the cotton spinning business. They say he can turn around an ailing mill, and keep his workforce happy at the same time.'

'One thing I learned at sea is how to manage people. I treat them fairly and prefer to reward rather than punish.'

'I also heard you are for ever investing in new machinery.'

Adam shrugged. 'That is right. I am not interested in quick profit. I am building for the future.'

'But the profits come anyway, I am told. You are worth a pretty penny.'

'I won't deny it.' He sipped his brandy, keeping his eyes on his companion. Giles was staring moodily into the fire. At last Adam broke the silence.

'I read of Edward's death. And Mother told me of Jamie too. I am very sorry.'

'Thank you. But Jamie's death is not confirmed, and until it is—will you believe me if I say I would give anything to find him alive?'

'Of course. I know you never wanted the title.'

'True, but I do not want to see it pass out of the family.'

'Ah. I heard there is a claimant. You fear an imposition?'

Adam waited, knowing Giles was debating with himself.

'Yes,' he said at last. 'There is something not quite right about the woman claiming to be Jamie's widow. She knew him, I am quite sure of that, but...' He broke off again, and after an agonised moment he burst out, 'I cannot believe Jamie would have married her. Oh, I have nothing against the woman, but she is not the sort of woman who attracted him.'

'But who can tell what will attract a man?' Adam said slowly, an image of Amber Hall clouding his thoughts. 'One may see a woman and suddenly it is as if a man-o'-war has delivered a broadside.'

'Not Jamie,' said Giles firmly. 'He was wedded to his work.' He jumped up and fetched the decanter to refill their glasses. 'I would just like to know the truth!'

'What is the family doing to investigate?' asked Adam.

'We have made enquiries, of course, and Harry has gone to Spain to see what he can discover. There was a witness to Jamie's death, apparently, but whether he is still alive—' Giles looked up suddenly, a haunted look in his eyes. 'What if the woman is genuine, Adam, what if I am denying my own nephew his birthright?'

'You are trying to discover the truth, Giles. No one can hold that against you.'

Giles rubbed a hand across his eyes.

'M'father is already convinced the boy is his grandson. I hate to think what it will do to him if we prove him an impostor.'

'Well, you can do nothing until you have more proof. Until then this woman...Lady Hatherton... is living at the Dower House, is she not?'

'Yes.' Giles nodded. 'Everett told me you have moved into the keeper's lodge—damn it, Adam, you know we could have found a room for you here!'

'I think not. That might be thought presumptuous.'

Giles cast a quick, searching look at him.

'If the rumours are to be believed you're almost as rich as a nabob.'

'But breeding, dear boy, breeding.' Adam's lip curled slightly. 'Nothing as common as trade must sully the portals of Castonbury Park.'

And not only trade. That they might be half-brothers was something they both knew, but never discussed. Adam saw it in Giles's eyes, and his brow creased; he lifted his hand, as if in denial, and with a shrug Giles threw himself back into his chair.

'Breeding be damned,' he said cheerfully. 'If you are so wealthy I could introduce you to a dozen ladies of the *ton* who would be glad to catch themselves a wealthy husband. Times are changing, my friend. Many of the old families would be more than happy to welcome you.'

Adam pulled a face.

'Welcome my fortune, you mean. No, I thank you. I have no wish to pour my money into some impoverished lord's coffers—your own family excluded, of course. The uncertainty over who will inherit must be playing havoc with your finances.'

'We shall come about,' said Giles shortly.

'I am sure you will. But in the meantime, if there is anything I can do—'

Giles shook his head.

'No. You are too much a friend to be embroiled in our affairs.'

His look said the subject was closed and Adam did not fight it.

'As you wish. Let us talk, then, about something far more pleasurable. I believe congratulations are in order.'

Immediately Giles relaxed.

'Yes, I am betrothed. To Lily Seagrove.'

'The parson's daughter? I have not seen her since she was a babe. When is the happy marriage to take place?'

Giles waved his hand.

'In a few months, I hope.' He looked up. 'You will come, of course.'

'If I am invited.' Adam grinned. 'Your wedding is the reason I cannot prise my mother away from Castonbury immediately.'

'Quite right too. She and Lumsden run this place like clockwork.'

'Well, you had best look for another house-keeper, because I shall be taking her off to a life of leisure once your wedding is out of the way.' Adam drained his glass and rose. 'I must go. I have to settle Bosun in an outhouse before I can retire for the night. Heaven knows what he will think of his new berth!'

'If he objects too much you can always stable him here.' Giles walked to the door and opened it. 'Goodnight, Adam. And it is good to see you, even though I have spent the best part of the time boring you with my troubles.'

'They are genuine concerns, Giles, and I am

happy to listen.' Adam put his hand on Giles's shoulder. 'Don't worry. These things usually have a way of working themselves out. I will keep a weather-eye on the Dower House while I am here and if I see anything suspicious I will let you know.'

'Thank you, Adam, another opinion would be welcome.'

It was nearly midnight when Adam rode back to the keeper's lodge. He passed the Dower House, a black shape against the night sky, and thought of all Giles had told him. He shook his head. What with a possible impostor at the Dower House and the threats to Amber Hall's business, all was definitely not well in Castonbury.

Chapter Five

Amber rose the next morning, determined that Frederick should mind the shop that day. However, by the time she had broken her fast she had changed her mind. It was her practice whenever possible to be on hand to talk to her customers. Many were lifelong friends who would think it odd if she was suddenly too high and mighty to talk to them. Besides, Frederick was needed to help Jacob in the warehouse. And if those were not reasons enough, she would not for the world have Adam Stratton think she was afraid to meet him.

Thus, when Adam walked into the shop at ten o'clock, Amber was prepared. She schooled her features into a polite welcome, but his first words threw her off-balance.

'I thought you might leave your clerk in charge of the shop today.'

'I—that is, I would never—' She took a deep breath, and drew herself up, saying with as much dignity as she could muster, 'I see no need to avoid you, Mr Stratton.'

'I was not thinking of that.' His mocking eyes told a different tale. 'You might have wanted a male presence here in case you had any more, er, difficult customers.'

Amber bit her lip, knowing she had given herself away. It could not be helped, however, so she would ignore his taunting.

'I do not expect any more trouble, especially when the street is so busy. And if they did return, I am ready for them. What can I do for you, sir?'

'I have come to choose a cloth for my every-day coat.'

She indicated the bolts of fabric lined up on the counter.

'These would be my recommendations for you, sir. They are all wool, suitable for the coming summer months and—' She stopped herself just before admitting that she had chosen the shades of blue and grey to match his eyes.

'Which one would you suggest?'

'Me, sir? I have no preference.'

He moved along the line, fingering the soft

wool, holding it to catch the best of the light, and Amber watched him, taking in the firmly sculpted lips, the strong line of his cheek, noting the way his hair fell forward over his brow. She wanted to lean across the counter and brush the silky locks back into place. Instead she clasped her hands tightly together, holding herself rigidly upright, awaiting his decision.

'I think this one, the kersey. What think you?'

He unwound a length of grey-blue cloth and held it up against his chest. Amber kept her gaze fixed rigidly upon the material.

'An excellent choice,' she said briskly. 'Kersey is hard-wearing and weather-proof. I will give you Mr Leitman's direction and he will take your measurements and let me know exactly how many yards he will require.'

'You do not want any money now?'

'Mr Leitman will deal with everything. Besides, we agreed yesterday, I owe you a coat. The bill will be sent here for settlement.'

She concentrated on writing the tailor's details upon the back of a trade card. She was determined she would not look at Adam.

'Very well. I had best go and see him. I will be back later—'

'No!' Amber had been thinking her ordeal was at an end and her voice came out as a squeak. 'There is no need for you to return, Mr Stratton.'

'Oh, but I want to.'

She shook her head.

'I am sorry, but we shall be closed this afternoon.' He raised his brows and she was obliged to explain. 'I am going to Buxton to collect more material to replace what was damaged yesterday, and I am taking Frederick with me. There will be no one to mind the shop.'

'I see. You need more staff, Mrs Hall.'

'I know, but at present that is impossible.'

'Because of the threats?'

Her eyes flew to his face, then she remembered that she herself had told him about her troubles.

'Yes.'

'Perhaps I can help.'

'You?'

His smile set the butterflies rioting inside her again.

'Yes. I could work for you. I know a little about cloth.'

'But you do not need to work. You told me yourself you are a man of means.'

'That need not concern you.'

Amber shook her head.

'Out of the question. I could not possibly employ you.'

'Why not?' His reasonable tone flustered her. She shut her eyes, trying to muster her arguments, but he forestalled her. 'You know why I came here, but my mother is not yet ready to leave the Park.' He spread his hands, saying with a rueful grin, 'I rather took her by surprise, so I shall have to stay here for a few weeks. Until she becomes more accustomed to the idea of living with me in Lancashire. I shall need an occupation while I am here. I know something about cloth, I could help you.'

Amber's brain was in turmoil. She was desperately short of staff and the idea of having someone like Adam on hand, someone not easily intimidated, was very tempting. But what of her own attraction to him? Would she be able to cope, seeing him every day?

Of course she would. Amber told herself that the sooner she really got to know Adam Stratton, the sooner her infatuation would fade. She ignored the tiny voice in her head that whispered she might be fooling herself.

'A few weeks, you say? I could use another pair of hands....'

'Then why not try me? Let me go to Buxton for you.'

'And wages?' She forced herself to ask, praying he would not make some lewd suggestion. To her relief he answered her quite seriously.

'Whatever you pay your other warehouseman.'

Amber bit her lip. It was a risk. What did she really know about this man? Her body cried out that she knew all she needed to know about Adam Stratton, but she must not allow her heart to rule her head.

'Very well,' she said slowly. 'You may go with Frederick to collect the extra stock from Buxton. He is leaving at noon, can you be ready then?'

It was growing dark by the time Adam turned the dray horse into the yard of Ripley and Hall that evening. A chill wind had sprung up, reminding him that it was not yet summer. He was glad he had sent word to his mother that he would not be able to join her for dinner. It would be some time yet before he could get away. He smiled to himself. If his mill managers could see him now they would be amazed to find him working at such a menial post and for a pittance. His inward smile grew. He would have refused any payment at all if he had thought she would agree to it, but he had a pretty fair idea that Amber Hall would not accept charity.

As he drew up she came into the yard, a paisley shawl wrapped around her shoulders.

'I did not think you would be so late.'

'There was some confusion over the order,' said Fred, jumping down. 'We had to wait for the two rolls of fustian to come in on the Leeds coach.'

'So you had no problems on the journey?' she asked anxiously. 'Did you see anyone?'

'It was peaceful enough. We did not need this.' Adam pulled the shotgun from the footwell and passed it down to Frederick. 'You can put that away now, Fred.' He jumped down, smiling at Amber. 'We are back safely with everything on your order.'

'Good,' growled old Jacob, shuffling to the back of the wagon. 'Then let's get it all unloaded and we can have our supper!'

Amber was trying to look unconcerned, but Adam noted the added colour in her cheeks.

'I always cook supper for Jacob and Frederick. You may join us, if you wish.'

It was grudging, and he was sure she wanted him to refuse, but the thought of the empty keeper's lodge was not attractive. He nodded, touching his forelock.

'I'd be delighted to join you, mistress.'

The darkling look she threw at him told Adam she was not fooled by his subservience.

They took supper in the large kitchen to one side of the shop. Amber and Maizie served the food, then joined the three men at the table.

'This is very good, mistress,' mumbled Jacob, helping himself to another piece of chicken. 'But I thought you said you'd finished all the old birds last month?'

'This one had stopped laying, so I decided she should go in the pot.'

Amber avoided looking at Adam. Heaven forbid he should think she had made a special effort on his behalf!

'There's no denying the mistress is an excellent cook.' Fred sat back with a satisfied sigh. 'That was very good, Mrs Hall, I thank you.'

She acknowledged him with a brisk nod.

'You know I don't expect you to work late for nothing, Fred.'

When the meal was over everyone helped to

clear the table, then Jacob announced he would make his final round of the warehouse.

'I likes to make sure everything is locked up right and tight.'

'I'll come with you,' said Adam, pushing back his chair. 'You can show me what you do.'

Jacob looked to Amber. 'Is that all right with you, missus?'

'Of course. Adam…' She stumbled over using his name, but to call him anything else would raise him above the others, and she could not do that. 'Adam needs to know, so that he can lock up for you, Jacob.'

The two men left the kitchen and Fred turned to Amber.

'So how long is he staying?'

'Only a few weeks.' She frowned a little. 'Is anything wrong, did you not get on today?'

'No, no, he was very easy. Knows his cloth too. I merely wondered why you should employ him, if he isn't going to be around for very long.'

'You know we need more help, Fred. And as you say, he understands cloth.'

'Aye, well, I'm not sure I want him knowing all our business!'

Amber stared at him, hands on hips.

'Fred Aston, what is the matter with you? I thought you would be glad of some help!'

Fred's thin frame hunched even further.

'Aye, well, I am, but I don't know why a man like that should want to work here, unless...'

'Unless what?' Amber knew what was coming, even before Fred screwed up his courage and blurted it out.

'Unless he's trying to court you! It's happened before, mistress, you know it has. Even Mr Parwich—'

Amber stopped him, saying curtly, 'I don't think you should compare Adam Stratton with Mr Parwich, Fred.'

'Maybe not, but what do we know about him?'

'He's Mrs Stratton's son, and that's good enough for me.'

'Aye, well, Mrs Crutchley says he's the duke's—'

'That is enough!' She cut him short, her anger flaring.

Fred's face turned bright red, and she bit back a further retort, saying quietly, 'We need an extra pair of hands, Fred, and Adam Stratton is all I can get for the moment.'

'Aye, I know.' He nodded, not looking at her.

She put her hand on his arm.

'You should go home now. It has been a long day.' She gave him a gentle push. 'You need not worry that Adam Stratton is going to replace you as my head clerk, Fred. You have my word that will not happen.'

He gazed at her for a moment, as if he would say something more, then with a slight shrug he collected his hat and coat and left by the kitchen door.

'You know 'is trouble,' opined Maizie, busily scrubbing at the dishes. 'He's sweet on you. Oh, yes.' She grinned over her shoulder at Amber. 'Can see it a mile off. He watches you like a lovesick puppy.'

'Oh, poor Fred.' Amber sat down at the table again. 'I don't think I have ever given him any reason to think that I—'

'Ooh, no, mistress, but it don't stop 'im worshipping you.'

Amber dropped her head in her hands.

'Don't you worry, mistress.' Maizie picked up another pan. 'Look at it this way—at least there's no chance of Fred being lured away by Matthew Parwich.'

Amber's head shot up.

'Oh, has he tried?'

''Course he has.' Maizie's reply was matter-of-fact, but no less alarming for that. 'He was round here on Thursday last, when you was gone off with the wagon. I was in the back, cleaning, but the door to the shop was open and I heard Mr Parwich asking Fred how would he like to come and work for him. Fred told him straight that he wouldn't be leaving. "I'll be here with Mrs Hall as long as she needs me," he says. "Well, that might not be very long," says Parwich. "Her days in business is numbered." So Fred tells him he'd better leave. But that's why he was so worried when you didn't come home that night.'

'Yes, I see. Oh, why didn't he tell me?'

'Probably didn't want to worry you. All of us—me, Fred and Jacob—we all love working for you, mistress, and we don't want the business to close.'

Amber was cheered by this display of loyalty. When the kitchen was tidy she sent Maizie to bed and went off to make her final inspection of the shop. She did not really need to do so. Fred would have put everything ready for the next day and Jacob was more than capable of locking up and making sure that the lamps were properly extinguished, but she liked to walk around the empty room, comforted by the fully stocked, tidy shelves and the neat boxes of threads and ribbons. Everything here was hers; it was what she had worked for, to provide for herself in the future.

When she returned to the kitchen she found Adam sitting at the table.

'Oh.' She stopped in the doorway. 'I thought you had gone, Mr Stratton. Where is Jacob?'

'At home by now, I would think. And I preferred it when you called me Adam.'

She realised her mouth had gone dry, and she was very conscious that they were alone. His presence filled the room, even if she turned away she was aware of him.

'Why are you still here?'

He gestured towards the kitchen door.

'There was no one to shoot the bolt after me.'

'Then I will do so now.'

He rose from the table and she quickly backed away towards the door, determined to keep as much distance as possible between them. She picked up his hat and held it out to him. Their fingers brushed as he took it from her and memory seared through her body. She thought bitterly how right she was to be cautious. She had to concentrate really hard to stop her hands from clutching at him, as if he could save her from disaster. She fought down the feeling. The disaster would be if she allowed him to undermine her independence.

'Would you like me to stay?'

His voice, slow and deep, was like a salve to her burning skin. It was so tempting to give in. He could take her in his arms and she would forget everything, become a slave to her passion once again. He was her weakness, but she knew she could not afford such a thing.

Amber drew herself up, forced herself to meet his eyes.

'Let me make it quite clear, *Adam*.' She stressed his name, hoping it would set him in his place as her employee. Unfortunately it made her remember when she had used it to cry out in ecstasy. Nervously she ran her tongue across her lips, then regretted the action when she saw how his eyes darkened with desire. She straightened her shoulders and tried again, saying icily, 'Please understand that while you are working for me you will be treated the same as my other employees.'

She held her breath. It was almost a physical effort not to lean into the space between them, to reach out for him. Her hands clenched into fists at her sides, nails digging into the palms as she fought against an attraction so strong it almost overwhelmed her.

'Amber—'

'I am Mrs Hall to you!' He flinched and stepped back, as if the words had been a whiplash. Her lips tightened against an apology. She must not show weakness. 'Please, go now.'

Adam stared at her, his eyes hard and angry, his mouth a thin line. She kept her own gaze fixed somewhere beyond his shoulder. Her body was rigid, her control as brittle as glass. Could he see the effort she was making? If he touched her now those fragile defences would crumble. She prayed that he did not realise the power he held over her.

After what felt like an eternity he seemed to come to a decision. Without a word he jammed his hat on his head and walked out.

Adam stepped out into the night. It was all he could do not to slam the door behind him. The woman was impossible. When he had offered to stay it had been out of concern for her safety, nothing more, but was she grateful? Not a bit of it! She withdrew behind an icy reserve and spoke to him as if he was the lowliest of her employees.

Which he was. And foolishly he had put himself in that position.

Adam's hectic stride slowed. He had to be honest with himself; it was not merely to protect her that he had offered to stay. He wanted to carry her upstairs and make love to her all over again. He could not believe she did not feel the attraction. Why, the air positively sizzled between them. Or perhaps it didn't. Perhaps it was all in his mind. He was so painfully aware of her, the tilt of her head when she was concentrating, the soft cadence of her voice.

She was right to send him away. The night they had spent under the stars had been the result of their extraordinary situation. To continue their liaison would bring no credit to him and could seriously compromise Amber's position in Castonbury—and he knew better than anyone just how gossip flew in the village.

Adam collected Bosun from the barn behind the warehouse and set off along the main street at a sharp trot, narrowly avoiding a red-haired man who had just come out of the Rothermere Arms. He swore as he dragged his horse out of the way, his anger resurfacing.

'What idiotic sense of chivalry made me offer to work for the woman in the first place?' he muttered savagely. 'I do not need her work, or her money! She wants to be independent, so let her look after herself!'

An image rose before him: Amber at the ford, fighting off her assailants. Then he recalled the suspicious characters in the shop. Who knows what damage they might have done if he had not come in.

He shook his head.

'It is none of my concern. She has Fred, and old Jacob. Let them jump to do her bidding. I'll be damned if I will!'

A sliver of moon was rising, giving barely enough light to see his way and he turned his attention to guiding Bosun into the narrow lane leading to the old keeper's lodge. The outline of the building came into view. It was a long time since he had slept in such a lowly place—even longer since he had taken orders from anyone, let alone a woman. He exhaled softly and looked up at the sky.

'You had best face up to it,' he addressed the silent moon above him. 'She's got under your skin and you don't like that one little bit!'

Chapter Six

Amber was at the small desk in the warehouse, totting up the orders with Fred, when Adam came in the next morning. She saw him through the little peephole window beside the door, and used the extra moments to compose herself. Thankfully Fred was doing the talking, so she had only to maintain a look of interest while her brain and emotions ran riot. After their parting last night she had not expected Adam to return and her first reaction was overwhelming relief. It was closely followed by anxiety. Could she face him again? As Fred came to the end of his report she knew the answer. She had no choice. Steeling herself, she gave Fred his instructions, then turned to Adam.

Heavens but he was attractive, with his chiselled features and his athletic body that positively exuded energy. Such thoughts did her resolution no good at all and she quickly buried them and addressed him in a cold, businesslike tone.

'If you are come to work, Jacob will show you what needs to be done.' She marvelled that she could speak so normally.

He dipped his head.

'Thank you, mistress.'

Fred closed the order book and went off to put it away, leaving her alone with Adam. She watched him hang up his coat and suddenly the words would not be denied any longer.

'I did not think you would come back.'

'We made a bargain,' he said shortly. 'I am not one to walk away as soon as we run into a squall.' His voice was cold and when he turned to her she could read nothing from his expression. 'If you'll excuse me I'll go and find Jacob.'

She watched him go, her pleasure in seeing him dimmed by his cool tone, but what else should she expect, when she had spoken to him so harshly last night? She had panicked when she had found herself alone with him, afraid that he wanted to kiss her again, and even more afraid that she would not be able to resist. Now she shook her head. She must put aside such ideas and think about the day ahead, but Amber found it difficult to concentrate. She felt restless, unsettled, and eventually she decided that only hard, physical work would dispel her mood. She threw a plain linen apron over her pale gown and took one of the rugs from her sitting room into the yard, hung it over the clothesline and gave it a beating.

The exertion had its effect. As the dust was beaten from the carpet so her sense of calm and purpose returned. Adam Stratton was an employee; he would take her wages, just like the others, and he would make himself useful. She paused to tuck a stray lock of hair behind her ear. That was an end to it. Now she could relax and get her mind back to business.

'Well, well. Reduced to cleaning your own rugs, Mrs Hall?'

The drawling voice made her look around, her lip curling.

'Matthew Parwich. What are you doing here?'

He ignored her question. He was standing at the open gate, leaning on his silver-topped cane as he watched her.

'If you sell the business to me, you can hire a maid to do that for you.'

'I have a maid,' she retorted, adding sweetly,

'Besides, when I am wielding the beater, it is your face I see in the rug, Mr Parwich.'

His leering smile widened. He walked into the yard.

'I love your spirit, Mrs Hall. Perhaps, instead of selling, we should consider a partnership....'

'With you? Never!'

He laughed. 'Now, now, my dear, you should not dismiss the idea until you have given it some thought.'

He stepped closer and ran his fingers down her bare arm. Amber jumped away, bringing the carpet beater down on his sleeve, where it left a dusty imprint on the dark cloth. Immediately the leer turned to a scowl. He raised his stick.

'Why, you—!' He broke off, staring past Amber.

'Do you need any help, ma'am?'

She looked over her shoulder. Adam was standing in the warehouse door. He had rolled up the sleeves of his shirt and the sun glinted on the fine golden hairs of his muscled arms. Slowly Matthew Parwich lowered his hand.

'I heard you had hired a guard dog.'

There was the hint of steel in Adam's blue eyes, but he said mildly, 'Nay, I'm merely the new warehouseman.'

Matthew's gaze switched back to Amber, his brows raised. She lifted her chin a little. There was no doubt that having Adam standing close by increased her confidence.

'An extra pair of hands is always useful, Mr Parwich. Now, perhaps you can tell me just what it is you want here? I am very busy.'

He waved one hand.

'I am merely being sociable, dear lady. I saw you in the yard and stopped to pass the time of day.'

'Well, you have done that, now you may be on your way again.' With that she lifted the rug from the line and carried it indoors. She stopped, just out of sight. Adam had stepped out into the yard to let her pass but she could see him, standing outside the entrance.

'Well, what are you waiting for?' Matthew Parwich's voice carried easily into the warehouse.

Adam's response was as calm as the other was irritable.

'To see you leave, as Mrs Hall requested.'

She heard Matthew give a short laugh.

'By God, you are a cool one! But you look a very useful sort of fellow. I could use you in my own business. What do you say to coming to work for me?'

Amber held her breath, only letting it go once she heard Adam's answer.

'I'm happy enough here.'

'There'd be more money in it for you.'

'Well, when I have grown tired of Ripley and Hall perhaps I might look you up.'

'Do. My name is Parwich, you will find my cloth business in Hatherton.'

His boots rang on the cobbles as he walked away and Amber leaned back against the desk, clutching the rug to her. She was still standing there when Adam stepped back inside. He stopped when he saw her and she gave him a brief smile.

'Thank you.'

He nodded silently and disappeared into the warehouse.

Adam rode back to the keeper's lodge well satisfied with his day's work. It would have been very easy to stay away, but he had never been one to resist a challenge, and Amber Hall was certainly that. Besides, she needed him, even if she would not admit it. The appearance of Matthew Parwich had confirmed his suspicions and he was thankful he had been there today. Old Jacob had come in to tell him the man was in the yard with

Amber, and it had not taken Adam long to get his measure. Parwich was a bully, but his powerful frame suggested that he would make short work of Fred, should that young man try to stand up to him. No, Amber Hall might declare she did not need his help, but Adam thought differently. She had instructed him to work under Fred's direction. Perhaps she thought it might humble him, taking orders from that stripling. In fact, he thought, unsaddling Bosun and setting about rubbing him down, it was better for his own peace of mind if he did not see too much of the woman.

Once he had washed himself and brushed off his coat, he decided to walk across to the great house. It promised to be a fine evening, and after working indoors for the best part of the day he would enjoy the fresh air. He had not gone far when he saw someone before him, a diminutive lady, walking slowly behind a young child who was making his unsteady way along the path. When she saw Adam she made haste to pick up the child. Adam raised his hat to her as he stepped aside.

'After you, Lady Hatherton.'

Her blue eyes looked at him uncertainly.

'You know who I am?'

'Of course, madam, I have seen you in the grounds of the Dower House.'

'And may I ask what you are doing here?'

'I am presently staying at the keeper's lodge. My mother is housekeeper at the Park.'

'Ah. Mrs Stratton. She has been…kind to me.'

'And others have not.'

'Some are still unsure.' A rueful smile touched her lips. 'I cannot blame them for that.'

'And this is your boy.' Adam held out his finger and the toddler clutched at it. The woman regarded this gesture with mild approval.

'Yes. Crispin.' She added quietly, 'He is my life.'

'He is very like you.'

She sighed.

'It would be better if he looked like Hatherton.'

'Mayhap he will, when he is older.' He eased his finger free from the child's chubby grip. 'I must go. I am on my way to join my mother at the great house. Is there any message I can take, anything I can fetch for you?'

She flushed.

'That is very good of you, sir, but no, I have all I need here.'

'Then I will bid you good day, my lady.' He touched his hat and strode on. So that was the woman Giles feared was an impostor. It was difficult to say. He gave a mental shrug. He would keep an eye on the Dower House, as he had promised Giles, but that would not be so easy now he was working at Ripley and Hall every day. And he had an idea that Mrs Amber Hall would not prove an easy taskmaster.

It was amazing the difference a little sunshine made to one's mood. Amber stepped out onto the street and looked about her, filled with a feeling of content and wellbeing. The cloudless blue sky promised a fine, sunny day and even the wind had lost its wintry bite, replaced by a balmy breeze that spoke of a fine spring to come. She hummed a little tune to herself as she began to unfasten the shutters. The faint clop of hooves made her look around and she saw Adam approaching on his grey horse. The bubble of happiness inside her swelled a little more as she went back to her task. This lightness of spirit had nothing to do with the man. She would not allow it.

'Good morning, mistress.'

His voice sent a pleasurable shiver down her spine, but she answered him calmly enough as she lifted the first shutter from the window.

'You should not be doing that,' he told her. 'Where is Fred?'

'Fred is out. And I am perfectly capable—'

She was glad of a reason to be indignant, but his deep chuckle cut across her retort.

'Oh, I am sure of *that*, madam, but nevertheless I will do the rest for you.'

He jumped down and held out the reins to her.

'Here, hold Bosun for me.' When she hesitated he grinned. 'I know. You would very much like to refuse my help, would you not?'

'Not at all,' she lied, taking the reins. 'After all, I am paying you to do such tasks.'

The gleam in his eyes challenged her and she raised her chin defiantly. Without a word he walked to the window and took down the remaining shutters, his size and strength making an easy job of it. Amber stroked the horse's nose and watched him in reluctant admiration.

'Bosun,' she said, when he turned to her again. 'A reminder of your seafaring days, I suppose?'

'Yes. My tribute to the many courageous men I knew back then.'

'You do not regret leaving the sea?'

'Not at all.'

He held his hand out for the reins but she ignored it, giving her attention instead to the horse.

'He is a fine animal.' She shot a quick, piercing glance at him. 'His keep must take every penny that I am paying you.'

'Perhaps it does, I had not considered it.'

She looked up at him then, frowning a little.

'So why are you working for me, Adam Stratton, if you do not need the money?'

Amber's heart began to beat more heavily. Having asked the question she was not at all sure she wanted to hear his answer. His blue eyes rested thoughtfully upon her for a moment and she found herself praying frantically.

Dear heaven, do not let him say anything untoward or I will have to turn him off.

The understanding in his gaze brought a flush to her cheeks. He answered lightly.

'Perhaps I am a spy, come to learn the secret of your success.'

Relief made her laugh.

'There is no secret, only hard work and honest dealing.' She pushed the reins into his hand. 'So stable your fine horse and get you to the warehouse, sir. There is work to be done!'

She heard him laughing as she went back into

the shop and she allowed herself a smile. Undoubtedly Adam Stratton made the sun shine a little brighter for her.

The days fell into a pattern: Adam would arrive at the warehouse early and work tirelessly. Amber kept her distance, issuing her orders through Fred. It was only sensible, she told herself. Fred was her clerk, her second in command. There was no need for her to concern herself with the day-to-day running of the business.

Soon the building was looking tidier than it had done for years. Repairs that had been outstanding were carried out, such as replacing the missing tiles on the roof and securing a broken shelf. Adam also suggested to Fred that a bell-pull should be installed in the shop beside the counter, so that Amber could summon help from the warehouse when it was needed. He learned the work quickly and proved himself equally at home filling in the ledgers as he was carrying the heavy bolts of cloth. Amber was aware of the improvements he was making to her business and she was thankful for it. Everyone seemed happier, even old Jacob took to whistling while he was working.

Amber heard Jacob's rather tuneless whistle coming from the yard as she walked through the warehouse. He and Adam would be preparing the dray ready for Fred to make the morning deliveries and she was loath to call any of them away from their duties to deal with Mr Leitman's order. The tailor had sent a message asking her to supply him urgently with a length of mustard kersey. Amber decided she could find that and package it up without help. Gazing up at the tidy racks she thought that neither Fred nor Jacob had ever managed to keep the top tiers quite so neat, but Adam, with his extra height and strong shoulders, was easily able to lift the bolts of cloth onto the top shelves.

She made her way along the aisle where the bolts of kersey wool were stored. The mustard kersey was not a popular fabric and she finally spotted it on one of the upper racks. She hauled the stepladder into place and climbed up to reach it. There was much less than half the original bolt of fabric left but she still needed both hands to drag it from the shelf, which meant she had to let go of her skirts, which she had gathered out of the way while she climbed the stepladder. With the fabric clutched in her hands she would have to take care descending the steps, and she was gingerly feeling her way with the toes of one foot when Fred's shrill cry made her wobble.

'Oh, good heavens, madam, whatever are you doing?'

She quickly replaced her foot on the step and leaned against the ladder to steady herself.

'Why did you not call me?' he asked, hurrying up to her.

'I did not think I needed you to fetch such a small amount of cloth. Here.' She reached down. 'Take this from me and put it on the cart for Mr Leitman, if you please.'

'Should I not help you down?'

Amber laughed.

'No, indeed, I can manage perfectly well. I would much rather you set off on your rounds now. You have a lot of calls to make today.' She waved him away. 'Go on, Fred.'

For a moment she watched him, smiling, as he reluctantly turned and walked off with the bolt of mustard kersey wool on his shoulder. It would be easier to get down now her hands were free. All she had to do was pull her skirts close—

'Are you sure you do not want any help?'

Adam's voice made her jump and she let her skirts fall as she clutched at the sides of the stepladder. He was standing at the far end of the aisle, leaning against the racking, his arms folded. She took her time to regain her balance and her composure before answering him.

'No, thank you.'

Aware of his critical gaze, she began to gather her skirts tightly around her while keeping her ankles covered.

'You are very likely to break your neck doing that.' He walked forward and before she knew what he was about he put his hands around her waist and lifted her down.

Amber wanted to protest, but the sensation of being suspended in mid-air took away her breath. He placed her gently on her feet but her heart was beating such a tattoo that she felt quite dizzy. It was all she could do to manage a breathless 'Thank you.'

'Think nothing of it.' He picked up the ladder and carried it back to its place against the wall. 'Why did you not call one of us to fetch that down for you?'

She replied haughtily, 'I see no reason to ask a man to do everything for me.'

He turned, his eyes glinting down at her.

'You do like to be independent, Mrs Hall.'

'Why, yes, I do.' She eyed him, anticipating his mockery, but although there was amusement in his eyes, it was not unkind. She relaxed a little. 'Perhaps it was a little unwise, to try climbing in a skirt,' she conceded.

'But you would do it again?'

She felt the smile grow within her.

'Of course. Although I would not try to fetch down the full rolls of cloth. Those I know would be too heavy for me.'

'An admission indeed!'

'It would be unreasonable to call Fred or...or anyone, every time there is a small job to be done.' She looked at him as a sudden thought occurred to her. 'You have never told me exactly what your business is.'

'Manufacturing.'

'In Lancashire? Would that be cotton?'

His eyes were alight with laughter.

'It might be, among other things.'

'Then you know as much about cloth as I!'

He shook his head, disclaiming.

'Not this side of the business. Working here has been...'

She bristled, withdrawing behind a haughty look and he continued after the slightest of pauses.

'…an education.'

'It is important for me to know about my business,' she said seriously. 'I must know how it works. Everything, in fact, because as a woman I am constantly being tested.' She frowned a little. 'People—men—think I should not be doing this, but I have proved myself far better at buying and selling cloth than either my father or my husband.'

She lifted her chin and gave him a challenging look. After a moment he nodded.

'Do you know, Mrs Hall, I think I believe you.'

Amber stood a little taller. Jacob shuffled up, whistling, but neither Amber nor Adam moved, and after looking from one to the other, the old man wandered off again. Amber cleared her throat.

'I am cooking supper for Fred and Jacob this evening. Will you join us?' She had instructed Fred to issue the invitation each time she had prepared supper for them all. It was important, she told herself, that she treated him no differently from the others, but after that first disastrous time Adam had always declined. This time…

'Thank you, but I cannot stay. I am dining at Castonbury Park. With my mother.'

Amber nodded. She refused to acknowledge the

little stab of disappointment. It was quite natural that he should want to spend time with his mother, after all the years of separation. As she watched him walk away she told herself she was glad he would not eat with them.

Adam might not have been at supper, but Amber could not escape his presence. Jacob and Fred were discussing his suggestions for organising the racks of cloth. She had begun to notice that Fred was much more likely to take advice from Adam than from her on ways to improve the running of the warehouse and the shop. Fred was very jealous of his position, and it said much for Adam's tact that his ideas were accepted so readily. She had to admit they were good ideas, and she had no hesitation in giving her permission for them to be implemented. She would have liked to talk to Adam herself about the business, to ask his advice, but she dare not. It was *her* business, *her* concern, and she would not share that with anyone. Besides, he was not staying. Another week or two at the most and he would be gone. It would not do for her to rely upon him too much.

Her attempts to change the subject succeeded for a short time but then the men would begin to talk of work again and she could not help noticing how frequently Adam's name came up.

She told herself it was a good thing that they all got on so well together, but every mention of Adam was like a tiny pinprick, so that by the end of the meal her nerves felt quite raw. She almost hustled Jacob and Fred out of the house, declaring that she was too fatigued to tarry, but even when the kitchen was cleared and Maizie had been sent to bed Amber could not rest. Her mind was too wide awake.

Picking up her lamp she made her way to the shop and sat down at the little desk. She opened her accounts ledger. There was always work to be done and she preferred to be working than tossing and turning in her bed, thinking about Adam Stratton.

An hour later the ink had dried on her pen and the blank space at the bottom of the neat column of figures was still empty.

'Oh, blast the man! Why must he invade my thoughts so much?' She threw her pen down in disgust. 'This is quite ridiculous. I shall turn him off in the morning and have done with it.'

A light tapping at the street door made her jump.

'Mrs Hall. Is everything all right?'

Adam's voice. For a moment Amber had the wild fancy that she had conjured him by magic, but she quickly stifled the idea. She unbolted the door and opened it a fraction. Adam's shadowed figure filled the door frame.

'I saw the lamp burning,' he explained. 'With the rest of the house in darkness I thought perhaps it had been overlooked.'

She stood back to let him enter.

'No, no, I, um—I could not sleep.' She waved her hand in the direction of the desk. 'Figures that will not balance...'

He swept off his hat.

'Ah. May I look?'

Silently she nodded her assent, shutting the door while he strode across to the desk.

'I thought you were dining at Castonbury Park this evening.' She watched as he shrugged off his jacket and placed it over the back of the chair. It was the coat she had mended for him, the one that had been damaged at the ford, when he had come to her aid, riding into the fray like Sir Galahad... She quickly dragged her thoughts away from that.

'I did dine there, but then I had to come back to the village.'

'So where is Bosun?'

'Tied to the yard gates.' He was poring over the ledger, the lamplight glinting on his fair head.

Amber's mouth dried as she felt that now familiar ache of desire wrenching at her insides. He should not be here. It was wrong. She turned away, clutching at the edge of the counter. This was her punishment for that one night of weakness. If she did not know how it felt to be in his arms, to be loved by this man, then she would not be suffering this terrible longing now.

Unable to resist looking at him she turned back, watching his lean fingers curled around the pen, remembering those same fingers caressing her skin…

'Ah, I see what it is, a badly scripted entry.' He picked up the pen. 'A seven that has been mistaken for a one. May I correct it?'

'By all means.' She added, as if prompted by some inner demon, 'Would…would you like a glass of wine?'

He looked up, surprised, and she heard herself saying quickly, 'I w-was about to have one, to help me sleep.'

'Then yes, ma'am, if you please.'

She lit a candle from the lamp and hurried to the kitchen, muttering angrily to herself all the way.

'Why, oh, why did you offer him refreshment? Now he will stay even longer.'

The demon on her shoulder merely laughed and told her that was exactly what she wanted.

Five minutes later she returned to the shop, balancing the glasses and the candle on a tray. When she put the wine down beside him he barely acknowledged her presence, concentrating on the figures, reworking the totals, double-checking his calculations. Amber drew up a chair and watched him, observing the way the lamplight played on his face, accentuating the lean jaw and smooth cheekbones, noting the lock of fair hair that fell forward over his brow. She clasped her hands around her glass lest she should be tempted to reach out and sweep it back....

'There. I think you will find it is in order now. That was the error there, do you see?'

Obediently she leaned closer, trying to concentrate on the changes he had made, while her brain wanted only to think about the way his skin smelled of warm tangy spices.

'Ah, yes,' she managed. 'Such a simple error.'

'And from what I know of you, Mrs Hall, quite out of character.'

She looked up quickly to find his eyes resting upon her.

'Y-yes,' she stammered. 'That was very careless of me.'

She knew she should not look at him again but somehow she could not resist. He held her gaze while every nerve shrieked at the danger of their situation, alone together in the dead of night. She swallowed.

'Thank you. You have been very helpful.'

'It was my pleasure.' His voice was soft, smooth—a contrast to the tumult she felt inside. 'Is there anything else I can do for you?'

'Wh-what? Oh, no.'

Oh, yes, sighed the demon on her shoulder.

Amber tried her best to appear at ease while Adam sipped his wine, watching her over the rim of the glass. Silence, taut as a bowstring, stretched around them. Abruptly she rose. She must end this, now.

'Well, then. If you have finished your wine I will show you out. The, um, the night air is cold. You will not want to leave your horse standing too long.'

'No.' He tipped back his head and emptied the glass. 'You are right, I should go.' His lips curved upwards. 'At least the books are balanced, ready for the morrow.'

Dragging up all her reserves she smiled back at him.

'Thank you. I shall sleep easily now.' She marvelled at how glibly the lie slid from her tongue. She doubted she would sleep at all, after his visit!

He did not reply but rose and donned his coat in silence. No innuendo or knowing looks. The perfect gentleman. Amber crossed her arms and hugged herself. What did she know of such matters? Her husband had called himself a gentleman, but his behaviour had been cruel and boorish. Adam's birth was at best a mystery, but he was much the better man. If only…

'I will wish you goodnight, then, Mrs Hall.'

He was at the door. Amber knew that one word would bring him back, but fear and blind panic kept her silent. To surrender to him again would be to lose everything, her name, her business… her heart.

Adam touched his hat and let himself out into the night. As he walked away he heard the bolts slide into place behind him. It was for the best. He wanted to sever his ties with Castonbury, not strengthen them, but every meeting with Amber Hall threatened to undermine his resolution.

He grinned to himself as he untied Bosun and scrambled up into the saddle. It was fortunate that Amber had not questioned him too closely on why he was in the village at that time of night. He had no good excuse to offer; in fact, it was quite idiotic. It was a clear night, and he had wanted to ride along the street where she lived.

Trade at Ripley and Hall was brisk. No suspicious characters loitered around the shop, and there were no more attacks upon the wagon. The local carriers were still wary, but Amber hoped that she would soon be able to persuade them to take her goods again. She began to feel more confident, as she had done before Matthew Parwich set up his business in Hatherton. Amber knew this was in no small measure due to Adam. His hard work and his ideas were all beneficial to her business, but she dare not tell him so, she dare not give him any hint of how much she was beginning to depend upon him. The attraction between them was too strong—she was drawn to him like a moth to a flame. And to get too close would spell disaster; it could result again in that lack of control that frightened her so. Therefore she kept her distance, but it did not stop her from thinking about him.

Adam Stratton certainly took far too much of her attention. She found that even when she was alone in the shop, poring over her accounts, her thoughts would wander back to him, remembering him in this very chair, the lamplight gilding his skin and his hair as he set her accounts in order. She was engaged in just such an unprofitable daydream when the shop bell tinkled and she reluctantly left her desk to attend to the customer. Her customary smile disappeared when she saw Matthew Parwich walk in. She gave him no greeting, merely waited for him to speak. He was in no hurry to break the silence and looked about him.

At last she said impatiently, 'Well, what do you want this time?'

He gave the complacent smile that never failed to irritate her.

'I am merely here to remind you of my offer.'

He casually lifted his cane and ran it across the ribbons hanging in the window. They shimmered in the light.

'Then you should leave now.' Amber was curt. 'I have already told you I do not intend to sell.'

'Are you sure?' His tone was smooth, but it held all the menace of a snake. 'You would be well advised to reconsider, Mrs Hall, while your business is in such a good state.'

'Are you threatening me, Mr Parwich?'

His unpleasant smile widened.

'Just advising you that circumstances can change, Mrs Hall. Customers can be very fickle, especially if you cannot supply what they want, and at a price they like.'

Her lip curled.

'If my customers wish to travel to Hatherton to buy goods more cheaply from you I cannot stop them, but admit it, you are losing money on those sales.'

He shrugged. 'I look upon it as an investment for the future.'

'I have no intention of giving in to you. My warehouse is full, despite your best efforts.'

He approached the counter. 'Oh, those were not my *best* efforts, I assure you.'

'Your threats do not frighten me,' she said coldly, reaching for the new bell-pull. 'Now I think you should—'

His hand shot out and grabbed her wrist.

'Oh, no, I do not think we want to call your guard dog just yet.'

'Let go of me!' She struggled to free herself, but he tightened his grip, his fingers biting into her skin.

'You think you have nothing to fear, with that new man of yours working here, but I have been making enquiries, my dear. Stratton is tolerated here, but Castonbury is a small place—he can never escape the slur on his parentage. It is no wonder that he does not want to remain here, where everyone knows about his birth. And when he leaves…' He gave a soft laugh and released her. 'I am a patient man, Mrs Hall,' he said, walking to the door. 'I can wait a little longer to buy your business. But I would advise you to consider my offer very carefully, while you still have a business to sell.'

He went out. For a long time Amber did not move. She leaned against the counter, rubbing her wrist. Her first reaction was to find Adam, to tell him what had happened, but that was exactly what she must not do. Matthew Parwich was right; Adam would be gone soon. She must find a way to deal with this herself.

The problem nagged at Amber until at last she

called Fred to mind the shop and she went off to see Mrs Crutchley. If anyone was looking for work, the butcher's wife would know of it.

'So you want a man to work in your warehouse.' Mrs Crutchley led her into her cluttered sitting room. 'I thought you were satisfied with Hannah Stratton's son.'

'I am,' replied Amber, trying not to blush. 'But he will be returning to Rossendale soon and I would like to take on another man and train him up, so that when Ad—when Mr Stratton leaves, we will not feel his loss.'

She was not being quite truthful there, thought Amber ruefully. She would miss Adam dreadfully, when the time came for him to leave.

'Well, there's no one lookin' for work that I've heard of.' Mrs Crutchley rubbed her chin. 'Mayhap one of the boys from the foundling school would suit.' She chuckled as Amber shook her head at that. 'No, you'd be looking for a man to fill Adam Stratton's shoes, would you not?'

'That is correct.' Amber gave her a wry smile. 'I want someone strong enough to move the rolls of cloth on and off the shelves, but I would also like him to be able to read and write. More than merely his name.'

'Well, I know of no one like that at the present time, Mrs Hall, but I will keep my ears open, and I am off to the Rothermere Arms later, so I will put the word out there too. But I have to say, madam, finding someone to take Mr Stratton's place will not be easy. He is such a fine young man, notwithstanding that he is a...well, notwithstanding his birth.'

'But that is only a rumour, surely,' said Amber, hating herself for prying. She remembered hearing the whispers when she was a child, but had paid them no heed. Adam had been the hero of her childhood and, in fact, the idea of him being the duke's son had only added to his attraction. That, of course, was when she was very young, and before he had disappeared from her life.

Mrs Crutchley folded her arms across her ample bosom.

'Well, the young man left Castonbury to go to sea nigh on twenty years ago, so no one talks of it now—not that anyone ever did say too much, out of respect for his mother. Hannah Stratton is a fine, upstanding woman, but it was always a mystery about her husband. Came to Castonbury Park as a widow, she did, but she's never spoken of her late husband—' she lowered her voice, although they were quite alone in the room '—and to my knowledge no one's ever seen any evidence that she was married. It was the present duke who brought her here, when his father was alive. Very unusual to take in a new servant with a babe in arms. That caused quite a stir, I can tell you. And of course the rumours started to fly from the minute she set foot in the great house. She never let it upset her though, and brought her son up just as she ought.'

'Oh, poor boy,' exclaimed Amber involuntarily. 'To have to grow up, never knowing your father.'

'Aye, but he's had more advantages than most,' said Mrs Crutchley. 'A good education and a comfortable home. That's more than many boys have, even those with two parents. And he's turned out very well indeed, despite it all. He'll make some young woman a fine husband.'

Mrs Crutchley's eye held a knowing gleam and Amber decided it was time to take her leave. She said all that was proper and set off back to the warehouse.

Adam's birth made no difference to the way she thought of him, except that perhaps it explained why he had not settled in Castonbury. She sighed. Mrs Crutchley was right, he would not be easy to replace, but Amber was well aware that he would not stay for ever, and Matthew Parwich's visit that morning had shown her that she needed *someone* at the warehouse.

At that moment the object of her thoughts appeared in the street before her. For a heart-stopping moment Amber wondered if he had been looking for her, but a moment's reflection told her that he had stepped out of the side lane that led to Mr Leitman's cottage.

Adam stopped and waited for her.

'Fred had a length of cloth to be delivered to Mr Leitman,' he said as she came up. He indicated the package beneath his arm. 'He has finished my new coat, so I have brought it away with me.' He fell into step beside her. 'I shall keep it for best though.'

'But I thought you had sent for your own clothes.'

'I did, but none of them are suitable for Castonbury.'

Amber was silent. From what he had told her, and his confident manner, she had thought him in possession of a comfortable living. Now she wondered if she was wrong. Perhaps he was a journeyman spinner, or a weaver. Perhaps the house he had bought for Hannah was no more than a tiny cottage. When she had asked him about his life he was very elusive. It was frustrating to think how little she knew of him.

'You are very pensive, Mrs Hall.'

She started out of her reverie.

'I was thinking about the warehouse. It is becoming apparent that I need more help there… more permanent help.' She flicked a shy glance up at him. 'I wondered if you might consider staying on.'

'Alas that is not possible.'

'I could increase your wages.'

He shook his head.

'I am flattered that you want me to stay, madam, but my life is not in Castonbury now.'

She dared to ask. 'Because of…the past?'

His brows snapped together.

'Why the devil should you think that?'

She felt the blush staining her cheeks but she had gone too far to stop now.

'The—the rumours. That the duke is…might be…'

'That I am his bastard?' She winced and her eyes fell before his frown. 'If it is so, it has never worried me.'

She hung her head.

'I beg your pardon. I should not have spoken.'

The silence hung between them. Amber wished she could think of something to alleviate the tension. Then, at last, Adam exhaled, the breath almost whistling through his teeth.

'No, you are right. It *did* worry me, when I was younger. That was why I was so eager to prove myself in the navy. I volunteered for all the most dangerous missions, took out a ship that was barely seaworthy filled with a crew of scurvy knaves, but I survived. Nay, I prospered. But when I decided to give it all up I knew I could not return here. I wanted to make a fresh start somewhere else, where no one knew me.'

'So you chose Rossendale.'

'Yes. It proved to be a good choice. My life is there now.'

So there was no possibility of his staying to work for her. Perhaps it was for the best. She could not believe that he would be content to take orders from her for the rest of his life. And if he should stay, how long would she be able to resist the attraction she felt for him?

No, despite the threat from Matthew Parwich, having Adam around was more likely to be her downfall than her salvation.

Chapter Seven

Adam worked hard every day, returning to Castonbury Park each evening in time to join his mother for a late dinner. His new coat from Mr Leitman was sufficiently fine for him to wear on these occasions, and it amused him to wear the jacket Amber had mended for him as his working coat. It was not what he had planned, but the clothes his valet had sent on to him were far too good for a warehouseman. He grinned to himself when he pulled out the watered-silk waistcoat and embroidered frock coat. He had asked Cardew to send him only his plain, working clothes, but it seemed the valet had his own ideas about what was considered everyday wear for his master. Consequently, the velvet coats, satin breeches and ornately clocked stockings remained untouched in the trunk.

He was glad the days were lengthening, for it meant that he could walk to the great house, and return before it was completely dark. His path took him within sight of the Dower House, and occasionally as he walked across to his dinner he observed Lady Hatherton wandering in the gardens. She was gone by the time he returned, although occasionally in the dusk he caught a glimpse of her manservant out of doors.

It gave him no little satisfaction to see that his efforts at the warehouse were making a difference to the business. Fred was a good worker, but it was impossible for him to take in all the deliveries of cloth, fulfil the orders and keep the warehouse shipshape. Jacob did what he could but his age was against him, and since he could barely read or write he was unable to mind the shop. It did not take Adam long to master how the warehouse was run and to suggest to Fred ways of improving efficiency.

He had to go carefully, for he was aware of an underlying animosity, as if Fred was afraid Adam intended to steal his position. There had been much the same rivalry between the younger officers on board ship, and when Adam was captain he had done his best to treat his subordinates fairly, promoting on merit, rewarding often and punishing only when necessary. Such tactics had served him well, and he had continued to use them with his mill workers. The first mill Adam had bought had spun wool, but since then he had purchased a linen mill and most recently he had built his own factory to break into the lucrative cotton trade.

He was interested now to see the end product and how it was used, storing up ideas for ways to expand his own business when he returned to Rossendale, as he must do in a few more weeks. He was in touch with his mill managers by letter, and although he prided himself that he had trained his officers well and was confident that they were as competent as he at running the manufactories, he knew the situation could not go on indefinitely. He mentioned the fact to his mother when he escorted her into church one Sunday.

'I have been here for three weeks, now, and must start thinking of going back.' He spoke gently, knowing that she would be disappointed. He saw the dismay in her face as she turned to him. They had arrived separately at St Mary's, his mother travelling to the village in one of the carriages that the duke insisted should be put at the disposal of his senior staff, while Adam rode alongside on Bosun, and it was as he was walking with her to the church door that he made this remark.

'Must you go yet?' She put her hand on his arm. 'I was hoping that you would stay for Lord Giles's wedding.'

'Whenever that is to be.' Adam smiled. 'The date has not yet been set. I shall return for it, of course,' he replied, 'but I have my own affairs to attend to in Rossendale.'

'Yes, of course, but I thought, now you are working for Ripley and Hall…'

'That was only ever a temporary arrangement, Mother.' He paused. There had been no incidents since he had started work there, but perhaps before he left he would make sure that Amber had a replacement warehouseman, even if he had to hire someone suitable himself. His mother spoke again, pulling him out of his reverie.

'Then I suppose I must let you go.'

He heard the sigh in her voice and squeezed her hand.

'It will not be for long, Mother. You will soon be coming to live with me.'

'And I am looking forward to it.' She smiled. 'I

am not getting any younger, and I admit it would be pleasant not to have to work so hard.'

'You shall not work at all when you come to Rossendale unless you wish it,' he assured her. A movement on the road caught his eye and he looked up. 'Who are those men, Mother, on the roadside?'

'Do you mean Sir Nathan Samuelson? He owns Grantby Manor.'

'And the other man, the one with red hair?'

Hannah frowned.

'I *think* his name is Webster. He works for Sir Nathan but he has not been in the area very long.' She glanced up and observed his pensive frown. 'Is anything wrong?'

'I am not sure,' he answered slowly. 'I thought I had seen him recently at the Dower House.'

'I did not know you had called there.'

'I haven't, but there has been a man in the grounds on a couple of occasions, when I have been going home from the great house.'

'After dinner? But it is growing dark by then. If you saw anyone it will have been Foster.'

Adam shook his head.

'I know Foster, he was at the great house when I was a boy, so he must be sixty if he's a day.

This man was younger. I'd swear it was that fellow. There is something about his walk, the way he carries himself.' He shrugged. 'It is of no moment, except that it would not look well for the lady living at the Dower House to be receiving such a caller, late at night. I should mention it to Giles, perhaps.'

'I would rather you did not,' his mother said quickly. 'At least, not until you are sure. There could be a perfectly reasonable explanation, and a lady's reputation is at stake.'

Her anxious look persuaded him and he nodded, smiling.

'Very well, I shall say nothing until I am sure.'

He was still smiling as he looked up to see Amber Hall standing on the far side of the churchyard. His first thought was how charming she appeared in her high-crowned bonnet with her dusky curls peeping out. She looked away immediately and hurried into the church, the skirts of her rose-green walking dress billowing out behind her. His stomach clenched, as it always did at the sight of her. Perhaps he should bring forward his departure, for no matter how often he saw the woman the tug of desire did not lessen, and it was doing him no good at all.

He was in complete accord with Amber that they should keep apart. After all, he would be leaving Castonbury soon and no more than she did he want to become embroiled in a passionate affair. He supposed he would have to marry one day, but his future wife would be a comfortable, biddable sort of woman, not an independent virago with a will of iron. He recoiled from the idea. What was he doing, even thinking about marriage? Amber Hall had made it quite plain to him that nothing was further from her mind.

Amber might be his employer but they rarely spoke; in fact, she deliberately avoided him. This, of course, was exactly what he wanted. She directed all her instructions to him through Fred, but nevertheless the warehouse was alive with her presence. He could smell her perfume in the air and occasionally he would hear her singing in some distant part of the building.

She was a siren, a seductress who had tempted him once and now he could not forget her. He looked up at the church looming ahead of him and tried to be charitable. In his youth he had used women in the same way Amber had used him—a night of passion that they had both enjoyed before going their separate ways. All he could say in his defence was that they had all been women of the world; he had never taken advantage of any innocent young lady. If any of those former lovers had suffered the same aching regret that he now felt, then he was truly sorry for it. Shaking off such lowering thoughts he escorted his mother into the church.

It was many years since he had attended a service at St Mary's, but he remembered coming here with his mother as a child. One memory in particular was very clear: in the biting cold of each New Year they would make the journey to the little church with a small posy of winter evergreens and Christmas roses. They would leave the posy on the small shelf beneath the white marble memorial on the south wall. He had been too young to read the inscription at first, but later, he realised it was a memorial to a Captain Soames, who had perished at sea.

Looking back, he wondered if his mother had thought of it as some sort of peace offering to the gods, asking them to protect him when he eventually became a sailor. He glanced down at his mother and his heart swelled with affection. She had worked so hard for him, given him so much. The memories continued. He was eight years old, standing beside her once again as the short winter's day drew to a close.

'Who was this man, Mother?' He tugged at her sleeve. 'Was he a great sailor?'

'Yes, my love. A very great man. Not only was he very brave and very honourable, but he was kind, too, and generous to those less fortunate than himself.'

'Then I want to be just such a man, when I grow up.'

She had knelt then, so that her face was level with his.

'I can think of nothing that would make me more proud of you, my son.'

And he remembered seeing the glint of tears in her eyes.

'Well, my dear, what did you think of that?' Hannah said, as she left the church on Adam's arm. 'Reverend Seagrove's sermons are always so uplifting, I find.'

Adam's response was non-committal. He had not attended to the vicar's sermon. Amber had been sitting some little way in front of him, and he had spent most of the service trying not to stare at her while all the time thinking about her beautifully straight back, her slender neck and how elegant her long fingers looked, encased in their soft kid gloves. Occasionally she turned her head a little, and he caught a glimpse of her profile, the straight little nose, the soft plumpness of her lips and that determined little chin, that always seemed to be raised challengingly whenever she confronted him. Yet there had been no challenge in her eyes the night they had lain together under the stars, only desire.

'Reverend Seagrove, do you remember my son, Adam?'

He was obliged to drag his thoughts back to the present. The Reverend Seagrove welcomed him warmly and introduced him to his daughter, Lily. Adam said everything that was proper, but was all the time aware of Amber, who had preceded him out of the church and was now standing a short distance away, talking to a thick-set gentleman with ruddy cheeks and bushy side-whiskers. Adam recognised him as Sir Nathan Samuelson. There was something in the way he hovered around Amber that set Adam's teeth on edge. He turned away, prepared to escort his mother back to the carriage, but she touched his arm.

'My dear, poor Amber Hall has been cornered by Sir Nathan. Do let us go and rescue her.'

Adam's jaw tightened.

'Perhaps she enjoys being...cornered.'

'No, no, my dear, no one could enjoy that man's attentions! Poor girl, she looks positively harassed. Come along.'

He could do nothing but follow his mother, who routed Sir Nathan with such tact that he ambled off quite happily in search of another quarry.

'There.' Hannah smiled at Amber. 'You can be comfortable again now, my dear.'

Amber was far too conscious of Adam standing beside his mother to do more than murmur her thanks.

Hannah chuckled and patted her arm. 'That man cannot resist a pretty face.'

'Yes, he is tiresome, but he means no harm, I think.' Amber's glance flickered towards Adam. 'Mr Stratton.'

He touched his hat.

'Mrs Hall.'

'Adam tells me he has been helping you at the warehouse,' Hannah continued, blissfully unconscious of the constraint between her two companions.

'Yes.' Amber eyed him warily, unsure just what he had told his mother. 'He—he is a great asset.'

They were walking towards the road, where the Castonbury coaches were waiting to take the family and servants back to the Park, when Hannah stopped.

'Oh, dear, Sir Nathan is standing by the lych gate. I am sure he is waiting to waylay you again, Amber dear.' She put her hand on Adam's arm. 'My love, there really is no need for you to ride alongside the carriage. Perhaps, instead, you would escort Mrs Hall to her home?'

'Oh, no, no, I could not take him away from you, Mrs Stratton. It is your one day together....'

'Nonsense, my dear, when I get back I shall be busy for at least an hour, organising everyone for dinner. Let Adam take you home. He may leave his horse safely tethered here for a little longer.'

Amber looked around her. There was no one she could call on. If she refused Mrs Stratton's offer, then she would surely fall into the clutches of Sir Nathan. She thought wildly that even that would be preferable to having Adam as her escort, but the smiling concern on Mrs Stratton's face told her that such a refusal would offend. A quick glance at Adam told her nothing at all.

'There, then that is settled.' Hannah stepped back. 'You need not hand me into the carriage, Adam. I shall wait here for Mr Lumsden and pass the time of day with any of my acquaintances who come by—Mrs Crutchley, for example, is approaching and she always enjoys a good gossip. But, Amber my dear, you will not want to be delayed. The woman can talk the hind leg off a donkey, as the saying goes. So, Adam, you had best be on your way now.'

Thus dismissed there was nothing for Amber to do but to put her fingers into the crook of Adam's arm and accompany him away from the church. Amber wanted to break the uncomfortable silence, and searched for something to say. It was strange, this man had worked for her for more than two weeks now, and she knew little more than he had told her on that first night, when they had shared confidences and so much more. She quickly dragged her thoughts away from the memory.

'I am sorry to take you out of your way, sir.'

'It is nothing.'

So cold, so distant. She tried again.

'How are the preparations progressing for the wedding? Life at the Park must be very busy now.'

'I believe it is.'

His brevity angered her.

'Come, Mr Stratton, I am sure we can do better than this. We must observe the distinction between us during the working day, but I think we can be a little less formal here.'

'I do not think so. I experienced your…informality, madam, the first time we met.'

She stopped.

'You think I meant—' She tore her hand free from his arm. 'Oh, how dare you!'

Amber turned on her heel and marched on.

'How dare *I*?' he demanded, catching up with her. '*You* were the one who acted like a stranger once we reached Castonbury.'

'And just what did you expect me to do? If word of that night got out—'

'Oh, of course. You have your reputation to consider.'

'I have my *business* to consider!' she flashed.

They had arrived at the warehouse. Amber knew that Maizie would not be at home so she strode through the yard to let herself in by the warehouse door. She ignored Adam, hoping he would go away now that he had done his duty.

But he was determined to pursue her. She heard his angry voice at her shoulder.

'Oh, your business—your business. That is all you care about.'

'As a matter of fact it is!'

Amber reached into her reticule for her key. She was shaking with anger, so much so that she could not fit it into the lock. Adam took it from her and opened the door.

'So what do you propose,' he demanded, following her into the building and slamming the door. 'During the day I call you "ma'am" and tug my forelock, and you will summon me back to join you in your bed whenever the mood takes you?'

'Get out!' She rested her hands on the desk to support herself. The shock of her anger had made her knees weak. He ignored her.

'If you want that sort of man I suggest you advertise,' he snarled.

'How dare you speak to me like that?' she raged, turning to face him. 'You are no gentleman.'

She could almost feel the anger sparking between their furious glances. His lip curled.

'Gentleman? Hah, what would you know about gentlemen? Your actions are not those of a lady, Mrs Hall, they are those of a—'

He never finished the sentence. She brought her hand up and slapped him so hard and so fast that his head snapped back. She was still trembling, only the desk behind her preventing her from collapsing to the floor. His slow smile mocked her and in a rage she brought her hand up again, but this time he was too quick and grabbed her wrist. Instantly she raised her left hand, only to have that, too, caught in an iron grip. He twisted her hands behind her back. She was imprisoned, her breasts pressed against his coat. She glared up at him.

'Let me go, you devil!'

His eyes narrowed.

'Devil, is it? Then let me show you how a devil behaves.'

Before she could turn away he swept down upon her, capturing her mouth with his own. It was hot, demanding, and it robbed her of any coherent thought. For a brief moment she was paralyzed by shock, but then she reacted violently, not to fight against him, but to return his kiss, matching his savagery with her own. He released her wrists and she grabbed his collar, holding him close. They collapsed back onto the desk, his weight pinning her down as he began to kiss her face, her eyes.

The muslin fichu around her neck was discarded and he placed his lips on her throat. She drove her hands through his hair, pulling him closer, moaning a little when he began to nibble at her ear. His hands were roaming over her body, exploring the contours through the layers of clothing. Impatiently she scrabbled with his neck cloth, wanting to rip open his shirt, to satisfy the desire that was overwhelming her.

'Heavens you are like to choke me,' he growled, deftly undoing the knotted muslin with one hand. He raised himself and she could barely suppress a whimper as he moved away from her. 'Let us continue this somewhere more private.'

Without ceremony he picked her up and carried her towards the inner door. She clung to him, nuzzling into his neck and alternately kissing and nipping the skin. His arms tightened as he almost ran up the stairs, hesitating at the top. Amber pointed to her bedroom door.

'In there.'

It was the work of a moment to push through it and he dropped her none too gently on the bed, quickly covering her with his own body as she reached up to pull his face down to hers. Their kisses grew ever more urgent; his tongue plunged into her and her body melted beneath him. She lay pliant, almost swooning, as he released the buttons running down the front of her walking dress. He struggled with the strings of her skirt and she roused herself sufficiently to help him. They scrabbled out of their clothes while exchanging hot smouldering looks that fired the blood. Coat, waistcoat, skirts, petticoats, chemise, stockings—their clothes were discarded and thrown off to litter the floor until they were both stripped bare. Only then did they pause.

Amber lay back on the bed, her heart thudding against her ribs and her eyes fixed upon Adam. The hot desire in his eyes inflamed her as much as the sight of his aroused, naked body kneeling over her. She reached out to touch his chest. It was smooth and hard, the muscles quivering to life beneath her roving fingers. She saw a shadow of uncertainty cross his face.

'I cannot—Amber, I will not do this if you are not sure.'

Her spirit was flying. She felt all-powerful and she reached out for him, drawing him down on top of her, feeling the heat of their bodies combining.

'I *am* sure. More so than anything else I have ever done,' she murmured, before kissing him with all the passion that was within her.

They explored, worshipped, caressed each other with hands, mouths and tongues, driving each other to the brink of ecstasy again and again. Amber had experienced nothing like it before. She had only her instincts to guide her, and Adam's reactions to her touch. When he groaned with pleasure her own excitement grew, until he pushed her hands aside and subjected her body to such intimate and detailed attentions that she writhed beneath him, crying out she knew not what.

At last, when she thought she could bear nothing more, he moved back on top and entered her. He clasped her buttocks, holding her firm while he caressed her, his movements slow and rhythmic, gradually increasing her pleasure until she was bucking and thrashing. Still he held on, stroking, caressing, the intensity of feeling mounting steadily. She dug her nails into his shoulders as he carried her even higher until she was gasping, almost sobbing with the pleasure of it. She heard him cry out, felt him tense as he took her over the edge into a shattering, shuddering, explosive climax and she felt as if she was falling in a million little pieces.

Amber lay with her eyes closed, listening to the steady tick-tick of the clock on the mantelpiece. This was not a dream. She could feel the warm length of his body against her skin. All through the protracted church service she had been aware of him, felt his eyes on her back; her body had ached with the tug of attraction. She had resolved not to give in to it, to ignore him. If only his mother had not insisted that Adam should see her home.

No, she must not blame Hannah for her own weakness. Nor would she blame Adam. He moved against her now, wrapping his long limbs around her curled back, one hand cupping her breast. Immediately her body responded, leaning into him, delighting in his presence.

'Where is Maizie?'

He whispered the words even as he nibbled her ear. Amber almost purred with pleasure.

'She goes to visit her mother on a Sunday.'

'If she had been here, do you think it would have stopped this?'

'Yes—no. I doubt it.'

'Ah, so you do not deny the attraction between us?'

He murmured the words between the butterfly kisses he laid across her shoulder.

She sighed as the little darts of pleasure shot through her.

'I have never denied it,' she murmured, 'but I cannot allow it.'

The kisses stopped.

'You just did.'

'I know, and I am very sorry for it.'

'I am not.' His hand cupped her shoulder. 'Amber, there is no reason to keep me at bay.'

She pulled away from him and sat up.

'You will be leaving soon, to return to your home.'

'You might come with me.'

'No. My home, my living, is here. It could never work.'

'You make it sound as if I lived in the Americas, rather than a mere fifty miles away.' He trailed his fingers down her spine and she arched her back, fighting the urge to lie down with him again. He continued, 'I am a single man, you are a widow. I see no reason why we should not—'

'It cannot be.' She turned to him, trying to stretch her mouth into a smile, but failing miserably.

'Then you must tell me why.'

He put his hand on her hip. It was the lightest

touch, but it effectively anchored her to the spot. She gave a little shake of her head. They hardly knew each other. How could she explain? His grip tightened a fraction. He said softly, 'I think you owe me that much.'

'Because, when I am with you, I cannot help myself.'

He grinned.

'I do not see that as a problem.'

'But it is.' Amber got up and scooped her wrap from the back of a chair. It would be easier to explain if she was not naked. She turned back to see that he was watching her, stretched out on the bed, his head propped on one hand and the sheet draped over his lower limbs like some Greek sculpture. She turned away from the distracting image. 'Whatever my resolve, it crumbles when you are near. You only have to touch me...' Her hands twisted together as she forced out the confession. 'I have never felt like this before. I have never, willingly, been so much in anyone's power. I am quite, quite *helpless* when I am with you. I cannot help myself. It frightens me, to be so weak, so lacking in control.'

There, she had said it. She put her hands to her cheeks. Would he gloat now he knew his power over her? She did not turn when she heard the bed creak and the soft pad of his footsteps on the bare boards.

'Does it help to know that it is the same with me?' He was standing so close she could feel his breath on her cheek. 'I have never felt like this about any woman before. When I am near you I want only to touch you, and when I do, I am lost. You are my mistress in the truest sense of the word. You have enslaved me.' He put his hands on her shoulders and turned her to face him. 'If we feel like this about each other, then we should not ignore it. Marry me, Amber.'

Adam caught his breath at the enormity of what he was doing. It had been his intention to carry his mother away from Castonbury and sever all ties with the village. To return to his new life in Rossendale, where no one knew his past. He had always expected to find a bride from amongst the manufacturing families in Lancashire. A meek, biddable wife who knew her place, not a strong, independent woman like Amber Hall, who would doubtless challenge his authority at every turn. But the words were out, spoken with no consideration for all the plans he had made, plans based on logic and reason, as befitted a man of the Enlightenment. Yes, the words were out and he was surprised to realise just how much he meant them.

Amber turned to look up at him, searching his face. An offer of marriage, was he teasing her? His eyes were perfectly serious.

'I…cannot.'

'Cannot?' He raised his brows. 'I think after what has just occurred it is almost obligatory.'

His gentle teasing brought tears very close. She struggled to speak.

'I cannot give up all this. My life, my business. If I marry, then all I have worked so hard to build up will be lost to me.'

'I do not covet Ripley and Hall, Amber, believe me. I told you, I have my own business. I would leave you to run this one—'

She shook her head.

'It is the law, Adam, we both know that. When a woman marries she becomes a chattel, her husband's possession. To be loved, possibly. Or ignored, or beaten…' She added quickly, 'I am not saying that is how you would act, but if I marry you I lose all rights to my business, my money… my life even.'

She turned to him, willing him to understand. 'I have been my own mistress for years, Adam. I have fought hard to be a person in my own right. It has taken a long time for people to accept that *my* handshake will seal a bargain, that they can do business with *me*, and not with my husband or my father. Why, even now, I have heard you talking to Fred in the warehouse, and he is much more willing to accept advice from you than from me. If I married you, everything would change. People would look to you for decisions. I would once more be a mere adjunct.'

'I do not think that is very likely, my dear. You are far too successful at your business to be over-shadowed by me.'

She shook her head. 'I am not ready to let it all go, to give up everything to my husband.'

She paused. And what of love? The word had not been used by either of them. Love was the warm, comfortable affection her parents had shared. It was not the desperate infatuation her father had felt for his mistress, just months after her mother's death. Nor was it the lascivious fumblings Bernard had inflicted upon her. Was what she felt for Adam—what he felt for her—so very different from either of those? How could she be sure? She added, 'Besides, we know so little of each other.'

'That would change, given time.'

Time. With Adam living in Rossendale, more than fifty miles away. What time could they have together, how would they get to know each other, to love each other?

Adam took her hands. 'I must leave here soon, but that does not mean we cannot write, and I will come back, just as soon as I can. Pray say you will consider my proposal. We will draw up a contract. Ripley and Hall can remain under your control. We would need someone to run it, of course. Fred, perhaps.

'We come to this as equals, Amber. Well, what say you?' He took her chin in his hand and forced her to look at him.

She searched his face. His blue eyes had never looked more serious, but there was something else, a hint of uncertainty that she longed to kiss away.

'Equals.' She felt a smile welling up. 'I like the idea of that. I will think about it.'

'Good. Then let us waste no more time arguing.' He bent his head to kiss her and immediately the flame of desire leapt up again, stronger than ever. He tugged open the ties of her wrap. 'What time does Maizie return?'

Her arms slipped around his neck, murmuring her words against his skin.

'Not until supper.'

'Then we need not get dressed just yet....'

Adam rode back to the lodge an hour later with an unaccustomed lightness to his spirits. His head was full of images: Amber beneath him, her eyes dark and lustrous, Amber laughing in delight at something he had said, making him feel like the wittiest being in the world, Amber sleeping beside him, her hair tumbled over the pillow like a billowing dark cloud.

She completed him. He laughed aloud as the phrase came into his head. How odd. He had never noticed the lack, but having met Amber, it was as if he had found another part of himself. She had said she would consider his proposal, and when he thought of the passion they shared, the enjoyment they found in each other, how could she not accept? He left Bosun at the keeper's lodge and set off on foot for the great house, glad to make use of the restless energy that consumed him.

'So, Captain, you are leaving us soon.'

Hannah had invited Lumsden to join them for

dinner in her sitting room, a rare honour, but one that precluded Adam from discussing his thoughts about Amber Hall with his mother.

'I have business in Lancashire that requires my attention, yes,' he said. 'I must be gone within the week.'

'But you will come back for Lord Giles's wedding,' said his mother.

'Perhaps sooner.'

Adam smiled. What had happened with Amber Hall had changed all his carefully constructed plans. It seemed Castonbury would not let him go quite so easily. He would go back to Rossendale, make what arrangements were necessary, then return to the village to continue wooing Amber. For the first time he was impatient for the evening to end, so that he could be alone to think about his future.

By the time he left the dining table Adam had made a decision. His courtship of Amber Hall would succeed, he was certain of it, and when at last she agreed to marry him he would give her no chance to change her mind. He would obtain a special licence. It would probably take some time so he would write to his man of business tonight and tell him to organise it. Good heavens, he paid the fellow enough, it was about time he earned his fees with something other than contracts and bills of exchange. He strode out of the kitchen wing, already mentally composing his letter and imagining the flutter it would cause amongst his staff in Rossendale. On the path he hesitated, then turned back to the house.

'Good grief, Stratton, can't a man enjoy a solitary drink before retiring?'

Adam grinned as Giles berated him. He had taken the liberty of coming into the house unannounced and he knew that his friend would have been within his rights to send him packing, but when he entered the study, Giles merely unwound his long frame from his chair and lounged over to the side table to pour him a brandy.

'I beg your pardon for disturbing you so late,' said Adam, taking the glass. 'I wanted your advice.'

Lord Giles raised his brows.

'That sounds serious. Perhaps we should sit down.'

Adam shook his head.

'No, no, I will not delay you more than necessary. I have to be abroad early in the morning.'

'So, too, do I,' retorted Giles. 'Out with it, then, man.'

Adam hesitated. Now that the moment was here

he was not sure where to start. In the end he decided to be blunt.

'I am getting married.' He saw the shock in his friend's eyes and his lips twitched. 'Well, perhaps that is not strictly true. I intend to marry, and by special licence. My lawyer will go to London and organise everything, but once it is obtained I need to have it to hand very quickly. I am returning to Rossendale shortly, but will come back here as soon as may be, and to avoid delay I would like to arrange for the licence to be sent here, for your attention.'

'The devil you would,' exclaimed Giles. 'Are you sure the bishop will grant you your licence?'

'I do not see why not.' Adam's eyes narrowed and there was an edge of steel to his voice as he continued. 'So far I have only used my wealth to advance my business. Now I plan to use it for my own comfort. I shall pay whatever is necessary to succeed in this.'

Giles laughed.

'By God, I believe you will. Well done, Adam, 'tis about time you found yourself a mate. By all means have the licence sent here and I will keep it safe for you. May I know the name of the paragon who has captured your heart?'

'For the moment I think I should keep that a secret.' Adam grinned. 'She does not even know of my scheme yet!'

The waxing moon was bright enough for Adam to walk back to the lodge without the need for a lantern and he used the time to indulge himself in thoughts of Amber. She was an independent lady and he thought he understood her fears about marriage. He tried to put himself in her shoes. Would he willingly give up ownership of his mills, his fortune? The answer was no, of course not. It was something else his lawyer must devise, the contract that would allow Amber to retain her own business when they were married. She should see that he was a man of his word. And she should have shares in his mills too. He wanted her as his partner in all things. He would talk to her about it again, but not yet. That could wait until he returned to Castonbury, once his affairs were in order and he had obtained the special licence. Then he would court her relentlessly and put to rout all her arguments. He could wait a week or two.

He was thus pleasantly engaged when he saw the lights of the Dower House in the distance.

There was nothing unusual in that, but his keen eyes caught a figure crossing the light. Someone was in the garden. Adam did not hesitate. He turned off the path and headed towards the Dower House. A low hedge separated the grounds from the parkland and Adam approached it silently. A low murmur of voices was carried across to him on the soft breeze and he drew back into the shadows of a nearby chestnut tree.

The diminutive figure of Alicia, Lady Hatherton, appeared, a shawl wrapped about her shoulders, and walking beside her was a stocky gentleman who was talking to her in a low voice. In the pale light of the half-moon it was impossible to identify the man, but his head was turned towards Alicia and he was gesticulating, as if to make some forceful point. Not a servant, then, Adam concluded. They walked to the front door where they parted, and as the lady entered the house the light from the open door washed over her companion standing on the drive. There was no mistaking the red hair or rather florid features of Hugh Webster.

An odd time of day for a social call, thought Adam, as Webster turned away from the house. The path lay a short distance from where Adam was concealed in the shadows. Webster would pass within yards of him. Adam wondered if he should confront the man, but decided against it. From what he had heard of Lady Alicia this was a delicate matter. He would talk to Giles about it in the morning.

Adam was an early riser, but his visit to the great house the following morning was unproductive. Lumsden informed him that Lord Giles had gone away and was not expected to return until Thursday. He set off at a canter for the village, but even so his detour had cost him time and when he entered the warehouse he found Fred waiting for him, looking pointedly at the clock as Adam walked in.

Adam meekly begged pardon for being late and Fred sent him off to harness the dray horse to the wagon.

'Mrs Hall and I are off to Hatherton to collect a number of deliveries from the coaching office,' Fred told him, when Adam drove the wagon into the yard a short time later. 'You will need to mind the shop while we are gone....'

'Actually, I have decided that Adam can drive me to Hatherton.' Amber came out into the yard, tying the ribbons of her straw bonnet under her chin as she talked.

'But, madam, you said on Saturday—'

'I know, Fred, but I have changed my mind. The landlady from the Rothermere Arms is calling this morning to collect the linens and printed cotton she ordered, and since I cannot be here it would be best for her to deal with someone she knows.' Amber gave him a reassuring smile. 'You know there is no one I would trust more to look after my customers, Fred.'

The young man was very downcast, but he merely nodded and slouched away. Adam was about to jump down to help Amber into the wagon but she waved to him to stay in his seat and she climbed up nimbly beside him, affording him a glimpse of her exceedingly pretty ankle. He looked away. He must keep his mind on business, not on how smooth and neat that same ankle felt beneath his hands. Fred was standing by the gate and the look he threw at Adam was full of resentment.

'I fear he is not happy that I have taken his place today.' Adam guided the wagon carefully out into the street.

Amber glanced back.

'I know, but I wanted an opportunity to talk to you, after yesterday…' There was a delicate flush on her cheeks.

'We were very reckless,' he admitted. 'Do you regret it?'

He felt his spirits lift when she shook her head. 'No, I am glad.'

'So, too, am I,' he said cordially. 'I must go back to Lancashire soon, but when I return, I—'

Amber knew she must stop him.

'No.'

He glanced down, a crease furrowing his brow at the single word. It was an effort to continue, but she knew she had to do it.

'No,' she said again. 'When you return to Lancashire I will never see you again.'

'I thought we agreed—'

'I said I would consider all you had said. And I have. I have decided it will not work.'

The words hung between them. She waited, tensed against an explosion of anger. It never came.

'Would you care to tell me why?'

His quiet words should have made it easier for her, but they did not. Somehow the carefully reasoned arguments she had spent the night rehearsing did not want to be expressed.

'I have told you, when you are near me I am not...in control.'

'And I told you it was the same for me.'

'I know, which makes it all the more imperative that we do not see each other again.' She clasped her hands in her lap. 'I made up my mind long ago that I should never marry again, and...and although I was tempted by your offer yesterday, I cannot accept. My life is here, in Castonbury. My friends—they mean far too much to me. Neither can I be your mistress, Adam. My business would be ruined if word of that got out.'

'Perhaps you think I am not respectable enough for you,' he shot at her.

She blinked. 'I do not know what you mean.'

'You know very well.' She watched the muscles in his jaw working angrily. 'Some say I am the duke's bastard.'

'It makes no difference to me whose son you are!' Amber clutched her fingers together even tighter. 'I hope you will believe that the rumours about your birth had no bearing on my decision that we should part.'

'No? I have seen the sly looks that come my

way. I have no doubt the gossipmongers have commented to you on my presence.'

'If they have you may be sure I gave them short shrift.'

'But having a bastard in your employ is very different from marrying one. In Rossendale no one knows or cares about my birth.'

'Then go and pick a bride for yourself there!'

'That was my intention, until I met you.' He exhaled, a long, weary sigh. 'Forgive me, I did not mean to lose my temper. If you are dead set against marriage with me, then I will not press you further.'

Tears stung her eyelids. She preferred his anger to this sudden calm acceptance. Perhaps he, too, had spent a sleepless night, only in his case he had been regretting his rash proposal, issued in the heat of the moment. Now he could walk away with no ties, no regrets. How perfectly convenient she had made it for him. The cart trundled on in silence.

'Will you tell me why you have decided not to marry again?' he asked at last, not taking his eyes from the road. He added, when she did not speak, 'I would like to know why you are rejecting me.'

'It is not just you. I will not marry any man.'

He laughed, a hard, humourless sound.

'And you have had dozens of offers, I suppose!'

She raised her chin.

'Yours is not the first offer I have received since I have been a widow. Papa hoped that I might marry again, but either I didn't like the gentlemen or the gentlemen did not like the trade. Besides, I wanted to run the business myself.' She felt the memories crowding her and said quietly, 'You have no idea what it is like to be a chattel, sir. A mere bauble to decorate a man's house. I was brought up in this business, I could see what was going wrong but I was not allowed to do anything about it. My ideas were dismissed as foolish nonsense, first by my father, and then by my husband.' A shiver ran through her. Bernard's method of dealing with anything he saw as criticism was brutal, and inflicting bruises and cracked ribs upon her had somehow roused other passions in him. Eventually she had learned to keep her opinions to herself.

Shrugging off the memories she continued. 'I fought hard for the independence I now have, and I vowed I would never surrender it again. After you had gone yesterday—'

'You panicked.'

'I did not!'

'You do not trust me.'

'I think you are sincere when you say we will be equals, but as soon as there is a decision to be made, if our views differ, then you will override my wishes.'

'I suppose it would be useless to remind you that I have suggested ways around this?'

She sighed. 'Yes, it would. Please, Adam. Do not try to persuade me otherwise. We have known each other for only a few weeks, it is better that we end it now.'

'I do not agree, but I will not try to change your mind. Not yet.'

'Not ever,' she corrected him, and found his eyes upon her again, a disquieting glint in his own.

'By the way,' he said, 'I need to give you notice that I will be leaving at the end of the week.'

Her spirits dipped still further, but this was what she wanted, was it not?

'Very well. I will have your wages ready for you on Friday.'

'You are happy for me to continue working until then?'

'Yes. I must set about finding a replacement. It will not be easy.'

'I hope it will be nigh on impossible.'

She turned her head and found herself gazing into his smiling blue eyes. Despite the sadness in her heart she could not prevent herself smiling back at him. If there was anything needed to convince her that he was dangerous to her peace of mind it was the way his smile held her transfixed; the creases around his eyes deepened and his look was a tangible caress. She would never forget, even though she would teach herself to live without it. He took her hand and lifted it to his lips. She felt his kiss through the soft kid of her glove. Another memory to store away.

She realized they were driving into Hatherton and resolutely drew her hand away, hoping Adam's tender gesture had gone unseen, but there were several people on the street, and one man was raising his hat to her. She kept her eyes averted, but she had already recognised the man as Matthew Parwich.

Chapter Eight

Amber's business in Hatherton was soon concluded and when the various packages were loaded onto the wagon they set off again for Castonbury. She had seen nothing more of Matthew Parwich. She suspected it was Adam's presence that had prevented him from approaching her. She was sorry he had seen Adam kiss her hand, but whatever he made of that was not important, since Adam would be gone by the end of the week. The thought of Adam's leaving was a lowering one, but she kept up a cheerful flow of small talk during the return journey. Adam responded in kind, for which she was grateful, and by the time they were back in Castonbury they were once again conversing with some semblance of normality.

'I do not like to think of you without protection when I am gone,' said Adam as they drove along the street towards the warehouse. 'Parwich is likely to increase his bullying tactics when he knows you are alone.'

Amber wondered if he had heard of Parwich's last visit to the shop, but a moment's reflection told her this was impossible. Perhaps she *should* tell him; he might then change his mind about leaving her.

No! Quickly Amber slammed the door shut on the temptation and said stoutly, 'I am not afraid of Matthew Parwich.'

He reached out for her hand.

'But I am afraid for you.'

'You should not be. Sooner or later he will realise I have no intention of selling. Besides, there is business enough for both of us.'

Adam was silent for a moment.

'I do not think Parwich is the sort to compromise over the business,' he said slowly. 'There must be good men, ex-sailors and soldiers, who would not easily be intimidated. Let me find—'

'No, thank you, Adam.' She interrupted him. 'I am quite capable of finding someone.'

'You had not done so when I came along.'

'That is because I was looking for someone local. I will take your advice and advertise wider afield. As you say, a man from the army or navy would suit very well.' She frowned at him. 'Your look says you do not trust me to do this, but I will, Adam. I give you my word I will take on a man to replace you.'

'Will you write out the advertisement today?'

'I will do it as soon as I have a free moment. First I have to sort out all this cloth and organise my deliveries. But it will be done before the end of the week, I promise.'

'Good. In the meantime, let us tell no one I plan to leave. I do not want to give Parwich notice that you will be alone on Monday.'

'Thank you.' Her fingers turned beneath his covering hand and gripped it. 'I shall miss you.'

He turned to grin down at her.

'That is what I am counting on. It is my fervent hope that after a few weeks apart you will admit that you cannot live without me!'

They turned into the yard and Adam ran around to lift Amber down from the wagon. She need not have waited, she could easily climb down unaided, but it was too tempting to be in his arms again, and if he held her a little longer than necessary, and if she returned his smile with one equally tender, what harm could it do? It would be the last time.

'So you are back.'

Fred's tone was uncharacteristically sullen.

'Oh, dear, have you had a hectic day here?' she asked, conscience-stricken. 'We made very good time coming back, and I had hoped the shop would not be too busy today.'

'No, it has been very quiet,' he conceded, following her indoors. 'Miss Seagrove came in to enquire about the material she had ordered, to make coats for the Poor School.'

'We fetched the fustian from Hatherton today so we can fulfil her order. And we collected the shot silk and the velvets, too, as well as the silk trim for Mrs Crutchley's new bed-hangings. If we get everything packed up today you can start to deliver the packages tomorrow. Give me a moment to remove my coat and bonnet and we will set to work.'

A week of hectic activity stretched ahead of them. The order book was consulted, parcels made up and Adam and Fred were kept busy delivering to the nearby households until late into the evening for the next two days. Amber persuaded Adam to take dinner with them at the warehouse, but she made sure they were never alone, and they took formal leave of each other, their fingers barely touching. Amber knew that if she allowed him any closer her resolve to keep him at arm's length would crumble. At least the onset of her monthly cycle was some relief. Twice now she had given herself to Adam and not considered the consequences. Such madness could not be allowed to happen again.

Adam accepted this arrangement and made no attempt to persuade her, which proved to her that either he did not care, or he was truly a gentleman. Whichever of these was the truth, it made her misery even more acute. As for finding someone to take his place, Amber kept putting it off. Somehow she did not want to acknowledge that he was actually leaving her.

Amber welcomed her sleepless nights, for they allowed her to think about Adam, to relive their time together, each look, each soft word, but eventually exhaustion caught up with her. On Thursday morning she woke from an uneasy doze to find she had allowed her morning hot chocolate to grow cold. She summoned Maizie, scolding her for not coming back to wake her.

'You should have come up to see why I had not rung for you to help me dress,' she admonished her sternly.

'Nay, Miss Amber, if you was asleep 'twas 'cos you needed it,' retorted Maizie, not a whit abashed. 'I've seen those dark rings beneath your eyes and although it's not for me to say what's causing 'em I can guess well enough.'

'I am quite sure you cannot,' snapped Amber, scrambling into her gown. 'Pray fetch my shawl for me, I must go downstairs.'

'Not before you've broken your fast,' said Maizie firmly. 'I've set your tray in the sitting room, as usual.'

Adam heard the soft rumble of voices above stairs. Amber had slept late. It was not for him to blame her, although he was impatient for her to come down so that he could see her, watch the way her eyes lit up when she smiled at him, listen to that soft musical note in her voice. It was not what he wanted, of course. If he had his way he would sweep her up into his arms, covering her face in kisses before carrying her back upstairs to spend the morning making love to her. But Amber had decreed that could not be, and much as his instinct cried out against it he would honour her decision, certain—almost certain—that given time she would realise they belonged together.

Just thinking of her made his body harden with desire, and it took a supreme effort to turn his mind back to his work. He moved to the shelf by the door, where the orders they had made up last night were waiting, packaged and labelled, ready to be delivered. Fred was in the shop, so Adam began carrying the parcels to the wagon. It was easy work, but any physical activity was welcome. He heard his name and looked up to see Matthew Parwich standing by the open gate. His carriage was behind him, and two footmen standing to attention, their wigs and lace neck ruffles contrasting ill with their battered faces. They would have looked more comfortable stripped to the waist in a prize fight than waiting upon a cloth merchant. He frowned. They looked vaguely familiar, but before he could put his mind to it Parwich beckoned to him, and Adam moved to the gate.

'A fine morning,' called Parwich, leaning on his Malacca cane.

'Aye,' returned Adam cautiously. 'I'd wager this is no social call.'

'My, but you are a suspicious fellow.' Matthew Parwich smiled, but his eyes held only a cold, calculating look. 'I was in the area and thought I might call upon Mrs Hall.'

'Then you should present your card to her maid, not to me.'

'But you have more influence over the lady, I hear.'

Adam regarded him coldly.

'What is it you want?'

'I would like you to use that influence.' Matthew Parwich pulled a fat purse out of his pocket and held it on his palm. 'Persuade your mistress to sell the business to me.'

Adam's lip curled as he regarded the bag of coins. Bright red leather, as coarse and ostentatious as the man himself.

'Put your Judas purse away, Parwich. I will not touch it.'

'Perhaps you hope to get the business for yourself.'

'Perhaps I do.'

Parwich took a step forward.

'I have nothing against you, Stratton,' he said, putting a hand on Adam's shoulder. 'But I would advise you to distance yourself from Mrs Hall. I mean to have this business, or destroy it.'

Adam knocked his hand aside. 'Be careful, then, that it does not destroy *you.*'

He went back into the yard. Jacob was standing by the wagon.

'What did Parwich want?' he demanded.

'He was just warning me off.'

Jacob grunted and spat on the ground.

'Aye.' Adam nodded with a grim smile. 'My sentiments precisely. Now, let us get this wagon loaded.'

Amber hurried to the sitting room, knowing it would be useless to argue with her handmaiden. She did not sit down, but picked up a piece of bread and butter and carried it to the window, which overlooked the yard. Adam was loading the wagon. She looked down at him. The sun was already at its peak, and it glinted on his head, turning his hair to gold, burnished with a hint of flame-red. Like a breathtaking sunset. He had discarded his jacket, revealing the close-fitting waistcoat that hugged his chest and followed the tapering line of his waist to the narrow hips encased in buckskin. A light breeze fluttered through the full sleeves of his shirt, making his shoulders look impossibly broad.

Her mouth dried and the bread was hard to swallow. How could she let him walk away from her? He had offered her marriage. Was that not what every woman wanted? A sudden draught chilled her and she rubbed her arms. She had tried marriage and vowed never again. The thought of Bernard's brutish behaviour still made her shudder, even after all these years. The beatings and the bullying had left her very wary of all men. Part of her argued that being Adam's wife would be a very different experience, but how could she be sure? The law said a wife was the property of her husband and Bernard had often reminded her of the fact. Was it any wonder she was afraid to commit herself to another marriage, to relinquish her freedom?

Adam had talked of a solution, of giving her control of Ripley and Hall, but could she trust him? Once they were married would he not want to manage her life and her business? She had told him she did not want a husband and she would not consent to be his mistress. What did that leave, a platonic friendship? The thought was almost laughable. They had only to be in the same room for the attraction to be tangible. She suspected even Fred had noticed, although he had said nothing. No, a complete break was the only solution, and the sooner she stopped thinking of Adam Stratton, the better.

Giving up on her breakfast Amber went downstairs. She was too late to speak to Fred, for the wagon pulled out of the yard even as she reached the door. With a nod of greeting to Adam and Jacob she went back inside, determined to lose herself in her work.

She spent the morning rearranging the display of cloth in the shop window, delayed only when Mrs Crutchley walked by and, seeing her thus engaged, dropped in for a chat. She should be grateful, she told herself as she pinned on her smile and listened to all the local gossip. The distraction helped her to keep her resolution not to think about Adam, but it was nearly noon before the butcher's wife finally departed and Amber could finish her work.

Adam heaved the last of the bolts of cloth into place and climbed down the ladder, dusting his hands. He stood beside Jacob, looking up at the high shelves.

'Well, will that do?'

'Aye.' The old man nodded approvingly. 'We'll not be needin' those heavier wools 'til the end o' the summer, when everyone starts thinkin' about their winter coats. That's a good job jobbed. I haven't been able to do that for years now, those heavier rolls is fearsome difficult to handle for someone without your muscle.'

Adam laughed and patted the old man on the back. 'But your knowledge of the stock is equally important, Jacob. I would not know where to find half the cloth here.' He paused a little, judging if it was a good time to make another suggestion. 'I wonder if we should think about putting new labels on the shelves, so even those of us who don't know our moleskin from our twilled cotton might find it easier.'

'Don't you try to gammon me, Adam Stratton,' growled Jacob. 'You knows as much as me about what's on them shelves.' He fixed his rheumy eyes upon Adam. 'If I was a betting man, I'd say you'd been involved in the cloth business afore now.'

'Well, yes,' admitted Adam, 'but until I came here I knew more about the spinning side. I have learned a great deal during my time here.' He broke off as he heard a familiar light tread approaching.

'Jacob, where is the order book?'

Amber appeared in the aisle. She was dressed

soberly in a plain, high-necked grey gown, her glorious hair scraped back, no frivolous curls to distract, but still her beauty shone through, illuminating the shadowed aisles of the warehouse.

'I ain't seen it today, mistress. It should be in the drawer at the back o' the shop, as usual.'

'It is not there.' The faintest line creased her brow and immediately Adam wanted to kiss it away, to carry her off from all these troublesome worries. Those luminous dark eyes turned to him. 'Have you seen it, Adam?'

He dragged his thoughts back from the delightful daydream.

'The order book? No. I used it last night to check all the orders, then it was returned to the drawer.'

She smiled, and fluttered one white hand.

'No matter. I expect in his rush to get out Fred has put it aside somewhere.'

But when Fred returned and was questioned, he looked blank.

'Is it not in the drawer?'

'No, it is not,' declared Amber, hands on her hips. 'We must find it.'

A hunt ensued, Amber setting everyone to look and look again. After an hour they reconvened by the warehouse desk.

'Well?' she demanded.

'We've looked everywhere, missus,' said Jacob.

She tapped her foot impatiently. 'But it must be here. One cannot lose such a large ledger.'

Jacob rubbed his chin.

'I do reckon that villain Parwich has stolen it, he was hanging around the gate this morning.'

Immediately she was alert.

'When was this?'

'When we was loading the wagon, missus. He drew up at the gate in his fancy carriage.'

'What did he want?'

The old man shook his head.

'I dunno. Adam here spoke to 'im.'

'He merely repeated his threats,' said Adam calmly, distracted by the way a few strands of dark hair had escaped and now curled riotously around her face, accentuating her flawless complexion.

'But the shop was locked then,' she murmured, frowning. 'He would have had to come in through here.'

'That he did not do,' Fred assured her. 'I was in here all morning, and Adam and Jacob were filling the wagon. No one could have entered the building without being seen.'

'Well, we have searched everywhere in here,' said Amber.

'Not quite.' Fred looked towards the pegs by the door where Jacob's faded coat and Adam's jacket were hanging. 'Perhaps, mistress, you should check the coats?'

Adam shook his head.

'Why should we have put it there?'

'I know, a preposterous idea,' murmured Amber.

'But we have tried everywhere else,' muttered Fred, lifting down the two coats and holding them out.

Amber took Jacob's greatcoat and shook it.

'This is looking positively threadbare,' she said, smiling as she returned it to its peg. 'I am sure I have a length of worsted that would…' Her words trailed away as Fred gave her Adam's coat and she found it unexpectedly heavy. She turned to him. 'May I look?'

'By all means.'

He watched her reach into the first pocket and pull out a large red leather purse.

'What is this?'

Her puzzled look mirrored his own.

'I have no idea.'

'I have,' said old Jacob, his chin jutting pugnaciously. 'I saw Parwich carrying that self-same purse this morning.'

'Yes, but—' Adam's brows snapped together.

'Now it makes sense,' muttered Fred.

Adam said nothing. Amber's eyes were still fixed upon him.

'It is not necessarily the same one,' she spoke quietly, but he could hear the desperation in her voice. 'Is it your wages, perhaps, saved for your journey to Lancashire?'

'Wages!' Frederick had taken the purse from Amber and opened it. 'Six months' wages would not amount to this!'

'I do not know how it came to be in my pocket,' said Adam, steadily returning her gaze.

'I do,' snapped Fred. 'He has sold your order book to Parwich.'

'Adam?' She was still looking at him, her eyes pleading with him to explain. 'Is that true? If you needed the money—'

'No!' He ground out the word, holding his temper. 'I have told you I am not penniless—'

'But we have only your word for that.'

He ignored Fred's interruption. The look in Amber's eyes was cutting him to the quick.

'I do not know what has happened to the order

book,' he repeated. 'Neither do I know how that purse came into my pocket. Let us sit down and—'

'By heaven, you do not expect to remain here after this?' exclaimed Fred. 'Mrs Hall, you cannot let him stay. He is working for Parwich!'

'That is a lie!'

'Is it?' Fred's thin face was suffused with anger. 'How convenient that you should be on hand to rescue Mrs Hall from attack, and that you should then be free to work here, worming your way into her affections. Hah, do you think she could ever trust you, when we don't even know who your father is—'

The jibe went too deep to be ignored. With a growl Adam lunged towards Fred, his fists balled and ready to strike.

'Enough!' Amber threw herself between them, saying angrily, 'I will not allow you to start a brawl on my property.' She glared at them both before turning to Adam and saying icily, 'I think you should leave now. Fred, give him his purse, and his coat.'

'It is not my purse, I tell you!'

The stricken look on her face silenced him. She swallowed, her lips quivering a little as she struggled to speak.

'Until we know more it is best that you go.'

Adam looked around. Jacob was shaking his head sadly, Fred was holding out his coat and looking at him with undisguised loathing. He tried once more.

'Amber—'

She turned away from him, her back rigid with distress and disapproval. She said pointedly, 'Come, Fred. If Matthew Parwich has that ledger he will use it to undermine us. He may even now be calling upon my customers. We will have to recreate as many orders as we can from memory, then we must write a list of everyone we can think of....'

Adam took the coat, but pulled the heavy purse from the pocket.

'Very well, I will go, but this stays here. You will not force that money upon me!'

He swung out of the door and crossed the yard, not seeing anything around him as he made his way to the barn to saddle Bosun. He could understand Amber's suspicion, but it still hurt him. If someone wanted to cause a rift between them they could not have found a more sure way of going about it. He walked Bosun through the yard, noting that the warehouse door was firmly shut against him. No one was watching him through the peephole window.

Amber applied herself ruthlessly to listing every customer and order she could recall, watching as Fred wrote them onto a fresh sheet of paper. Knowing how much Fred resented Adam's presence at the warehouse she was surprised that he made no attempt to discuss the theft, but she was relieved too. She could not bear to talk about it, although the thoughts whirled around in her head, making it difficult to concentrate on anything else. After an hour she excused herself and went up to her room. Her self-control lasted only until she had closed the door, then she sank onto her bed, trembling.

Adam had betrayed her. No sooner had she told him that she would not marry him than he had stolen her order book. Perhaps he had been working for Matthew Parwich all along. At that moment she did not care very much why he had taken it, only that he had betrayed her trust. He knew how much the business meant to her; there was nothing he could have done that would have hurt her more. She stared across the room, seeing nothing, her eyes painfully dry and an ache in her throat. She wanted to cry, but could not. She merely felt numb.

* * *

Adam tried to think clearly as he trotted away. It was not easy; Fred's taunts echoed in his brain. He should have known better than to return to Castonbury. With a muttered oath he shook his head, forcing his brain to concentrate upon the missing order book. The shop had been locked that morning. Either he or Jacob had been in the yard the whole morning, until Fred had taken out the wagon. How could someone have got in unseen? As he passed the Rothermere Arms he pulled on the reins and turned Bosun towards the inn yard. The landlord was carrying out an empty barrel as Adam arrived, and he stopped to watch this potential customer dismount, wiping his hands on his apron.

'Good day to you,' said Adam pleasantly. 'I wonder if a Mr Parwich called here this morning?'

'Ah, you mean that grand clothier from Hatherton, with his coach and four?' The landlord grinned. 'Aye, he did. There's a man set up in his own self-importance, if you don't mind my saying so. My missus told him weeks ago that we don't buy our cloth from anyone other than Ripley and Hall, as we've always done.'

'How long did he stay?' asked Adam. 'Did he meet anyone?'

The landlord rubbed his chin.

'He took a cup of coffee in the lounge, but no—' he shook his head '—he was alone.'

'Are you sure?' Adam persisted. 'Were you with him the whole time?'

'Yes, I was, more or less, until I came out to meet Mrs Hall's wagon. The missus was waiting for a delivery so I came out to fetch it. And Mr Parwich followed me out, so I am as sure as I can be that he didn't meet anyone. I went indoors then, and he drove away a few minutes later.'

Adam thanked him and went on his way, a furrow creasing his brow. Fred might have spoken to Parwich if they were both in the yard together. He could have smuggled the order book out and he would have had the opportunity to put the purse in Adam's pocket. He remembered it was Fred who had suggested checking their coats. But why? Fred was devoted to Amber. He shook his head. It made no sense to him.

He was no nearer an explanation when he reached the south gate to Castonbury. Giles was riding towards it from the opposite direction.

Adam waited for him to come up, glad to have a momentary distraction. He touched his hat.

'Good day to you, my lord. You have been away?'

'Aye.' Giles gave him a slight smile. 'Estate business. Everything has fallen to me, for the time being at least.'

They turned their horses and proceeded together into the Park.

'A heavy responsibility,' remarked Adam, wondering about his own responsibilities. How were his mills faring without him? He should return to Rossendale and leave Amber Hall and her cloth business to its fate. An idea no sooner thought of than dismissed.

'That reminds me,' he said. 'You asked me to keep an eye on the Dower House, so there is something I should tell you.'

Briefly Adam described seeing Hugh Webster on Sunday night. Giles listened, grim-faced.

'And what did you make of it?'

Adam shrugged.

'He did not go into the house, but to be calling upon a lady alone…'

'I know. It does not look good.' Giles took out his watch. 'This might be a good time…will you come with me now? We will confront her with this.'

Adam hesitated, but only for an instant. His own affairs would not be harmed by a small delay and he could then go directly to see his mother; she would not object if he did not change his coat.

'Of course I will come with you. Lead on, my lord.'

They followed the path to the Dower House, where they were informed that Lady Hatherton was in the garden. They found her sitting on a rug beneath a shady tree, her baby on her knees.

Alicia rose as they approached, picking her child up and holding him close. Adam thought it was almost as if she was afraid Giles might tear him from her arms. However, to Adam's ears there was nothing menacing about the tone in which Giles addressed her.

'Good day to you, madam. You know Capt—I mean, Mr Stratton?'

'Good day, Lord Giles, and yes.' She turned her blue eyes towards Adam. 'I have met Mr Stratton.'

'I am concerned, ma'am, for your safety,' Giles continued. 'Have you had any unwelcome callers recently?'

'Unwelcome…no.' She looked from one to the other, a faint crease in her brow.

'Mr Stratton saw someone in your garden on Sunday night.' Giles paused. 'A man.'

'A man? No, I do not—'

'Mr Stratton saw you talking with him.'

'I was on my way back from the great house,' added Adam quietly. 'It was quite late.'

'Oh.' She shifted the baby a little higher in her arms. 'Oh, that—that would have been Mr Everett. He has been very good, fetching firewood for me.'

'So late, madam? I cannot see my estate manager doing anything so improper.'

Adam shook his head. 'It was not Everett. It was Hugh Webster.' He added, anticipating her objection, 'I saw him quite clearly. There can be no mistake.'

A shadow crossed her face and her blue eyes darkened. Was it guilt? wondered Adam. It looked much more like terror. She swallowed nervously.

'Oh, yes.' She licked her lips. 'Yes. He—he brought me a note. F-from Sir Nathan.'

'Samuelson!' exclaimed Giles. 'Is he dangling after you?'

'I—'

Giles did not let her finish. 'I think in the present circumstances it would not be wise to encourage his attentions, madam.'

'I am not encouraging him,' she replied with great dignity.

'No, well, perhaps you would like me to have a word—'

'No, that will not be necessary,' she said firmly. 'I am quite…quite capable of dealing with Sir Nathan.'

'Aye, well, I think you should,' growled Giles. 'And you should discourage him from sending his messenger to call upon you!'

He inclined his head and strode off. Adam did not follow him immediately.

'Lady Hatherton, if Sir Nathan is importuning you—'

She shook her head quickly.

'No, no, it is n-nothing like that, I assure you.' She managed a nervous smile, her hands clutching her baby to her. 'Thank you for your concern, but, please, go now.'

'So it turned out to be nothing more than a storm in a teacup,' remarked Giles, when Adam caught up with him again.

'I think she is afraid.'

'I did not mean to frighten her.'

'No, not of you—at being found out.'

'Well, that is not surprising, if she has been carrying on a dalliance with Samuelson.'

'What do we know of this Webster, the messenger?'

Giles shrugged.

'Nothing more than that he works for Sir Nathan.' He waved an impatient hand. 'I have too much on my mind at the moment to worry about whether the woman has an admirer. But what of you, Adam? You are not usually abroad at this time of day. Have you given up on Ripley and Hall?'

'Something like that.' Adam's response was brief. He would not add to Giles's worries with his own tale of woe.

Giles grinned suddenly. 'Perhaps you would like to try your hand as stable master? Old Tom needs someone to take over from him and I have had nigh on half a dozen since Christmas, but none will stay!'

'And nor would I,' retorted Adam. 'I fear I am growing weary of Castonbury, and long to get back to my spinning mills. They are not half so troublesome!'

They parted at the stables and Adam made his way through the servants' wing, his own concerns surfacing as he approached his mother's quarters. He did not want to worry her and initially decided that he would say nothing of the events at the warehouse, but when at the end of their dinner together she remarked that he was very quiet, he changed his mind. He meant to keep it light, but his tone grew more serious as he recounted his tale.

'Parwich must be behind this. He is trying to force Amber out of business and he will use her order book to approach her customers and undercut her prices.'

'And by planting the purse in your coat he is also hoping to destroy Amber's trust in you.'

'Exactly.'

'Only a very deep trust could withstand such a blow. Tell me, Adam, does Mrs Hall return your affection?' She met his startled gaze and smiled. 'My dear, it is as plain as day to me that you are in love with her.'

'How can you say that? We have never—'

She reached across for his hand.

'My love, it is in your voice whenever you speak

of her, and in your eyes. But how does she feel about you, does she love you?'

'I don't know.' Adam stopped. His jaw tightened and he said quietly, 'No, how can she, when she is prepared to believe I have betrayed her?'

'I doubt if she *wants* to believe it, but from what you have told me the evidence is quite…damning.'

He rubbed his hand across his eyes. He felt incredibly tired.

'It is. I have my suspicions, but…' He sighed. 'It makes no sense.'

'Then you must *make* sense of it, Adam.'

Her vehemence drew a reluctant smile from him.

'You are right, of course, Mother. I will go back to the lodge and get some sleep. Perhaps something will occur to me by the morning.'

He collected Bosun from the stables and rode back to the keeper's lodge. His thoughts should have been on the missing order book and the red purse, but instead he was thinking of what his mother had said. He was in love with Amber Hall. How had he not realised it? Just thinking of her warmed his heart, and whenever she walked into a room it was somehow brighter. He liked her, yes. He desired her. He had even asked her to marry him. A logical solution to that desire, he had thought. But love? Was what he felt for Amber that all-encompassing passion that made him want to keep her by his side, to love, honour and cherish her all the days of his life? It was something of a shock to realise that, yes, that was exactly what it was. Why had he not seen it, why had he not told her he loved her? He knew some men found it easy to talk of love, but he had never done so. Perhaps it was because when he thought of love he thought of his mother, living alone for so many years.

And what of Amber? She desired him, that he knew, but surely if she loved him she would not want to send him away. With his new-found insight he wondered if she was afraid to love him, to surrender herself to that grand passion.

You may never know.

The words were in his head, yet as clear as if he had spoken aloud. They taunted him, echoing through his brain as he rode up to the lodge.

'I have to go back. Tonight,' he muttered, bringing Bosun to a stand. 'I have to make sure she understands it was not I who betrayed her.'

Turning Bosun away from the keeper's lodge, he dug in his heels and cantered off into the night.

Chapter Nine

A distant bell was chiming as Adam rode into the high street, announcing that it was ten o'clock. Knowing the warehouse and its barn would be locked up he decided to leave Bosun at the Rothermere Arms. It was a busy coaching inn and its yard was alive with noise and bustle night and day. He set off to walk to the warehouse. As he expected, the gates were shut and the building was in darkness when he arrived, but a light was burning at an upstairs window, so he walked around to the kitchen and beat a loud tattoo with the knocker. When it went unanswered he tried again. This time the upstairs sash was thrown up and Maizie leaned out.

'Who is it, beating on our door at this time of night?'

'Adam Stratton,' he called up. 'And it is not that late.'

'It is when the mistress has spent all day writing out 'er order book from memory,' retorted Maizie. 'Get you gone, Mr Stratton. She doesn't want to see you.'

'Just five minutes. Ask her to spare me that.'

Maizie ducked back into the room, her head reappearing a moment later.

'You have a nerve, turning up here, after what you have done,' she called out. 'The mistress will not see you. She says if you persist she will call the magistrate and have you arrested for thieving.'

A shadow fell across the window and he guessed that Amber was standing behind her maid. He raised his voice.

'Pray tell your mistress that I have done nothing amiss, but she needs to beware. Tell her to take care—'

He heard a murmur, a woman's voice coming from the room.

'Aye, I'll tell 'er,' muttered Maizie. 'Now be off with you!'

The sash slammed down. Adam raised his hand to knock again, then let it fall. She would not see him. Well, he was not finished yet.

Ten minutes later he had arrived at a small cottage at the end of a lonely lane. At first he thought it was in darkness, but as he walked up the path he perceived a glimmer of light through the shuttered window. Encouraged by this, he knocked loudly.

Fred Aston opened the door. When he saw Adam he tried to shut it again but Adam was too quick for him. He forced the door wide and easily dealt with Fred's attempts to bundle him back out into the lane.

'You can't come in here,' Fred protested. 'My mother is asleep.'

'Then we had best not wake her.'

Adam stepped into the small sitting room while Fred stood by the door, gazing at him with sullen defiance.

'What do you want?'

'I want to know what you have done with the order book.'

Any lingering doubts Adam might have had were dispelled by the sudden expression of fear that flashed across the young man's features.

'That is a question I should ask you,' said Fred, recovering. 'Mrs Hall and I have spent the day trying to recall each and every order outstanding.'

Adam waited. Fred met his eyes defiantly for a few moments, then looked away.

'We both know I did not take the order book,'

said Adam quietly. 'You smuggled it out of the shop and passed it on to Parwich when you stopped at the inn, did you not? And Parwich gave you the purse to slip into my pocket.'

'Stuff and nonsense!' Fred's laugh was not convincing. 'You will never get Mrs Hall to believe that.'

'No?'

'No!' Fred glared at him. 'You come along and—and *bewitch* her with your grand talk about protecting her, but she doesn't need you, Stratton. Jacob and I are all the protection she needs!'

'If that is so, then why did you give the order book to Parwich? You know how that will damage the business. Do you want to ruin her?'

'N-no, I would never do anything to hurt Mrs Hall!'

'Then where is the order book?'

'I don't know.' He flung his arms wide. 'Why do you not search the house? You will not find it. I do not know where it is, I tell you.'

'Do not lie to me, Fred. You were the only one with the opportunity to take it.'

'Apart from you!'

'Yes, apart from me,' agreed Adam. 'But I know I did not take it.'

'You cannot prove anything,' Fred declared, retreating behind a chair. 'And who is Mrs Hall most likely to believe? Me, or a man she has known for less than a month?'

Adam looked at him.

'How much did Parwich pay you?'

'Nothing! As if I would take a penny—'

Adam frowned. He said slowly, 'So was it all an elaborate charade to get rid of me?' When Fred did not answer he continued, 'Just what do you think Parwich will do with that order book, Fred? He is the real villain here, not me.'

Fred licked his lips.

'If—if it was not you who took the book, then— then I am sure it will turn up again.'

Adam's lip curled.

'Is that what he promised you, that he would give you the book back? And you were fool enough to believe him? He will use it to try and steal away your mistress's customers. He wants to destroy her, and you are helping him!' He added more quietly, 'Come, Fred, admit it, and I will go with you to see Parwich. We will recover the book, before it is too late.'

Adam waited, watching the emotions flit across the young man's face. At last Fred shook his head.

'I told you,' he muttered stubbornly. 'I know nothing about it.' He threw another sullen look at Adam. 'And if you think you can beat a confession out of me, you won't do it.'

'No, lad, that is not my way.' Adam's last flicker of hope died. 'But I will get to the truth, believe me. I am not done yet.'

He left the cottage and strode back to the inn. Everything he had heard convinced him that Fred had taken the book, but they both knew Adam could prove nothing. When he reached the Rother-mere Arms he spoke to the servants, but although it was confirmed that the two coaches had been in the yard at the same time that morning, no one remembered seeing Matthew Parwich speak to Fred. Frowning, Adam went inside, calling for a mug of ale.

Due to the lateness of the hour the coffee room was empty, which suited Adam perfectly. He took his drink to a table by the window and sat down to think what he should do next. His options were limited. If Fred would not confess, his only chance was to find the order book and return it to Amber. He had just decided that he would have to turn housebreaker when a burst of laughter from the taproom opposite interrupted his thoughts. He glanced up. The door of the coffee room stood open, and across the passageway he could see the remaining stragglers in the taproom. Hugh Webster's distinctive red head caught his attention. The man was finishing his drink, one hand on a comrade's shoulder. He showed every sign of being about to depart. Webster took leave of his companions and glanced into the coffee room as he stepped into the passage, giving Adam a long, considering look before slouching out into the night.

Adam looked out onto the street and watched the man pause to button his coat before setting off in the direction of Grantby Manor. He had not gone far when a figure broke away from the shadows and approached him. Adam sat up. His first thought, that it was footpads, was quickly dismissed. This was a single, cloaked figure.

And it was female.

Adam frowned. The cloak was all-enveloping, but he saw one white hand come out to grip Webster's sleeve and as the woman looked up her face was momentarily visible. Adam grabbed his hat and raced out of the inn. The pair were moving into the shadows. Adam crossed the street, as if heading in the other direction, but once he had reached the shelter of the buildings he turned back, using the darkness to move closer. He may not be able to find a solution to his own problems, but he might just be able to help Giles. He was still not close enough to hear what they were saying when they parted. Webster moved away and without a backward glance strode off. The cloaked figure remained watching him, unaware of Adam until he spoke to her.

'Good evening, Lady Hatherton.'

The figure started, one hand going to her mouth to stifle a scream as she turned to look at him. Her blue eyes were wide with terror.

'A little late for you to be out alone, is it not?' he remarked cheerfully.

Alicia, Lady Hatherton, clasped her hands together.

'It is,' she agreed cautiously. 'I must get back.'

'Then let me accompany you.'

'No—there is no need.'

'Oh, but it is no trouble,' said Adam. 'I could not possibly let you walk back unattended.' He looked around. 'You are alone, are you not?'

'Yes, I—I came out for a little air.'

'To walk over a mile in the dark, for a little air is, to say the least, unusual.' She made no reply and he said gently, 'Come, my lady, tell me the truth. I saw you talking to Webster.'

'Y-yes, I, um, I came to tell him that he must not bring me any more notes from Sir Nathan.'

'Would you not have been better served communicating that to the master, rather than the servant?'

'I would, I suppose, but I do not wish to embroil myself in any way with Sir Nathan, so writing to him is out of the question. I thought a word to his man would suffice.'

She spoke with quiet dignity. Perhaps she was telling the truth.

'You are probably right,' he answered, prepared to give her the benefit of the doubt. He held out his arm to her. 'We are fortunate that we have a moon to light our way back.'

It was more than a mile to the Dower House but the lady was not inclined to dawdle and they covered the ground quickly. Adam's attempts to draw her out failed signally. She was nervous of him and he could not blame her. However, when they reached the gates of the Dower House she turned to thank him. The moonlight enhanced her ethereal beauty and glinted in her blue eyes. There was a time when he would have been enchanted by such a vision, and would have taken the opportunity to flirt a little, perhaps even to steal a kiss, but he was impervious to her charms, his mind full of a much darker beauty and a pair of lustrous brown eyes.

He took his leave of Lady Hatherton and watched until she was safely indoors, then he turned towards the lodge. He could leave Bosun at the inn until the morning. However, the closer he came to the lodge the more restless he became. He did not feel in the least tired. It was not yet midnight, he would walk back and collect his horse. Perhaps by the time he had reached the village again he would have worked out a way to prove his innocence. He shook his head and gave a little grunt of frustration. He did not seem able to think straight, and since he knew he would not sleep, perhaps the exercise would do him good. During his days at sea his ship would have foundered, lost with all hands, if he had been so besotted over a woman.

He strode through the darkness, only the occasional cry of a fox breaking the silence. The village street was as he had last seen it, shadowed and deserted. The night air was cool, but it had been a fine spring day and he was a little surprised at the faint smell of smoke in the air—until he raised his eyes and saw a pall of grey smoke rising against the black sky. His heart contracted. It was at the far end of the high street. The warehouse.

He broke into a run. The village was in darkness, save for the inn, and he dashed there to raise the alarm, shouting orders to the startled ostlers before going on to the warehouse. As he approached his worst fears were realised. The smoke was belching from the building and the flames were already beginning to lick around the windows. The shop was shuttered, so he ran to the kitchen door and hammered upon it. There was no response. He ran back to the yard gates. They were locked. He could scale them easily, but thinking of the help he prayed was following him he charged the gates, the old wood splintering against his shoulder, as he had expected.

The warehouse was well alight, smoke and flames licking around the roof tiles and seeping out under the door. A glance through the broken peephole window showed him nothing but grey smoke and the occasional flash of red flame. He put his hand against the door and it swung inwards, surprising him. A wall of smoke and intense heat belched out. Flames darted over him and he leapt back, dragging the door closed again.

He stepped back, surveying the building. Flames were beginning to appear through the roof of the warehouse, but thankfully the shop and the rooms above it were relatively untouched.

He dashed to fetch the ladder from the wall of the barn and settled it against an upstairs window, which he guessed to be the living quarters. Even as he did so the sash was thrown up.

'Oh, thank heaven!' Maizie hung out of the window, wringing her hands. 'Quick, quick, the smoke is coming up the stairs!'

Adam leapt up the ladder and without ceremony he grabbed Maizie and threw her over his shoulder.

'Where is your mistress?' He grunted the words even as he carried the maid to the ground.

'She is gone downstairs. I told her not—'

Adam heard no more. He scaled the ladder again and tumbled through the window into the black, smoky room.

It was like going back in time. Suddenly he was at sea again, below deck where the air was thick with smoke and the smell of gunpowder. Men were shouting orders, curses, screams, as a cannonball ripped through the wooden hull, killing some, maiming even more. Fire quickly spread through the ship, feeding greedily on the tar and wood. And there was no escape. Most sailors could not swim; those that were not burned to death perished in the water....

Adam shook his head. He must dispel those images and concentrate on the present. He could taste the smoke in the air but that was all. This end of the building was not yet alight. He fumbled his way through the dark to the landing, where smoke was swirling up the stairs like thick fog.

'Amber!' The acrid fumes burned his throat. He shouted again, then his eyes caught a glimpse of something pale and wraith-like at the bottom of the stairs. He ran down, his eyes smarting in the smoke. Amber was in the narrow passageway, using a blanket to beat at the flames that were even now licking around the bottom of the warehouse door. Again the nightmare of fire on board ship filled his mind, the burning hold, the smoke seeping out between the timbers. If there were men in the lower decks they could not survive. To lift the hatch would only speed the fire's progress.

'Don't open it!' He pulled Amber away as she

reached for the door. Her white nightgown floated around her ankles and he feared that at any moment it might catch fire. He took the blanket from her and stuffed it against the bottom of the door. 'This way. We must get out.'

He drew her into the kitchen, shutting the door behind them. The smoke was still in the air, but much less dense. Amber struggled against his hold.

'I can't leave. I must put it out!'

'Impossible from here.' A little light filtered in from the window and showed Adam the way to the door. He could hear shouts and cries coming from the street now. 'Let's get outside. Once you are safe we will see what can be done.'

There was loud crash, followed by a low rumble that shook the building. The rafters were collapsing. Instinctively he pulled Amber into his arms.

'We must get out.'

'But my stock, my shop…!'

Ignoring her protests he almost carried her to the outer door, his fingers scrabbling to pull back the bolts. Finally they were outside, coughing and gasping as the night breeze hit them. Adam was still gulping the cool, fresh air into his lungs when Amber twisted out of his grip and headed for the front of the building. He followed her. A crowd had gathered, many of the villagers in hastily donned day clothes, others with coats or cloaks thrown over their nightgowns. Some were bringing buckets of water, others had broken open the shop door and were carrying what they could to safety through the smoke. He ran over and directed them to take everything into the barn which lay on the far side of the yard, out of reach of the fire.

Adam looked back at the main buildings. Only wisps of smoke were coming from the rooms above the shop but the warehouse was a furnace. Part of the roof had gone and the flames leapt unhindered to the sky, sending glowing red sparks upwards with the smoke. The very walls of the building seemed to glow red-hot. The buckets of water the villagers had brought were useless against such heat.

Fred Aston ran up and Adam snarled at him.

'Is this your doing too?' he said savagely.

'No, no, I swear—we put out every light, I am sure of it.' Fred gazed in horror at the roaring, burning monster.

Even as they watched there was another deafening, splintering crash as the remains of the warehouse roof collapsed. Fred backed away, whimpering.

'Oh, dear heaven, surely he would not have— no, no, it was nothing to do with me!'

Amber stared at the inferno. Her eyes were stinging and her nightgown was scorched and blackened. She forced her numbed brain to think and was immediately overwhelmed with fear.

'Maizie?' she cried out frantically, not knowing which way to run.

'I'm here, Mrs Hall.' The maid came towards her, a red woollen shawl wrapped around her shoulders.

'Thank heavens!' Amber hugged her.

'How did it start?' Albert Moffat, the landlord of the Rothermere Arms, came puffing up with Jacob at his side. Their faces were streaked with dirt and Jacob was still carrying one of the rolls of cloth he had rescued from the shop.

'Someone fired the warehouse,' said Jacob. 'You knows, missus, we checked that every lamp and light was out before we shut up fer the night. We always do.' He scowled at Adam. 'What are you doing in Castonbury at this time o' night?'

'It was Mr Stratton who raised the alarm,' put in Albert Moffat.

'That don't mean he didn't start it.'

Amber peered around. She did not recognise the voice, but there were two men she did not know in the crowd, although in the dark it was difficult to be sure, and they had a young boy with them. Travellers, staying at the inn, perhaps.

'No,' said Fred, his eyes wild. 'No, Mr Stratton didn't do this.'

'I heard as how he had been turned off,' shouted the other stranger. 'P'raps he had a score to settle.'

'That's preposterous.'

Amber tried to be reassured by Adam's calm reply, but she was finding it difficult to think properly. She put a hand to her head.

'No,' she said. 'No. He rescued me.'

'Aye, well, that might've been to cover his tracks.' The stranger raised his voice. 'After all, what do we know about him? He's only been here a few weeks.'

The villagers were nodding and a few were muttering now.

'And he come bangin' on the door earlier,' added Maizie, 'demandin' to speak to Mrs Hall.'

Albert Moffat raised his hands. 'Now is not the time to think about this. We'll put it to Sir Rufus tomorrow.'

'He'll have cut and run by then. Lock 'im up, I say.'

Amber was beginning to hate that voice from the crowd.

'Of course I won't leave,' retorted Adam impatiently. 'I have nothing to hide.'

Maizie pulled Amber out of the way as the crowd surged forward and gathered around Adam. Voices were raised, people were nervous, muttering that if this could happen to Ripley and Hall, what next might be set alight? She heard Adam's voice, calm and authoritative.

'Very well, lock me up if you wish, but you are making a mistake. Fred, will you tell them what you know?'

Fred was looking on, his face ghastly in the ruddy glow of the fire.

'I—I don't know anything. I only came out when I heard the commotion.'

The crowd had turned into an angry mob, their shouts and cries rising to fever pitch. Amber closed her eyes and rubbed her fingers against her temples.

'What do you say, Mrs Hall?' The landlord touched her arm. 'I think we had best lock him up for his own safety. I'll get the magistrate to question him tomorrow at the inn.'

'Yes, yes—do that.' Above the heads of the crowd she met Adam's eyes, just once before they bundled him away. She tried to read the message in them. Was he blaming her, was he telling her he was innocent? Her heart wanted to believe that, but in the smoky darkness he might as easily have been saying, *Forgive me.*

'Fred's going to make sure the barn is safely locked up,' said Maizie, coming back to Amber and putting an arm around her. 'And Mrs Crutchley has said we can stay with her tonight. It's all right, mistress.'

Amber dragged her eyes away from the mob escorting Adam to the gaol and looked at the burning wreck that had been her home and her business. All right? It would never be all right again.

Chapter Ten

The lock-up was black and chill. When the door was first bolted behind him Adam could see nothing, but gradually his eyes adjusted and the narrow slit of a window allowed in sufficient moonlight to show him a small, square room. He had to fight down his impatience at being imprisoned. His only comfort was that Amber and Maizie were safe.

His mind and body still tingled with restless energy and he paced up and down in the confined space, going over everything that had occurred since he came upon the fire. The warehouse door had not been secure. That could not be a coincidence. He frowned. The little window beside it was broken too. It was possible that someone had squeezed through there and unlocked the door. Then there had been the men in the crowd, very anxious to put the blame upon him. He had not recognised them, but he had noted that they were fully dressed. It was possible they had been at the inn, but he did not recall seeing them in either of the public rooms when he had called in there. And there had been a young boy with them. He would surely have remembered if there had been a child in the taproom.

He frowned in an effort to bring the men's faces to mind. They had both been wearing caps and mufflers, a little overdressed for the mild night. As soon as he was free he would look into that. And he would speak to Fred again. The lad was frightened and might well be persuaded now to tell him the truth. But until then the long night stretched before him.

His throat was raw from the smoke, but there was no water in the cell. Nothing save a wooden bench that ran the length of one wall, just long enough for Adam to stretch out. He made himself as comfortable as he could and settled down to wait for morning.

The Long Room of the Rothermere Arms had been used for many years as a meeting place, and it was packed the following morning when

Adam was brought in by the parish constable. He supposed he should be thankful that he was not in chains like a common felon, but he suspected he looked little better than one, for his clothes were dirty and creased, his hair was uncombed and a rough stubble shadowed his cheeks. Adam squared his shoulders and held his head high as he walked in. He spotted his mother immediately. She was dressed in her best grey gown, and Lord Giles was standing behind her. His eyes raked the room until he saw Amber. She was very pale and wearing a loose gown that looked much too large for her—most likely borrowed from some good neighbour. A quick glance around showed him many familiar faces, but the two strangers who had been so vociferous the previous night were not present.

A number of tables had been brought together at one end of the room and a gentleman in an old-fashioned bag-wig sat behind them.

'Sir Rufus Eglington, the magistrate,' muttered the constable, ushering Adam towards the centre of the room.

'Well now, well now,' said Sir Rufus testily. 'What is all this.' He glared at Adam from beneath his bushy eyebrows. 'You set fire to a building.'

'No, sir, I did not, but someone did. The warehouse door was unlocked.'

Sir Rufus gazed down at the papers in front of him.

'When the constable searched your person, he found a flint, a steel and some matches.'

'Of course. I use them to light the candles at the lodge.'

'You were in the village last night. You called upon Mrs Hall.'

'I tried to do so.' Adam's eyes flickered towards Amber. 'She would not see me, however.'

'So you came here, drank yourself into a rage and went back for your revenge.'

'No.'

'He was in here, sir,' declared Hugh Webster, stepping forward. 'I saw him. He was sitting alone, brooding over his ale, when I left at around eleven o'clock.'

'Yes, I was here,' agreed Adam, 'but I left soon after you.'

Sir Rufus consulted his notes again.

'But that would have been a good hour before you came back to raise the alarm.' He fixed Adam with a stony gaze. 'Where were you?'

An expectant hush had fallen over the room. Adam swallowed. Hard.

'I would rather not tell you.'

A murmur ran around the room, like the ripple of breeze through a wood. Sir Rufus sat back and folded his arms.

'I think you must, Mr Stratton.'

'I cannot.'

'And why?'

Adam hesitated, painfully aware that Amber was watching him closely.

'It involves a lady.' Another murmur, louder this time, and Adam raised his voice to speak over it. 'You will hardly expect me to divulge a lady's identity in so public a place, Sir Rufus. I am willing to tell you, in confidence, but no one else.'

The look he received from beneath those bushy brows was piercing, but Adam met it calmly.

'Very well,' barked the magistrate. 'Clear the room!'

There was much chatter and scraping of chairs as everyone filed out. Amber approached the magistrate.

'I would like to stay, Sir Rufus.' She added quickly, 'I think I am entitled to hear what he has to say, since I am bringing the prosecution against this man.'

Her words hit Adam like a body blow. Did she

really believe he would betray her like this? Good heavens, as a sailor, and now as a mill owner, he knew better than anyone the devastation a fire could cause.

'You have a point, madam. You may stay.' Sir Rufus gestured to the constable. 'Shut the door behind you, Huggins, but do not go far away. I will hear what Mr Stratton has to say. Well, sir? Explain yourself.'

Adam's heart sank. Amber was the very last person he wanted to hear his story. He was well aware how flimsy it would sound. 'When I left here I found a lady...an acquaintance...in the street, alone. I escorted her back to her home, then returned here for my horse.'

'And what was this lady's name?' growled Sir Rufus. His brows snapped together when Adam did not speak. 'Come, come, sir. The charge against you is a most serious one. We need the lady's name!'

Sir Rufus was tapping his fingers impatiently on the table. Amber kept her gaze fixed resolutely on the floor. Adam cleared his throat.

'Lady Hatherton. I escorted her back to the Dower House.'

'Lady Hatherton?' The magistrate frowned.

'The lady claiming to be Lord James's widow? What would she be doing abroad at that time of night?'

'She would have to tell you that herself.'

'Hmm. Very well, I will ride out immediately to see her.' Sir Rufus got up. 'In the meantime, you will go back to the lock-up. Huggins!'

As the magistrate went to the door, shouting for the constable, Adam was left alone with Amber. It was his only opportunity to explain and he took it.

'This is all wrong,' he said urgently. 'Someone is trying to—'

She interrupted him.

'Did you make love to her too?'

'No! Amber, I swear—'

She put up her hand.

'Please, no more. There have been enough lies.'

He had never known her so dispirited. It tore at his heart.

'I have never lied to you! How can I convince you?'

He put out his hand but she flinched away from him.

'You cannot. I trusted you, Adam, and this is the way you repay me.' Her chin went up and a flicker of anger lit her eyes. 'You must hope that

Lady Hatherton's testimony is sufficient to save you, because I intend to hire the finest lawyer to prosecute you through the courts for this. I intend to ruin you, Adam Stratton!'

She turned and hurried away. Adam went to go after her, but the constable blocked his way.

'Not so fast, Mr Stratton.' He nodded towards Giles, who was standing in the doorway with Hannah. 'His Lordship is standing bail for you and Sir Rufus has agreed I can hand you into his custody.'

'Thank heaven for that!'

His mother came up and took his arm.

'Let us go, Adam. Lord Giles has his carriage waiting.' She added, seeing his hesitation, 'You have no need to worry about your horse. His Lordship has sent one of his grooms to ride him back to the Park.'

Once they were safely in the carriage and bowling back towards Castonbury Park, Adam turned to his mother.

'Tell me, how is Mrs Hall, has she lost everything?'

'We do not yet know. She was insured, which is a blessing, and she has already sent an express message to her insurers.' His mother was holding his hand tightly, as if afraid he might disappear if she let go.

'What is going on, Adam?' Giles demanded. 'I do not believe for a moment that you are guilty, but how do you come to find yourself in such a fix?'

'Mrs Hall has a competitor who wants to buy her business.'

Giles nodded. 'Matthew Parwich. I have heard from several people this morning that he has been undercutting her prices in an attempt to lure away her customers.'

'Quite. Before I came he was making life very difficult for Mrs Hall. He saw me as a serious threat and I believe he stole Mrs Hall's order book and put the blame on me. I also believe he arranged for someone to set fire to the warehouse. It is no secret that I am living alone at the keeper's lodge, easy enough to set it about that I wanted revenge upon Amber for turning me off. I think the men who actually set fire to Mrs Hall's property were in the crowd last night. When they saw me, they turned it to their advantage.'

'But you do have someone who can vouch for you?'

'Yes. Lady Hatherton.'

'What!'

Adam managed a grim smile at Giles's exclamation.

'Webster was in the taproom last night, and when he left she accosted him. They spoke for no more than two minutes, but then he went off, leaving her to make her own way home alone. Even if I had not wanted to know what they had said to each other I could not have done other than escort her back to the Dower House.'

Giles grinned.

'Chivalrous to the last! So what did she have to say?'

'Our meeting with her yesterday had some effect. She told Webster not to bring her any more notes from Sir Nathan.'

'And you believed her?'

'Why not?'

Giles frowned. 'Damned havey-cavey way to go about things, but I suppose it might be true. But enough of that for now. I have stood bail for you, my friend, you will remain within the Park grounds until this matter is sorted out.'

'That will suit me very well. All I really want now is a wash, and a shave!'

* * *

Amber hurried out of the inn and allowed Maizie to escort her back to the butcher's house. The gown she had borrowed from Mrs Crutchley swung limp and heavy around her ankles. It was far too wide, but the extra material sagged almost to the ground, which was all that was required to maintain a lady's modesty. She nodded distractedly to those who pressed their sympathies and good wishes upon her but in truth she barely heard them. Her head was still reeling with the events of the past twenty-four hours. When she had walked into the Long Room the sight of Adam, dishevelled and exhausted, had almost overpowered her. She did not want to believe he had stolen the order book, and she could not accept that he had set fire to her warehouse and then come back to save her. There must be another explanation. She had not dared to look at him, but listened intently, waiting for him to explain it all. Instead she had been dragged even deeper into the quagmire of misery when he declared he had been with Alicia, Lady Hatherton.

Was he villain enough to seduce Alicia and persuade her to vouch for him, or was he innocent of arson and merely the worst kind of libertine?

Amber could not decide. Her tired mind shied away from even thinking about it. She felt numb, exhausted.

'Dear me, Mrs Hall, but you look fit to drop!' Mrs Crutchley's words elicited no more than a faint shake of the head from Amber. The butcher's wife ushered her into the house and sat her down in an armchair overflowing with cushions. 'Let me fetch you a glass of wine, my dear. You are as white as your neckerchief.' She bustled around, dispatching Maizie to the kitchens to warm some soup while she pressed a glass of wine upon Amber. 'There, my dear, drink that and you will soon feel better. And not another word from you about bespeaking rooms at the Rothermere Arms. Crutchley and I are only too delighted to have you stay here for as long as you want.'

'Thank you, ma'am, you are very kind.'

'Kind! As if we wouldn't look after one of our own at a time like this. And I shall go over to the great house to see Hannah Stratton later. It doesn't matter to me whether that son of hers is innocent or guilty—she has been a good neighbour for the past thirty years and the poor woman will be out of her mind with worry, I don't doubt. Maizie will sit with you, I'm sure, while you eat your broth or—my dear, you look so tired. Would you prefer to go to your room and sleep?'

Amber let the flood of words wash over her, only taking in the last phrase. Sleep. Yes. She wanted to go to sleep and never wake up.

Hannah remained at the keeper's lodge with her son, telling him that she had arranged everything at the big house and she would not be required to return until dinnertime. He left her clearing up while he shaved himself and changed his clothes. His linen cuffs were torn and singed past repair, but he put the shirt aside for laundering. The jacket reeked of smoke from the fire, overlaid by a dank mustiness, the result of his night in the cell. He should get rid of it, he had many everyday coats much better than this, but when he looked at the odd buttons and remembered the events leading up to Amber sewing them on for him, he found himself reluctant to part with it. He would hang it outside. A good airing might freshen it.

Adam was glad of his mother's company and even more thankful for the basket she had ordered to be sent over from the great house.

'I guessed no one would feed you while you were in that dreadful lock-up,' she had told him, unpacking the contents onto the table. 'If only I had known, but word did not reach us until this morning, then Lord Giles insisted upon coming with me to the hearing.'

She sat with him while he broke his fast, as she had done when he was a boy, making sure he finished his meal. She listened intently while he told her all that had happened the previous evening.

'And you are convinced it is Matthew Parwich who is behind all this?' Hannah frowned. 'He would go to such lengths to drive Amber out of business?'

Adam nodded.

'Amber supplies most of the families around here and Hatherton—including Castonbury Park. Her customers are very loyal and having found that he can't beat her by fair means, Parwich has resorted to foul ones.'

'But that is terrible. What can be done about it?'

'We will fight him.' He flushed at the knowing smile in her eyes. 'I know Amber thinks she is alone, but I will help her, once I am free.'

'But will she let you?' mused Hannah. 'She does not trust you.'

'I know, but as soon as my innocence is proven—'

He was interrupted by a heavy knocking on the door. He opened it to find Sir Rufus standing there.

'So you *are* here, Stratton.'

'As you see,' Adam responded calmly. 'I gave my word to Lord Giles that I would remain.'

He stood back and the magistrate entered, removing his hat and nodding to Hannah as he did so.

'I have just come from the Dower House,' he barked. 'The lady denies everything.'

Hannah's face paled,

'But you explained,' said Adam. 'She need not tell you why she was in Castonbury…'

'Lady Hatherton says she did not leave the Dower House Thursday night.' The bushy brows twitched together. 'It leaves you unable to account for yourself, Mr Stratton, at the time the warehouse was set alight. I have no option but to commit you to trial for arson. Until that time, since His Lordship stands bail for you, I must insist that you do not leave the Park. And I advise you not to approach Lady Hatherton. It would go ill with you if I thought you were harassing her.'

'But how long will it take, to bring this to trial?' asked his mother.

Sir Rufus shrugged. 'A month, maybe three. Or more.'

'The devil it will!' exclaimed Adam. 'I have been away from my own business for far too long as it is. I cannot leave it another month!'

'You will have to do so.'

'No,' said Adam explosively. 'I have to get back. There are bills and wages to be paid. My people cannot draw such sums from the bank.'

'Well, that is a problem, sir, but it ain't mine,' snapped Sir Rufus. 'I shall send a man over to check on you, and if I find that you have moved by only a yard beyond the pale I shall clap you in irons!'

With that he stomped out. Adam stared after him, his jaw set hard.

'Oh, Adam!'

Hannah went to him and he put his arm about her.

'Do not fret, Mother. I will send for my own lawyer from Rossendale and we will soon have this resolved.' The image of Amber rose in his mind, the anger and hurt burning in her eyes was chilling. He had no doubt that he would be able to convince the courts of his innocence, but would he ever convince Amber Hall?

* * *

Exhaustion gave Amber the blessed relief of a long, dreamless sleep but when she awoke the leaden depression was like a dark cloud, enveloping her. Maizie and Mrs Crutchley had decided between them that they would not rouse her and it was almost noon when she eventually came downstairs. She forced herself to eat a little bread and butter, then announced her intention of going with Maizie to look at the warehouse.

Mrs Crutchley immediately advised against it.

'Now, my dear, you don't want to go worrying yourself over that just yet. Young Frederick Aston has been looking after everything.'

'I must look at it sometime, Mrs Crutchley.' She patted the older lady's hands. 'Fred told me yesterday that the fire did not take hold in the shop or the living area. If it is possible I would like to move back there. At the very least I want to look in the linen press. I am hoping some of my gowns may be wearable.'

'Aye, well, I can understand that, my dear. You will feel much more like your old self when you are dressed in your own clothes. Well, off you go, then, but do not overtire yourself, and when you come back you shall sit down with us to a nice lamb dinner!'

With these kind words echoing in her ears Amber went off to see what was left of her business.

'Oh, heavens.'

The first sight stopped her in her tracks. Only the walls of the warehouse remained, blackened and charred. The roof was completely gone and the windows were burned away, the gaping squares staring out at her like sightless eyes. A tiny curl of smoke wound up from the centre of the ruin, where the remains of the rafters were still smouldering. The shop and living quarters were still intact, although the shop door had been smashed when the villagers had broken in to rescue what they could of her stock. Maizie followed her into the yard, where they found Jacob picking through a mass of debris. He doffed his cap when he saw Amber and followed her shocked gaze towards the ruin.

'Aye, 'tis a bad business, missus. It would have been even worse if the roof hadn't fallen in and buried the fire, so it didn't take hold in the shop. We saved what we could, but 'tis precious little, and the warehouse is completely gutted. Like I told the gennleman this morning, it was burning like the very pits of hell.'

'Gentleman, Jacob?'

'Aye, missus. From Buxton, he was. A Mr Elliot. Spoke to Fred, he did. Said he was come to inspect it for the insurers.'

'Oh, yes, of course. Is he here now?'

'No, missus, he's gone off to make his enquiries. I told'n we had already found the culprit, though it pains me to think 'twas Adam Stratton did such a thing.'

'Don't talk of 'im to me,' said Maizie, her lip curling in disgust. 'He should be hanged for what he's done to my poor mistress.'

'Hush now.' Amber forced herself not to crumble at the mention of his name.

'Well, he should,' said her maid stubbornly. 'And there's plenty in Castonbury as would do it, too, given half a chance. I heard 'em last night, saying they should finish it now, and not wait for the law.'

Amber shuddered.

'Sir Rufus will deal with this.' She hoped her voice sounded confident. 'We will have no mob rule here. The people of Castonbury are not like that.'

'Oh, ain't they?' muttered Jacob. 'Get them stirred up enough and you'd be surprised at what they will do.'

Amber left Maizie outside talking to Jacob and stepped into the shop.

It was very dark, for although the shutters had been removed the windows were black with soot. The floor was littered with ribbons and threads that had been scattered in the rush to empty the shelves. At first glance everything looked black, but closer inspection showed little real damage to the fittings, although a thick layer of sooty dust had settled over every surface.

Fred was standing by the little desk at the back of the shop. He looked around when Amber came up and she saw the tear tracks cutting through the grime on his cheeks.

'I am so sorry,' he whispered.

She fluttered her hand, warding off his sympathy. Her spirit felt as dead and empty as the shop. She looked back to the counter, remembering when Adam had stood on the other side, smiling down at her. She forced herself to think back. Surely the warmth in his eyes had been genuine? And the way they had talked. Freely. Like equals. That was the term he had used when he was trying to persuade her into marriage. Was he so skilled at seduction that he knew exactly how to get beneath her skin? She closed her eyes. For the first time since the fire she felt the sting of tears behind her eyelids. She would not let them fall, however. She would not cry over Adam Stratton.

'All that work yesterday to write down every order we could remember.' Amber tried to summon a smile for Fred. 'If only we had left the list in the drawer here, as usual, instead of locking it in the desk in the warehouse. But I thought it would be safer there.'

Fred gave a gasp, then a sob and sank down onto the chair, putting his elbows on the sooty desk and dropping his head into his hands.

'Oh, mistress, this is all so dreadful, I can never forgive myself!'

She squeezed his thin shoulder.

The harsh, racking sobs increased. His grief was intense. Amber wished she could cry like that, release all her anguish, but the hurt within her was so deep-rooted it had split her very soul and she was determined not to shed a single tear over the man who had caused it.

'No, Fred, you cannot blame yourself. This is not your fault.'

'But it is!' he gasped, his voice choked with tears. 'I am so ashamed. I should never have done it.'

At first she only heard his grief, but then the meaning of his words seeped into her brain and made her frown.

'Never have done what, Fred? What are you talking about?'

'I t-took the order book.' He shrank lower onto the desk. 'I gave it to Mr Parwich and he g-gave me the purse to put in Adam's pocket. He p-promised me he would take care of it for a few days, just until Adam was gone.'

'And you believed him?'

Fred gulped, trying to fight back his misery.

'He t-told me he w-wanted to make you his partner, that the business would grow even bigger, stronger, if you worked together. He said you'd be able to open another shop, perhaps in Buxton, and I could be manager. Only...only he said Adam Stratton was getting in the way of that. He—he said you would go into partnership with

Adam and…and marry him, and there would be no place for me.'

'Oh, Fred.'

'I w-went over to H-Hatherton early this morning and saw Mr Parwich. I told him I needed the order book back now, so we could find out what we needed to buy in.' He raised his head and turned his red-rimmed eyes towards her. 'He laughed at me, mistress. He—he said he knew n-nothing about any order book.' He drew a sobbing breath. 'He s-said that if I told anyone about it he would have me h-horsewhipped for a liar.'

His head sank down on his hands again and he continued to cry, his narrow shoulders shaking with grief.

'So Adam did not take the order book.'

'No.' Fred's voice was muffled in his sleeve. 'He knew n-nothing about it.'

'And…' She hesitated. 'Do you think he started the fire here?'

'No.' Fred shook his head vehemently. 'No. I'm sure Mr Parwich did it. And I think…I think he will now use your order book against you. If only I had seen all this before. I have been such a fool!' Fred looked up. 'While you are still trying to get your business started again he will contact all your customers and offer to supply their orders.'

Amber regarded his distress and felt nothing. Perhaps if she could shake off this lethargy she might care about the orders. For now she just wanted to walk away from everything.

'And if that wasn't bad enough.' Fred's words were very close to a wail. 'Adam Stratton is being blamed for the whole. And Mr Crutchley said he'd heard men talking at the inn, mistress, saying how they'd take the law into their own hands if Sir Rufus didn't do his job.'

She frowned.

'Who were these men, Fred?'

'I don't know. Mr Crutchley said there were some of the villagers there, those who're easily led, but it was strangers stirring them up. Albert Moffat told 'em to stop, but it doesn't look good. If Adam is found guilty...'

'He will not be. He has someone to vouch for him.' Amber rubbed her arms, as if by doing so she could thaw the icy numbness that had settled over her. She must try. 'Sir Rufus was going to see...the person. I am sure Adam's name will soon be cleared. In fact, it may well be resolved by now.'

'Thank goodness.' Fred dragged out his handkerchief and mopped his face. 'But that will not repair your business, mistress. I have ruined everything.'

'Not quite everything. It was very brave of you to tell me the truth.' The weight on her spirits had eased, just a little. 'Shall we go upstairs to see the damage?'

He blew his nose and stuffed the filthy handkerchief back in his pocket.

'I suppose I will have to leave Castonbury,' he said miserably. 'You will not trust me to work for you after this.'

'No, I will give you another chance, Fred.' Her smile went dreadfully awry. 'After all, you and Jacob and Maizie are all I have left now.'

The rooms above the shop had suffered little more than smoke damage and Amber was able to carry away some of her clothes, with Maizie prophesying cheerfully that after a day or so in the fresh air, the acrid smell of smoke would disappear. Amber spent the rest of the day with Maizie, Fred and Jacob, cleaning the rooms, opening the windows and declaring her intention of moving back in as soon as possible. She worked hard, hoping that by pushing herself to the limit she might be granted another night of oblivion. It worked, and she awoke the next day feeling much refreshed. The fact that she could also wear one of her own gowns helped to raise her spirits even more. It was a Sunday, and after attending the morning service she returned to the ruined warehouse ready to believe that something of her business might be salvaged, after all.

Now the emergency was over, the villagers had gone, and Jacob was wheezing and coughing so much that Amber was worried that he had inhaled too much smoke and she sent him off to his bed. Thus the task of clearing the yard and starting an inventory of the stock that had been salvaged fell to her and Fred. He worked tirelessly beside her, as if trying to make up for his previous offence, but his eagerness to please made him overzealous, hovering around Amber, trying to predict her every wish, when what she really wanted was to be left alone with her thoughts. She was a little surprised that there was no word from Sir Rufus and she tried hard not to want Adam to come and see her. She might believe, as Fred did, that he was innocent of the charges, but the image of Alicia's golden beauty stood between them. His inconstancy could never be forgiven.

The sound of footsteps on the cobbles made her look up. A stranger was approaching, a tall, spare man in a black frock coat. He raised his hat to her.

'Mrs Hall? I am Mr Elliot, surveyor for the Twiss Fire Insurance Company in Buxton.'

His long face and keen dark eyes showed no signs of warmth or friendliness.

'Do you usually make your calls on a Sunday, Mr Elliot?' she asked him.

'I would have preferred to speak to you yesterday morning, ma'am, but I was told you were indisposed. I trust you are fully recovered now?'

She wondered if he was funning. They were surrounded by the ashes of her livelihood. She was not sure she would ever fully recover from that. She said coolly, 'I am well, Mr Elliot, thank you. You are here to make your report, I suppose?'

'I am, madam, and also to conduct my own investigation into the, er, conflagration.'

She waved her hand.

'It is as you see, sir. The business is all gone. We have a little stock that was recovered from the shop. It is in the barn over there, and is yet to be—'

'Yes, I came here yesterday and spoke to your clerk.' He nodded to Fred, who was standing a few yards away. 'Since then I have been making further enquiries.' He pulled a notebook from his pocket and flicked through the pages. 'I understand a suspect has already been apprehended.'

'Yes, but—'

'A Mr Adam Stratton.'

'But that was a mistake,' said Fred. 'He didn't do it.'

Mr Elliot did not look up from his notes.

'Sir Rufus has committed him for trial.'

'But that is impossible,' said Amber. 'He has a witness—'

The hooded eyes flickered over her briefly.

'Apparently not.'

Amber shook her head.

'It does not matter. I do not believe Mr Stratton is responsible. I have decided I shall not bring a prosecution against him.'

'I am afraid that is not up to you, Mrs Hall.' His sonorous voice had the sombre ring of a death bell. 'I was speaking with the butcher and his wife earlier today. They tell me Mr Stratton has already sent for his lawyer. From Rossendale.'

'What if he has?'

Mr Elliot put his notebook back in his pocket and put his palms together, as if in prayer.

'I am also informed that Mr Stratton has a business of his own in that area.' He saw her frown and added softly, 'Mrs Crutchley heard that from Mr Stratton's mother, who is housekeeper at Castonbury Park. One would imagine she would know such things, would she not?'

'Well, yes, but—'

'This started me thinking. You see, we—the Twiss Fire Insurance Company, that is—have recently been visiting areas northwest of here, looking for new business, you understand. I remembered that there are a number of mills in that area owned by a Mr Stratton. He is, in fact, the largest manufacturer in the area. Unfortunately he has already made his own arrangements regarding fire insurance, but—'

'Yes, yes,' Amber broke in impatiently. 'What has this to do with anything?'

The man's thin lips curved slightly, in the first signs of a grim smile.

'Whether or not it is the same Mr Stratton I have yet to discover, but it is very likely. And even if he is not, a man who can afford to summon his own lawyer to defend him is a man of substance, and can afford to pay for the damage caused here. We will prosecute Mr Adam Stratton.'

Amber took a step back.

'But he didn't do it. I know he did not.'

'And how can you be so sure of that, Mrs Hall?'

Amber glanced at Fred, who was listening white-faced to the exchange.

'I—I know the man. Having thought it all over I am sure he is innocent.'

'Then he may call you as a witness to his good character when we meet with the magistrate again on Wednesday morning. He will need you, Mrs Hall. From what I can gather the villagers are very angry about this crime. They are looking for a scapegoat.' He touched his hat. 'Good day to you, Mrs Hall.'

He turned and walked off, leaving Amber to stare after him.

'What does it mean, mistress?' Fred came up, his voice and face strained with anxiety.

Amber kept her eyes on the surveyor's retreating form and did not reply until he was out of sight.

'The insurers want to recover their money,' she said slowly.

'But not by convicting Adam. Not if he is innocent.'

'No, not if he is innocent.' The lethargy that had

overwhelmed Amber for the past days fell away. She said decisively, 'Get the wagon ready for me, Fred. I am going out.'

Chapter Eleven

Adam put down his axe and eased his shoulders. The pile of logs he had chopped for the fire was enough to last well into the winter. He just hoped he wouldn't be staying here that long. The restriction on his movements was beginning to irk him. He had not even been allowed to go to church that morning, so once he had fed and exercised Bosun in the Park he had looked for ways to work off his energy. The previous two days had been spent writing letters to his mill managers and his man of business, as well as his lawyer, but now all he could do was wait for their replies. He had already fixed the loose slates on the roof, and once he had filled the woodshed he wondered just what he would do to occupy his time.

Occupying his mind, of course, was not a problem. He thought constantly of the fire, wondering how Amber was coping. He desperately wanted to help her, but for the present he could not even help himself. He was not entirely surprised that Alicia had refused to corroborate his story. From what Giles had told him she was under considerable suspicion herself, the family at the great house reluctant to accept that she was really Jamie's wife. To admit that she had been walking with him, alone and late at night, would do nothing for her reputation. He had seen her in the Park yesterday, but she had turned back when he came into sight and he did not pursue her. What would be the point? He was not the sort of man to force her into telling the truth.

He tried not to think what would happen if he was found guilty of arson. It carried the death penalty and would mean transportation at the very least, and confiscation of his property. All he had worked so hard to build up would be lost. His head came up. Was that not what Amber had said to him when he had asked her to marry him? If this was how she felt, so helpless, so vulnerable, no wonder she was so reluctant to say yes.

A movement caught his eye. A wagon was approaching. Adam held his breath. He put up his hand to shield his eyes against the low sun and stayed thus as the wagon slowly lumbered up to him. There was no mistake; it was Amber, her figure in its close-fitting riding habit outlined against the sun. A number of greetings rose up in his mind. 'How dare you come here!' 'Have you come to gloat?' 'Do you realise now you have accused the wrong man?' 'You look wonderful.'

He said none of them, but remained watching as she carefully brought the dray horse to a stand just feet away from him.

'I came to warn you.'

He raised his brows. He had not expected that from her.

'Oh? What other charges are to be levelled at me?'

'None by me,' she said quickly. Now she was close he could see how pale she was, with dark circles beneath her eyes. Those same eyes met his gaze steadily. 'Fred told me about the order book. I know now what he did to you. He is distraught, and so very sorry.'

'So he should be.'

'He believes it was Parwich who fired the warehouse.'

'And you? What do you think?'

'I believe that too.'

It was as if a weight had been lifted from his shoulders. He took a step forward but she put up her hand.

'That is not the end of it. I have spoken to Sir Rufus and told him I no longer believe you are guilty, but the insurers have taken up the matter. They will bring a prosecution against you.'

Adam shrugged.

'Let them try.'

She was still for a moment, irresolute, then she said, 'Mr Elliot, the insurance surveyor, thinks you are a very rich man. That you own a number of mills in Lancashire. Is that true?'

'Would that make any difference to you?'

She gave the tiniest shake of her head. 'If you are so very wealthy, why did you work for me, at such a meagre wage?'

Because I wanted to be near you, to help you. Because I loved you, although I did not know it then.

The words filled his brain, but somehow he could not bring himself to say them.

'I was in Castonbury, and at a loose end...'

A shadow passed across her face. Was it disappointment? She looked away.

'Lady Hatherton is not standing by you?'

'You make it sound as if we are lovers.'

'Are you not?'

'Of course we are not!' he exclaimed 'Our meeting was purely accidental, but I cannot blame her for not wanting to involve herself in this.' He stared at her. When she remained silent he muttered curses under his breath. 'You do not believe me.'

'No.'

'It is the truth. I fear she has more to lose than I.'

'More!' For a brief moment he saw behind her icy mask. She was afraid for him, and his heart leapt. She gathered up the reins. 'You risk everything, Adam Stratton, including your life. This is my doing. I have put you in danger, and I must now do what I can to free you.'

Adam frowned.

'No,' he said sharply. 'I am bound on oath to Lord Giles not to leave here, but once my people arrive—'

Amber flicked her whip expertly at the horse's rump.

'It may be too late by then. I am afraid Parwich will try to raise the mob against you, unless I can prove first that he is the guilty party.'

'No, Amber, wait!' He grabbed the horse's bridle. 'I cannot let you put yourself in danger for me!'

Her icy glance swept over him.

'I do not do this for you, Adam Stratton, but for my own conscience.' She raised her eyes to look past him. 'Pray let me go now. I see the constable is coming, to make sure you are keeping to your word.'

'At least tell me what you are going to do.'

'I want to see justice done, that is all.'

The wagon moved off and short of jumping aboard and grabbing the reins out of her hands there was nothing he could do to stop her.

Amber drove away, ignoring Adam's calls. She could not forgive him just yet, not while there was still doubt about his meeting with the beautiful widow. Her own father had told her that no man could resist a pretty face, and she knew only too well that Adam was a red-blooded male! That thought made her sigh to be in his arms again, but she could not relent, not until she knew the truth. With no little trepidation she drove on to the Dower House.

Alicia, Lady Hatherton, stood before the window, her hands clasped before her. She looked extremely nervous.

'I heard about the fire,' she said without preamble. 'I am very sorry for it, but I have never ordered anything from you.'

'I am not here on business,' said Amber. 'At least, not directly. My visit concerns Adam.'

Alicia stared at her, frowning slightly. Then her brow cleared.

'You mean Mr Stratton.'

'Yes. He is accused of setting fire to my warehouse.'

'And what is that to do with me?'

'He says he was with you at the time.'

Alicia gave a little start of surprise.

'H-how do you know that?'

Amber kept her eyes on the widow's face.

'As the injured party, I was there when Adam told the magistrate.'

'And…how many other people know of this?'

'I was the only one present besides Sir Rufus. Adam said he was escorting you back to the Dower House.'

Alicia was very pale. She shook her head, making the golden curls dance.

'That—that is nonsense. I told Sir Rufus as

much. I d-did not leave the Dower House that night.'

'That makes a liar of Adam Stratton.'

Alicia hunched a shoulder and turned away.

'I cannot help that.'

Amber bit her lip.

'If his actions sprang from merely chivalrous motives you are repaying him very ill.'

'Who would believe me if I were to tell them as much?' She swung round, spreading her hands. 'My reputation—'

'Is your reputation worth more than a man's life?'

Alicia's cheeks grew white.

'It will not come to that.'

'Why not? If he is found guilty...'

'This is nothing to do with me. I was not there!'

'If you were meeting someone else in the village, you need not involve them.'

'Mr Stratton did not name anyone?'

'No.' Amber waited, but when there was no response she said impatiently, 'To deny seeing Adam is to place him in great danger. Please—'

Alicia put her hands over her ears.

'No, no, I shall not listen to you! I cannot be a

witness without risking my reputation. And I have my son to consider.'

'But you know Mrs Stratton, do you not?' Amber pressed on. 'Has she not always been kind to you? This is *her* son that we are talking of.'

'It cannot be helped,' declared Alicia, holding up her head. 'Pray do not importune me any further. I would like you to leave now.'

Amber looked at the rigid figure before her. There was a stubborn determination in that pretty face and Amber could find no words to fight it.

'Very well,' she said quietly. 'I will go, but I wonder how you will live with your conscience, if your silence brings about the ruin of an innocent man.' She walked to the door but before opening it she turned again. 'Will you tell me one thing, in confidence—one woman to another?' Alicia looked at her and Amber thought at first she would not answer, but at last she gave a slight nod and Amber forced herself to ask the question that was in her heart. 'What is Adam Stratton to you?'

Alicia's blue eyes regarded her.

'Nothing,' she said at last. 'He is little more than a stranger. A kind stranger.'

* * *

No one thought it unusual for Mrs Hall to be calling at Castonbury Park, but when she asked for the housekeeper, and insisted she would see no one else, the rumours began to fly. After all, had she not accused Mrs Stratton's son of burning down her warehouse?

Amber could feel the speculation around her as she was led through the narrow passages to the housekeeper's sitting room and she was acutely aware of the delay as the little maid left her standing outside the door while she went in to tell Mrs Stratton just who was here to see her. She breathed a sigh of relief when the maid came out and said she might go in.

If her heart had been thudding uncomfortably while she was at the Dower House, it was positively hammering now. She had no right to expect any sort of welcome from Hannah Stratton, but the housekeeper greeted her with her usual quiet dignity and invited her to sit down. Hannah's cheeks were very pink, and her blue-grey eyes overbright, as if she had been crying.

'I have come to tell you I have withdrawn my charges against Adam.'

Hannah nodded.

'One of the maids brought the news back from the village this morning. But that is of no import now, is it? The insurers will insist he stands trial.'

'I know. That is why I have come to see you. I am determined to prove his innocence.' Amber flushed as the housekeeper regarded her keenly.

'I thought you were determined to see him hanged.'

'No, I never—' She bit her lip. 'I was…angry.'

'A woman scorned?' For a brief moment Hannah met her eyes. 'Adam told me of his meeting with Lady Hatherton.'

'I was wrong about that,' said Amber quietly. She bowed her head. 'I think now I have been wrong about so many things.'

'You know he loves you.'

'Does he?' Amber looked up. 'He has never said so.'

She read the sadness in the older woman's eyes.

'He has learned to keep his feelings well hidden. It is only recently that I have realised just how hard it was for him to grow up here, without a father. You will have heard the rumours about— that he might be the duke's son?'

'Yes, but I never heeded them. It means nothing to me.'

'Adam said he never cared about them either, but I think he did.' Hannah sank down on a chair, her hands clasped before her. 'When he was a child he asked me about his father and I fobbed him off. I had pledged that I would never disclose the truth and in return I was allowed to live and work here, to keep Adam with me.'

'I do not doubt you thought it was for the best.'

'I did, but now I wonder if I have done him a grave disservice.'

Amber did not know how to reply. At last she said, 'Your son is a good man, Mrs Stratton. I am sorry I did not see it earlier.'

'It is often the way,' murmured Hannah sadly. 'We do not appreciate something, until we lose it.'

Amber's heart contracted. She might well have lost Adam's affection. If so she would learn to live with that, but it would not stop her doing what she could to clear his name. She raised her head.

'Did Adam tell you I had accused him of taking the order book?'

'He did.'

She met Hannah's gaze steadily.

'I did not want to believe it, but at the time I could see no other explanation. Now I know I was wrong and I want to do what I can to put that right. I know who has my order book. I want to get it back and…and hopefully find some proof that there is a link between its theft and the fire in my warehouse. If we can do that, then Adam will be freed.'

'We?'

Amber took a deep breath.

'I have a plan. But I need your help.'

The black ducal carriage with the Rothermere Arms emblazoned on the doors drew every eye as it rattled into Hatherton the following morning. Inside, Hannah shifted uncomfortably on the deeply padded seat.

'Is this not a little…ostentatious?' She addressed the maid sitting opposite her, a plump, unprepossessing creature with a grimy, pockmarked face whose red nose and cheeks suggested an addiction to gin. A few frizzy grey curls peeped from beneath her mobcap and altogether she presented such a slatternly appearance that Hannah thought she would never employ such a wench at Castonbury Park. The creature was quite repulsive, except for a pair of laughing dark eyes that twinkled incorrigibly.

Amber had been at pains to make her disguise

as thorough as possible. Maizie's mobcap covered her hair and the gown Mrs Crutchley had given her was padded out to hide her figure. She was glad she had moved back into her own quarters above her shop the previous evening. Not only had it spared her the necessity of explaining her charade to Mrs Crutchley, but she had found ample quantities of ash and soot to enhance her disguise. The ash had worked like hair powder on the few glossy tendrils she allowed to escape, while a little of the soot together with judicious use of the rouge pot had coarsened her features perfectly. When she had finished, she was quite proud of her handiwork, and certain that Matthew Parwich would not look twice at such an unappealing creature.

'That is the whole point,' she said now, fiddling with the well-worn mittens that covered her hands. 'To supply cloth to the Duke of Rothermere is something Matthew Parwich will not readily forego. You did very well to persuade His Grace to allow you the carriage at such short notice.'

A soft blush suffused Hannah's features and Amber wondered if she was still in love with the duke. After all, she had served him faithfully for more than thirty years. Surely she would not have done so if she blamed him for getting her with child, and that Adam was his son was an open secret. That is how it was in a small place like Castonbury, nothing could be hidden. She smiled to herself. At least that is what everyone liked to believe, which is why Alicia, Lady Hatherton, intrigued them all so much: was she, or was she not, Lord Jamie's widow? Amber lost all desire to smile. Since the woman refused to help Adam, she had little sympathy for her.

'We are here.' Hannah's soft words interrupted her thoughts. 'And you were right, this *is* a busy time. There are two wagons unloading in his yard.'

Amber peeped out of the window.

'Excellent, that is just as I expected. Let us hope his staff will be tied up with the deliveries for a good while yet.'

Hannah hesitated. 'Should I tell him my name? He might connect me with Adam....'

'Just say you are from Castonbury Park. I am hoping his greed for the business will help us.'

Straightening her mobcap, Amber stepped out of the carriage. It was hard not to compare Parwich's business with her own. Or rather, what her own had been. The shop front was brightly painted with a garish sign over the door, and a three-storey warehouse to one side. Keeping her head bowed and adopting a rather shambling gait, Amber followed Hannah into the shop and was at once struck by how cluttered and untidy everything was. Bolts of cloth had been fetched down from the shelves and lay abandoned on a bench, ribbons flowed from a partly opened drawer and any number of pins were scattered on the counter. To one side she could see a little office, strewn with papers and books. Amber took comfort from the mess and the clutter. If Parwich was as careless in his business affairs as in his shop, she might well uncover some damning evidence against him.

A nervous-looking clerk stood behind the counter, but almost immediately Matthew Parwich appeared from a passage, which Amber guessed led to the warehouse.

'That's all, Harris, you can go and check in the deliveries for me. I will look after the shop.' He pushed past the clerk, who retreated immediately. 'Good day to you, madam. How may I help you?'

He came forward, his oleaginous manner making it plain to Amber that he knew this might be an important customer. Hannah drew herself up and regarded him with a faintly supercilious air.

'I am come from Castonbury Park.' She introduced herself with admirable calm. 'You will know, of course, that our orders with Ripley and Hall cannot now be fulfilled.'

'Ah, yes, the fire. Such a sad affair.'

His sympathy was so blatantly false that Amber's fingers curled until the nails were biting into her palms.

'Quite,' said Hannah briskly. 'His Grace is anxious to bespeak the new bed-hangings and servants' livery for his son's forthcoming wedding, and since Ripley and Hall cannot supply it…' She let the inference hang delicately in the air.

'My dear madam, let me assure you that Parwich's warehouse can provide anything His Grace should desire.'

Amber kept a respectful distance behind Hannah, listening with admiration as Hannah reeled off the list of materials she required. Her tone was confident, with just enough reserve to imply that she was not convinced the warehouse could supply her needs. Matthew Parwich did his best; he pulled bolts of fabric from the shelves, opened drawers full of trimmings, but still Hannah demurred.

'It is all so difficult. We have dealt with Ripley

and Hall for so many years, and they always had such a vast amount to choose from. So many different fabrics, and such an array of colours! His Grace will be anxious to know we can rely upon you.'

'Madam, I can assure you that we can match anything you could get from them. If you can spare the time, perhaps you would like to look around our extensive warehouse facilities....'

Hannah smiled graciously. 'That might help. His Grace will certainly want me to report back to him.' She turned to Amber. 'You may wait in the carriage for me. We will be...?' Hannah paused, raising her brows and Matthew Parwich spread his hands.

'A half-hour at least, ma'am, if you wish to see everything of relevance to His Grace's requirements.'

'I shall certainly want to see everything,' declared Hannah. 'Lead on, Mr Parwich.'

Amber moved slowly towards the door, but as soon as she was alone she turned back and went directly to the little office. The clerk might return at any moment, and it was a struggle to make a methodical search. Every surface was covered with papers, trade directories and pattern books.

An old-fashioned walnut knee-hole desk was set beneath the window with a number of ledgers stacked on it, together with piles of papers and trade cards. She ran a finger across the spines of the books before pulling out the accounts ledger. Quickly she scanned the entries. If Parwich had paid someone to set fire to her warehouse she hoped there might be some clue here, but nothing stood out. The entries were made in meticulous detail, many referring to payments to carriers and tradesmen, names that were familiar to her. Then, turning the page, she saw two entries in a different hand, made on the Friday following the fire. By comparison with the rest of the ledger these entries were stark, no detail, just two names that she did not recognise, each with a payment of five guineas. She picked up a pencil and took one of the trade cards from the pile, quickly writing down the details from the ledger. The card was secreted safely in her pocket and she put everything back as she found it.

A sudden noise made her jump. She looked around, but the shop was still empty. Heart hammering, she glanced at the clock. Less than ten minutes had passed, so she continued her search, looking in each of the drawers in turn before reaching down to try the cupboard at the back of the knee-hole. To her surprise it opened and she gave a whispered cry of delight. There, on top of an untidy pile of papers, was her order book.

She pulled it out and carefully closed the door. She must leave now, to stay longer would be to risk discovery. She rose and was just stepping out of the office when she heard the noise again. It sounded like a bump behind the panelling in the shop. Amber froze. Her straining ears caught another faint sound, like a soft whimper. Intrigued, her eyes swept the room. The alcove beside the fireplace was filled with shelves above a small cupboard. Unusually, the cupboard door was secured by a large bolt. She took a step closer, but her curiosity was tempered by caution. It might be rats, or perhaps a savage dog. She should take the order book and leave immediately. Then she heard another sound, something very like a hiccup. She pulled back the bolt and opened the door.

Curled up on the floor of the cupboard was a young boy. He had a deep cut on his cheek and his eyes were red-rimmed from crying. He looked about ten years old, but he was so undernourished that he might well have been older.

'Oh, you poor child. What in heaven's name are

you doing in there?' She reached out for him but he drew back, regarding her with huge, frightened eyes. Amber let her hands fall and knelt down. 'Can you not come out?'

'No, he'll belt me again if I do.'

'Who, Mr Parwich?'

'Aye.'

'Are you his apprentice?'

The boy shook his head.

'Then why are you here?'

'Nowhere else to go. Me mam was his moll until she died o' the pox.' He scrubbed at his eyes with his grimy knuckles. 'He never used to hit me when she was here.'

'What is your name?'

'Billy.'

'And how old are you?'

'T-twelve, I fink.'

The clock chimed, reminding Amber that her time was limited.

'Well, Billy, you do not have to stay with him,' she said gently.

'I do.' The boy gulped. 'He says he'll come after me and kill me if I runs away.'

'Oh, no, he won't,' declared Amber, making a

decision. She held out her hand. 'Come along, Billy. You are coming with me.'

Hannah's tour of the warehouse took considerably more than half an hour. She made sure to stop and inspect every type of fabric, posing questions, asking for prices, and by the time she left the shop the duke's coach had been standing in the street for almost an hour. Matthew Parwich escorted her to the carriage, where Amber was waiting for her, the ample skirts of her borrowed gown billowing over a good half of the floor space.

Hannah climbed in, holding her breath until the steps were put up, the door closed and the carriage set off. Then she let out a long and heartfelt sigh.

'That was the most nerve-racking thing I have ever done in my life!' She sat up suddenly. 'Did you get it?'

Amber nodded and pointed to the large leather-bound book beside her.

'And I doubt he will notice it is gone for quite some time. He seems to be shockingly disorganised.'

Hannah subsided back against the squabs again.

'Disorganised or not, my heart was thudding the whole time, thinking I would be found out!'

'He did not look suspicious when he handed you into the carriage,' observed Amber.

'No, thank heaven. He is no doubt thinking of the substantial order he expects—not that I shall be buying *anything* from the man, my dear. He is the most odious little toad-eater. Even if you are not able to supply our needs, I will not use him. I shall order the cloth from London, if necessary. I do not know when I have spent a more uncomfortable hour.'

'Nor do we,' said Amber. She looked down and said in a slightly louder voice, 'I think it is safe for you to come out now.'

She twitched aside her skirts to reveal a small and distinctly grubby boy.

'Heavens,' exclaimed Hannah. 'What on earth is this?'

'This is Billy,' said Amber calmly, pulling the child onto the seat beside her. 'We are helping him to escape from Mr Parwich. No need to be afraid,' she added quickly, 'he tells me he is not an apprentice. And you can see that he has been very cruelly treated. I found him locked in a cupboard, and he tells me Matthew Parwich gave him the cut on his cheek. Do I have that right, Billy?'

The boy nodded.

'Aye. He belted me. Took 'is belt off and lashed me with it,' he added, seeing Hannah's blank look. 'He only meant to 'it me across the shoulders, but the buckle came round an' caught me cheek.'

'And these cuts on your arms,' said Hannah, her soft heart melting. 'Where did you get those?'

The boy pulled his ragged sleeves down, as if ashamed of his injuries.

'That was from the broken glass,' he muttered.

'Well, we shall not allow you to be hurt any more,' declared Hannah, shocked. The poor child looked so anxious that she gave him a motherly smile. 'And why did he lock you in the cupboard?'

''Cos he don't want me talking to the delivery men.'

'But why?'

''Cos I knows things.'

'What sort of things?'

The boy looked suddenly nervous.

Amber took his grimy hand in hers again.

'Come along, Billy. Tell us what you know.'

Chapter Twelve

Adam spent a restless night and was pleased to see the dawn, when he could rise and make his preparations for the day. The evening had been interminable and he was impatient for news of Amber. When she had left him, there had been a look of determination on her face that worried him. She was quite capable of trying to tackle Parwich alone, and he was almost sick with fear of what might happen to her. Love, he was discovering, made cowards of the bravest men. He hoped his mother might find time to visit him that morning, but by noon no one had appeared and he decided that he would have to break his parole and go in search of Amber himself. He was shrugging himself into his coat when the constable appeared, announcing that Adam was to accompany him to Castonbury.

'Oh? Has anything occurred, is there any news?'

'That ain't for me to tell you.' The constable sniffed. 'What I *can* say is that Sir Rufus is waiting for you at the Rothermere Arms, so if you would be so good as to saddle yer horse, sir, we'll be on our way.'

It was an unusually hot day, making the journey to the village uncomfortably warm. There was a tension in the air and heavy storm clouds were boiling up from the west. By the time they reached the inn a thick grey blanket of cloud had swallowed up the sun and covered the earth in a dusky gloom. The first spots of rain fell as they left their horses with a stable boy and the constable led the way upstairs to the Long Room, where he declared that the magistrate would be waiting.

There were three people behind the tables at the far end of the room, Sir Rufus sitting in the centre with a thin, long-faced man in a black frock coat on his left and a heavily veiled woman on the right. The magistrate signalled to the constable to leave, and as the door closed he addressed Adam.

'This is a matter of some delicacy, so we will discuss it privately.' He waved his hand at the stranger on his left. 'This is Mr Elliot,' he announced. 'He represents the Twiss Fire Insurance

Company.' He waited a moment, but no one spoke. After a quick glance to his right he continued. 'Lady Hatherton came to see me this morning.' He cleared his throat. 'She is prepared to swear on oath that she carried a message to the village on the night of the fire, and that you escorted her back to the Dower House.'

'That is correct,' averred Adam.

Sir Rufus scowled.

'Aye, well, I brought her here immediately to see Mr Elliot.' He stopped again, fixing the man with his bushy-browed stare.

'Yes, he did.' Elliot sat up, steepling his fingers. He paused to let a rumble of thunder die away. 'I have examined her, and with the other information I have gathered, I have concluded that there is not enough evidence to proceed with a prosecution.'

Mr Elliot's lugubrious countenance told Adam he was not pleased with this result.

'Aye,' growled Sir Rufus. 'You are no longer under arrest.'

'Thank you,' said Adam shortly. 'So I am free again to go where I will?'

'That's right.'

'Then the first thing I aim to do is to find out just who did start that fire!'

He was halfway to the door when it opened.

'Just a moment!' Matthew Parwich marched in, followed by two men, burly individuals that Adam knew he had seen before.

The constable followed them, looking harassed. 'I beg yer pardon, sir, but they insisted....'

'Yes, yes, just shut the door, Huggins. You may as well remain in here now,' muttered Sir Rufus. He raised his fierce eyes to Matthew Parwich. 'And who are you?'

'Matthew Parwich, from Hatherton,' he said, tucking his cane under his arm and pulling off his gloves. 'I have been following events here closely.'

'Oh?' Mr Elliot sat forward and subjected him to a keen-eyed scrutiny. 'And why should that be, Mr Parwich?'

'I, too, am a clothier, and if one warehouse has been burned down, what is to stop it happening again?'

'It won't,' snapped Sir Rufus. 'If we can catch the villain.'

'Which is why I brought these fellows to see you,' said Parwich smoothly. 'I have been making my own enquiries, you see, and came upon these two—they witnessed the whole thing.'

'Aye,' said one of the men. 'We saw it all.'

They shifted nervously before the magistrate. Perhaps it was the sudden flash of lightning that had put them on edge. Adam's eyes narrowed. He would swear now that these were the men from the crowd. He took another good look at them, trying to imagine them in livery, with full powdered wigs: it was possible they had been the footmen who had accompanied Parwich to the warehouse on that same Thursday. The rumble of thunder underlined the bolt of anger that went through him as another memory crowded in. These were the men who had attacked Amber at the ford.

'And what is your name?' barked Sir Rufus, raising his voice to be heard above the thunder.

'Jem Stills, Yer Honour.'

'And your companion?'

'Dan Fletcher, sir.'

'So you saw everything?' pursued Mr Elliot.

'Aye.' The man called Stills nodded. 'It was late on Thursday night. We was making our way back through the high street when I sees a movement in the warehouse yard. Dan and I watched someone climb out over the gate and run down the road to the inn. Next thing we knows the fire bell is clamourin' and the self-same fellow is racing back towards the warehouse.'

'And may I ask what you were doing in Castonbury at that time of night?' asked Sir Rufus.

'Looking for our boy,' said Dan Fletcher. 'Our little Billy. Run away, he had, but we heard as how he'd come Castonbury way so we followed him. Found him sleeping under a bush, so we was fetching him home. Ask anyone who was in the crowd that night. They would've seen us.'

'And who was the man you saw running away from the warehouse?' asked Sir Rufus.

Fletcher raised his finger and pointed at Adam.

'Him. No doubt about it. There was a lantern burning at the front of the building and we saw his face, plain as day.'

'Indeed?' Mr Elliot leaned back in his chair again. 'But we have a witness who says Mr Stratton was escorting her home at the time the fire started. He did not get back to the village until the warehouse was well alight.'

His eyes flickered towards Alicia.

'Perhaps the lady was mistaken.' Matthew Parwich stared hard at the veiled figure.

'She could hardly mistake a gentleman who was walking her home,' objected Sir Rufus.

'May we know the witness's name?' Parwich's request was greeted by an urgent shaking of the veiled head and he continued silkily, 'I see. Well, Sir Rufus, I have found you two independent witnesses who are prepared to swear to one thing, and you have a female who refuses to allow herself to be named....'

The inference was clear. Adam clamped down hard on the angry retort that sprang to his lips. The thunder rumbling around the skies seemed to taunt him. Suddenly his freedom was slipping away from him.

'Let it come to court, then,' he declared. 'I will prove my innocence there.'

Matthew Parwich turned to him, an ugly smile curling his thin lips.

'Will you now? And will your witness stand up in open court and vouch for you? I think not.'

Glancing at the wilting figure beside Sir Rufus, Adam doubted it too. Parwich continued, hardly able to keep the gloating triumph out of his voice. 'In fact, I am almost sure I could name her now. Is it not Mrs Hall, your lover, and accomplice in trying to defraud the insurance company?'

'How wrong you are, Matthew Parwich. Mr Stratton's witness is certainly not me!'

Amber's voice cut through the air and Parwich swung round, his eyes snapping angrily. She was standing in the doorway, one hand resting upon her closed umbrella, which dripped all the while onto the floor. Her cheeks were flushed and her hair was a little less tidy than usual, but she looked magnificent. Hannah was there, too, her voluminous cloak spread around herself and a small boy who was clinging anxiously to her hand.

Adam did not miss the wary look that flickered across Parwich's face. Fletcher started forward, exclaiming, 'Billy, my boy! Have you been running off again?'

'Keep your distance!' The end of Amber's umbrella caught him in the chest, holding him away. 'The boy is in my care now.'

'Nonsense!' snapped Parwich. 'He is my clerk, and I demand you return him to me!'

'A clerk whose only wages are blows?' Amber eyed him scornfully. 'He has signed no contract with you, and at twelve years old the boy is free to choose where he will live.'

'How did he get to you?'

'I found him at your shop this morning.' Triumph gleamed in the glance she threw at Adam. 'I disguised myself as Mrs Stratton's attendant. Very effectively, too, it seems.'

Adam grinned. 'The devil you did!'

'We would have been here sooner but we stopped at the shop for Mrs Hall to change back into her own clothes,' Hannah explained. 'And to clean the cut on Billy's face.'

Over the boy's head Adam looked at Amber. He hoped she could read in his gaze everything he wanted to tell her. The blazing triumph in her own dark eyes softened a little and his spirits climbed. Some demon of mischief made him murmur, 'I only wish I could have seen your disguise.'

A telltale blush suffused her cheeks.

'You would not have recognised me.'

Mr Elliot tapped on the table.

'I am sure this is all very interesting, Mrs Hall, but it has nothing to do with the case in hand.'

'Oh, but it does, Mr Elliot. I want you to listen to this boy's story.'

Jem Stills began to edge towards the door.

'P'raps we should be goin'—'

'Stay where you are!' barked Sir Rufus. He signalled to the constable to block the exit. 'Very well, proceed.'

Hannah removed her cloak and looked down at Billy, who shrank closer as another lightning flash lit the room.

'Come along now, dear, you must tell the gentlemen what you have told us.'

She pulled his cap from his head and put it into his hands, smiling encouragement. Outside the thunder rumbled ominously.

'Thursday last I was sleepin' in me cupboard—'

'Your cupboard?' Sir Rufus interrupted him.

'Yesser. In Mr Parwich's shop. He locks me in there every night.' He looked up at Amber, who smiled and nodded at him.

'Go on, Billy. There is nothing to be afraid of here.'

The boy swallowed.

'Anyway, he comes and wakes me up, and tells me to get me coat on 'cos I'm to go out with these two.' He waved his hand towards Stills and Fletcher. 'They took me to Castonbury and threw me over the gate into the warehouse yard, then they clambers over. Then they breaks the small window by the door and shoves me through.'

'Stuff and nonsense!' exclaimed Parwich. 'How much did she pay you to say all this, boy?'

'Quiet!' roared Sir Rufus. He fixed his eyes on Billy. 'Go on, lad.'

'I opens the door for them, and they says I'm to wait there. Then they goes off, and when they comes back I can smell smoke, and see flames comin' from the back of the building.' He looked frequently at Hannah and Amber as he continued to speak. 'We got back over the gate an' hid up the lane for a bit, 'til the flames was fair lighting up the building. Then the alarm was raised, and that man comes running up.' He pointed to Adam.

'And what happened then?' Amber prompted him gently.

'Then Jem says, "That's the cove what Mr Parwich bamboozled today, remember? Got him turned off for stealing that order book." "So 'tis," says Dan. "An' if I ain't mistaken he's the one as got in our way at the ford too. Well, we'll have our own back now."'

A curse from Dan Fletcher made him stop and shrink closer to Hannah.

'You need have no fear, lad,' said Sir Rufus, glaring at Fletcher. 'Tell us what happened next.'

'We waited 'til the crowd was around us, then Dan and Jem said as how they thought it was him—'

Mr Elliot interjected. 'You mean Mr Stratton?'

Billy nodded. 'Aye, they kept baiting the crowd 'til they turned on him, and he was taken off to be locked up.'

'A pack of lies, thought up by these two women,' declared Parwich. 'Sir Rufus, surely you do not believe any of this? Why, one is the man's mother, the other his doxy!'

Amber's face flamed, but even as Parwich spat out the word Adam flew at him, fists clenched. A clap of thunder coincided with Adam's punch to the jaw that sent Parwich sprawling on the floor. The constable stepped up and put his brawny arms around Adam to restrain him.

'Now, now, sir, you will do yourself no good by this.' The constable grunted as Adam struggled in his grip.

'You see the kind of man you are dealing with,' sneered Matthew Parwich, struggling to his feet. 'He is quick to anger, the sort who would take his revenge when turned off for thieving. Heaven knows why Mrs Hall should want to protect him, but they have fabricated everything, and the boy is their instrument.'

'Yeah, we've never seen this boy before!' declared Jem.

'But I thought you said earlier you had been looking for him?' purred Mr Elliot.

'No—I—that is, it was a different boy!' declared Dan, glaring at his accomplice.

The surveyor turned to address Billy.

'Do you know the names of these two men?'

'Dan and Jem.'

'Is that all?'

Billy nodded.

'He heard those names here in this room,' declared Matthew Parwich. 'The boy was snatched from my shop and is trying to blacken my name out of spite. I ask you, sir, I find two honest witnesses for you, they come here of their own free will and are then subjected to—'

'Sir Rufus,' Amber interrupted him. 'Have you been given the names of these two witnesses?'

The magistrate regarded his notes.

'Aye, I have them here.'

Amber was searching in her reticule. She pulled out a small paste card and handed it to Sir Rufus.

'I was at Mr Parwich's shop this morning, and I found these names in his ledger, a payment of five guineas against each, paid the Friday after the fire at my warehouse. Ask him to produce his accounts ledger, and you will see for yourself.'

'Well, well,' murmured Mr Elliot, leaning close to read the card. 'Fletcher and Stills. These, ah, *independent witnesses* appear to be in your pay, Mr Parwich.'

Sir Rufus rubbed his chin.

'Hmm, I think this, together with the boy's statement, is enough to—what—? Stop them!'

There was a sudden commotion. Parwich made a dash for the door but he was blocked by his accomplices, who were also making a bid for freedom. The constable lunged at Fletcher, who was leading the way. Parwich pushed Stills into the grappling men, sending all three of them crashing to the ground and leaving his escape clear.

In a flash Adam was after him. He jumped over the tangle of legs in his way and reached out to grab his quarry. As his hand closed on Parwich's shoulder, his opponent wrenched off the Malacca shaft of his sword stick and swung around. Adam sprang away but he was not in time to avoid the gleaming blade, which sliced through the left sleeve of his jacket. Almost immediately a dark stain began to seep over the cloth. Parwich bared his teeth.

'You have been a damned nuisance since you arrived here, Stratton. It is time I put you away.'

Amber looked about her. The veiled lady was the only one remaining in her seat, her hands clasped anxiously before her. Sir Rufus and Mr

Elliot had joined the constable and were holding Fletcher and Stills, who were struggling violently, and it was taking all their efforts to restrain them. There would be no help from that quarter. In a fury she turned back to Matthew Parwich.

'Shame!' she cried. 'How dare you attack an unarmed man?'

'Let him stand aside, then,' growled Parwich, the wicked blade waving menacingly. Adam stood between him and the door.

He won't do it, thought Amber, her stomach tightening. *He will die before he backs down.*

'Here!' Hannah threw her cloak to Adam, who quickly tossed it around his left forearm as he hurled himself forwards again.

Parwich lunged. Adam sidestepped, catching the sword in the folds of cloth even as his right hand came up and delivered a crashing blow to the chin. Parwich dropped unconscious to the floor.

A temporary silence replaced the mayhem of the past few minutes. Billy shrank against Hannah, watching the proceedings with round, frightened eyes. Having tied up Fletcher and Stills, the constable now approached Matthew Parwich while Adam stood over him, the sword stick in his right hand.

Mr Elliot moved back towards the table, brushing down his coat with hands that were not quite steady. The fracas had shaken him out of his usual cold placidity. The veiled figure leaned forward and murmured to him. He nodded and turned to the magistrate.

'You appear to have the situation under control again, Sir Rufus. We will discuss everything later, but the lady is distressed. With your permission I will take her away.'

'Aye, please do.' Sir Rufus nodded. 'Take my carriage. I will deal with the rest here.'

Mr Elliot helped the woman to her feet.

'Come, madam, I will escort you home.'

As they passed, Amber stepped into their path. A lightning flash penetrated the thick veil and she could just make out Lady Hatherton's pale features.

'I guessed it was you,' she said quietly. 'Thank you. Thank you for having the courage to do what was right.'

Silently Alicia bowed her head and allowed Mr Elliot to lead her away.

Sir Rufus held out his hand.

'I'll take that sword stick now, Mr Stratton.'

Adam handed over the sword, then held up the cloak, grinning at Amber. 'Excellent material, is it from your warehouse?'

'Yes, I— Adam, your arm!'

'What?' He glanced at his sleeve, where a dark stain was spreading. 'Oh. It is nothing.'

'Let me see.' She eased his coat over his shoulders. Beneath, the shirtsleeve was scarlet. She bit her lip as she pulled away the sodden linen to reveal a deep gash on his arm. 'We must stop the bleeding. May I use your neck cloth to bind it up?'

Even as she spoke her fingers reached for the knot, fumbling slightly. She met his eyes and saw the glinting smile in his own.

'Can you do it? You nearly choked me last time.'

She felt herself blushing. 'Adam, hush!'

'I do not care who hears me.' He raised his head. 'I love you, Amber Hall. I love you more than life itself.'

She gazed up at him. Had he really said those words? The truth was shining in his eyes and she felt herself grow weak.

She said quietly, 'And I love you, too, Adam. I think I always have, from that very first day when you came to my rescue.'

'I am very glad to hear it,' he declared, smiling down tenderly at her. 'Because I intend to marry you.'

Blushing, she sought for a distraction and realised she had not yet finished binding up his arm.

Parwich gave a crack of evil laughter.

'Marriage? Ha, that's rich!'

Amber ignored him as she tied Adam's neck cloth around the wound. It was more important to stem the bleeding than to listen to the man's vitriolic outpourings.

'Be careful how you speak of my future wife,' barked Adam.

'She'll never be your wife, unless you are too debauched to consider the consequences!'

'Parwich, I am warning you—'

'You are Rothermere's bastard!'

The venomous words filled the room, bringing a hush over everyone.

Hannah sank onto a chair, unconsciously pulling Billy towards her. Adam's brows rose. Amber almost smiled at the supreme indifference of his shrug.

'And if I am? If Mrs Hall does not object—'

Her heart swelled with pride.

'Of course not,' she replied, head held high.

'Adam Stratton is too much of a man to be diminished by an accident of birth.'

'Not diminished by his own parentage, perhaps, but what of *yours*, madam? Have you told him of your own "accident of birth"?' Matthew Parwich looked from one to the other. 'Or can it be that you do not know?'

Amber frowned. She did not like the man's sly tone. Her fingers trembled as she fastened the last knot and Adam covered her hands with his good one, looking past her to say, 'You are talking nonsense, Parwich. Sir Rufus, take him away with his friends and lock them all up!'

'Aye, come along now. Huggins, ask the landlord to spare me a couple of men to get these three to the lock-up.'

'First rule of business, Stratton, know thy competitor!' cried Parwich as he was bundled towards the door. 'I have been making enquiries about Amber Hall, née Ripley. *She is not John Ripley's daughter!*'

For the second time the room went still. A crash of thunder followed hard upon the words, as if the heavens themselves were pronouncing judgement. The rain began, building to a steady roar upon the roof. Sir Rufus nodded to the constable to take Stills and Fletcher away, then closed the door behind them, saying quietly, 'Perhaps we need to hear this out.'

Amber laughed and shook her head.

'There is nothing to hear. The man is deranged!'

'Am I?' His malevolent grin sent a shiver down her spine. 'I made it my business to find out about you, Mrs Hall, when it became clear that you were not going to quit Castonbury without a fight. If you had agreed to sell to me I would have not said a word, but you have brought all this on yourself.'

'All what?' said Amber, puzzled. 'What are you talking about?'

'You are another of Rothermere's bastards.'

Amber reeled back, the unexpected words were like a physical blow.

'That is a lie!'

'I have a signed deposition that says it is true. I put it in the same cupboard as your order book. If you had looked more closely you may well have found it. Your mother was a servant in Hatherton's household, was she not?'

'Yes, most families in the area have at least one child employed there....'

'Aye,' Parwich cut across her. 'My people turned up an old man, a servant who remembers your mother. He also remembers she was quite a favourite with Lord Hatherton—the old duke was still alive then, so your father was the Marquis of Hatherton— and that she left very quickly to marry a Castonbury man. Once I knew that I dug deeper. A little pressure, a few guineas here and there and people are only too willing to delve into the records, even those going back twenty-seven years. I discovered a draft on the Marquis of Hatherton's account for seven hundred guineas, payable to John Ripley on the day of his marriage.' His mouth twisted into a sneer. 'A large dowry for a chambermaid.'

'Lies,' declared Adam. 'The evil ranting of a guilty man.'

'Oh, I may be guilty of many things, Stratton, but in this I am telling the truth.' Parwich turned to Sir Rufus. 'When you search my premises for the accounts book, make sure you look in the knee-hole desk. I will make a gift of that deposition to my charming competitor.'

Amber felt the life draining out of her.

'No.' She stepped away from him, shaking her head. 'No, that cannot be true, because it would mean...'

She felt suddenly very dizzy but knew she must

not lean against Adam. She must not look for support there.

'Quite,' purred Matthew. 'Stratton is your half-brother. What do you think of him now, my dear? I hope your feelings for him are of a…*sisterly* nature.'

Amber's hands flew to her face. The drumming of the rain was surpassed by her own heartbeat pounding against her ribs.

'No,' she said again. 'I won't believe it.'

'Ask your vicar. He is damned close to the old duke, ain't he? And he was mighty disturbed when I asked him about your birth. Mighty disturbed.'

'Oh, my dear child!'

Hannah's anguished exclamation was too much. Amber felt physically sick. She had to get out of this room. Everyone was looking at her with a mixture of horror, sympathy and pity. She needed to think. She had to get away from here. Away from Adam.

'Mistress, are you ill?'

Billy's faltering voice forced her into action.

'No. Yes, but it is nothing serious.' She managed to look at Hannah. 'Can you take him…?'

'Of course. Billy will come back with me in the carriage,' Hannah said quickly. 'But, Amber—'

'No.' She shook her head. 'No more.'

Hannah reached out for her. 'Amber, wait. Let me—'

Amber shrank away.

'I must go. Excuse me!'

She almost ran out of the room. She looked neither right nor left, afraid of what she might see in people's eyes. The door had been closed, no one outside could have heard Matthew Parwich's revelation, but she *felt* so different. If it was true, if she was the duke's natural daughter, then she and Adam— She shuddered. No, no, she must not even think it.

The rain was sheeting down, bouncing off the cobbles in the yard and turning the street beyond to a brown muddy river. Amber had forgotten her umbrella, but no power on earth would persuade her to go back for it. Within moments of stepping out of doors the wet was seeping through to her skin. She broke into a run, thankful the street was deserted.

'Amber!' She heard Adam's voice behind her. His hand closed on her arm, forcing her to stop.

'Go away, Adam. I c-cannot be near you.'

'None of this is proved, Amber.'

'But what if it is true? What we have done…'

'No one knows of that.'

'*We* know of it.'

'And we must live with it—we *can* do so! Let me come with you to see the vicar—' She shook her head and he stifled a curse. 'Hell and damnation, Amber, I want to know the truth as much as you.'

'Then wait at the inn. I will send word there for you.'

'Can I not come—?'

'No. I would not have him know about you.'

'You cannot deny me!'

'I can. Adam.' A sob escaped her. 'I must.'

'No.' He gripped her arms, his voice shaking. 'I cannot lose you now—' He stopped, as if searching for the right words. 'I love you, Amber. I should have told you earlier, but I did not recognise it for what it was. You are my heart, my soul. My life. Don't go!'

He stood before her, hatless, his hair plastered to his head as the rain ran down over his face. It was as if heaven was crying for them. She lifted one hand and touched his cheek.

'Oh, my love, there is nothing else to be done.' Her own tears were mingling with the rain on her cheeks. 'What I feel for you...from the beginning the connection was so strong. Perhaps now I know the reason.'

He caught her hand and dragged it to his mouth, kissing her palm. Amber closed her eyes. Thunder cracked directly overhead but even that did not make her flinch. It could have been her heart breaking in two.

'I will not believe it,' he muttered savagely. 'There must be some mistake.'

'Pray that there is.' Tears choked her, she could barely speak. 'If all he said is true, then I can never see you again. I dare not. This must be goodbye.'

She looked away; the pain in his eyes was unbearable. It took a supreme effort of will to pull her hand out of his grasp. Even more to turn and walk away, leaving Adam behind her.

'Mrs Hall!'

The vicar's housekeeper beckoned her quickly into the hall, exclaiming at her foolishness in being out of doors in such weather.

'I need to see Reverend Seagrove, Mrs Jeffries.' Amber's teeth were chattering as cold and shock set in. Her heart sank when she received no reply. 'Is he not here?'

'Yes, he's here, dearie, but you'll not see him

like that. You will catch your death if we do not get you dry.' The housekeeper took her arm. 'Come along into the kitchen, by the fire.'

Half an hour later Amber was shown into the little parlour where the reverend received his visitors. Mrs Jeffries had found her a voluminous wrap to wear while her own clothes dried before the fire and her damp hair hung in a curling dark mass about her shoulders. When she was seated comfortably in a chair, he bent his kindly gaze upon her.

'Well, now, ma'am, what is it that has brought you to my door in this state? I have been acquainted with you long enough to know it must be serious.'

Amber did not reply immediately. She had to know the truth, but where to begin? At last, haltingly, she told him of Matthew Parwich's allegations.

'I have been going over and over it in my mind as I walked here,' she ended, wringing her hands together. 'It is true my father bought the warehouse and started his business at the time that I was born, but I always thought…that is, I never *thought* about it at all! Now, if what he says is true…'

The vicar sighed and took a turn about the room, his hands behind his back.

'I have been expecting this,' he murmured sadly. 'I am so very sorry. Mr Parwich came here a couple of weeks ago, asking if he might look at the parish registers, and he asked some searching questions about your birth. I said I could not help him, and hoped that was the end of it.'

'So, is it true, am I His Grace's n-natural daughter?'

The pause was barely a heartbeat, yet it seemed to stretch on for ever.

'I am afraid you are.'

'There can be no doubt?'

He shook his head. 'His Grace told me so himself.'

'I see.' She took out her handkerchief and wiped away a rogue tear.

The vicar walked to the window, saying with a sigh, 'This is in part my fault. His Grace confided in me years ago. He had reached that time of life when men begin to think over their past actions. He explained that he had been attracted to a servant, had seduced her.' He added quickly, 'His Grace was insistent that no blame should be attached to your mother for what occurred. She was an innocent and already betrothed to John Ripley, which made his actions all the more shameful. Realising how badly he had acted, he confessed the whole to Ripley and persuaded him to go ahead with the marriage. Ripley was eager to do so, and the money he gave him to set up his own business was more a sop to his own conscience than a bribe. He truly believed—and having seen you grow up I agree with him—that the marriage was a happy one.

'The duke told me he was minded to acknowledge you but it was I who advised him against it. You were newly married, the business was going well. I thought it could only do harm.' He sank into a chair, dropping his head in his hands. 'If you had been told then, this shock might have been avoided.'

Amber gave a little shake of her head.

'You were not to know. But it pains me to think my whole life has been a lie, a sham.'

He raised his head, saying vehemently, 'No! John Ripley and your mother were sincerely attached to each other, and devoted to you! There was no lie about that.'

'But he was *paid* to marry her, to take me in!'

'Yes, but he invested the money, so that you

might reap the benefit, and you have continued the business most successfully, have you not?'

'Yes, until the fire.'

'But you are insured. You will come about.'

Amber looked down at her clasped hands. Would she? Her future looked as grey and lifeless as the ashes of her warehouse. She did not think she had the energy to rebuild her business. Besides, Matthew Parwich's allegations would be all over Castonbury by the morrow, and who would want to buy from her then? A deep breath added a little steel to her crumbling form.

'Reverend Seagrove, do you have someone who can carry a message to the Rothermere Arms for me?'

Adam paced the floor of the small private parlour. It took less than four strides to cover its length but it helped to ease his frustration. A flagon of ale stood untouched upon the table and his damp coat hung over a chair before the hastily cobbled fire. Sir Rufus had taken Parwich off to the lock-up, the Long Room had been cleared and the inn had returned to normal, everyone going about their customary business.

Except Adam. How long had she been gone,

two hours, three? A glance at the clock told him that barely an hour had passed. His sigh, long and drawn out, echoed around the room. He needed activity, or he would go mad. He heard the thud and scrape of hasty steps, the door opened and a waiter stepped in.

'This has arrived for you, sir.' He proffered a tray, upon which lay a small note.

Adam reached out quickly, then pulled back his hand. Swallowing, he cautiously picked up the folded paper and broke the seal. His fingers trembled slightly as he opened the paper. It contained only four words.

"It is all true."

Chapter Thirteen

Adam rode back to the lodge, his face set, his mind a blank. He did not notice the steady rain that soaked through his clothes and ran down into his boots. He stabled Bosun and rubbed him down, glad that his years at sea had provided him with the discipline to keep working even when his world was falling apart. How much better would it have been if he had perished at Trafalgar, like Admiral Nelson?

Inside the lodge, letters from his factory managers and his man of business lay on the table—someone from the great house had collected his post for him—but he had no appetite for it now. All his achievements, his struggle to expand, to build new mills, to give hundreds, perhaps thousands, of people employment, a means of living, it all counted for nought if Amber was lost to him.

Nothing mattered any more. He glanced down at the growing puddle of water at his feet. The rain had drenched him to the skin. Mechanically he stripped off his clothes and dropped them into a pile. Perhaps tomorrow he would hang them out to dry.

Perhaps not.

He rubbed himself down with a cloth and climbed, naked, between the sheets of his cold bed. This would pass, of course. He had faced disaster before. He would go back to Rossendale, throw himself into his work. There was certainly plenty to do, he had been away so long, but for now he wanted just to mourn. He had not realised how much he loved Amber, until he had lost her.

There was a pounding on the door. His mother's voice was calling.

'Adam, Adam! Let me in. I want to talk to you.'

He ignored it. Time for talking tomorrow. He did not want anyone to see his grief, especially his mother. Another voice sounded. Deeper, more authoritative.

'Adam, open the door, damn you!' It was Giles. 'Let us in, man!'

Adam turned over and buried his head under

the pillow. At last the hammering ceased and silence fell again, save for the drip-drip of the rain off the eaves.

Amber lay between the crisp clean sheets in Reverend Seagrove's best guest bedroom. She had never fainted before, but after sending her message to Adam she had collapsed and the reverend had called upon Mrs Jeffries and Lily to help him carry her upstairs. The ladies had put her to bed, tucking her in with many soft words and placing a hot brick at her feet.

But despite the comfortable mattress and feather pillow she did not sleep. She kept reliving the events of the evening, hearing over and over again Reverend Seagrove's sad, gentle voice telling her there could be no doubt, she was the duke's daughter. Adam's sister. Yet while there had been gossip about Adam, and the tacit understanding amongst the villagers that he was the duke's son, her own upbringing had been swathed in a positive shroud of respectability.

Because she had been brought up by loving parents. Perhaps it was seeing Hannah struggle alone, hearing the whispers about her son, that had persuaded the duke to do something more for her own mother, to provide her with a husband and a means of support—nay, an investment that Amber had inherited and turned into the most successful business in Castonbury. Her thoughts turned to the ailing duke. She had rarely seen him and he had made no attempt to speak to her. He might be her natural father but he had proved a most unnatural parent.

By contrast, John Ripley had showed her nothing but affection. Her early life had been full of comfort and happiness. True, he had refused to acknowledge her ability to take over the business until ill health had forced him to do so, but there was nothing unusual in that. At least he had insisted her schooling should consist of more than needlework, music and the ability to read the Bible, all most parents considered sufficient for a daughter's education. The knowledge that she was Rothermere's daughter did not change her as a person, but it would, she was sure, destroy her business. Ripley and Hall would have to close. She had money, she would pay off Fred and Jacob—it was even possible that Fred might go into business for himself, although she was not sure he had the nerve for it.

Her world would change, but the grief of losing

her business was far overshadowed by the fact that she must lose Adam. She tossed restlessly in the bed. She had buried these, the most painful, thoughts, but now, in the darkest reaches of the night, she could avoid them no longer.

She was Adam's sister, but what she felt for him was no sisterly affection. Her body cried out for his touch, even while she mentally flayed herself for it. In an effort to relieve the pain she threw off the covers and jumped out of bed, pacing back and forth across the room. She wanted nothing more at that moment than to give up her life, to sink into unconsciousness and not have to face the daily, hourly torture of knowing that she must never see Adam again.

Amber threw open the window, wishing for the first time that she believed the old superstition that the night air was fatal to the human constitution. The balmy air mocked her. It was not even cold enough to chill, and the rain had ceased, so that she could not soak herself again in the hope that she might catch an inflammation of the lungs and perish. She had never understood what was meant by the sins of the father, until now. With a sob she dropped to her knees, clasping her hands together and praying with all her might for God to end her torment.

There was no immediate response, the heavens did not rend themselves apart with thunder and lightning as they had during the day, no thunder-ball came to smite her down, but gradually, as she trembled on her knees, recalling every prayer she had ever learned, the tears welled up and she gave way to heavy, body-racking sobs. They were followed by a flood of tears and she curled up on the floor and let them fall, crying her heart out for herself, for her parents and Mrs Stratton. For the duke. For Adam.

The morning sun shining in through the lodge windows did nothing to lift Adam's spirits. The pile of dirty, wet clothes on the floor bore witness to all that had happened. Once again his naval discipline came to his aid. He washed himself and dressed carefully in his clean linen, hesitating only when picking up the coat. He fingered the blue-grey kersey, remembering his visit to Amber's shop to choose it, the shy welcome in her eyes, at odds with her brisk businesslike tone. And her confusion when he had offered to work for her.

'Enough.' He barked the word aloud and threw the coat back onto the pile.

He went to the trunk and pulled out the first coat to hand, a blue superfine with a velvet collar. What did it matter to him now what he wore? He was fastening the buttons when he heard the carriage. Three steps carried him to the door and he opened it just as Giles was handing his mother from the coach.

'Your mother was determined to see you,' said Giles curtly. 'I thought she should not come alone. We did not know what state we would find you in.'

His mother put up her hand.

'Hush, my lord.' She cast an approving eye over her son. 'Good, you are dressed. A little pale, perhaps, but otherwise you will do.'

He had expected sympathy and soft words. Their lack surprised a small smile out of him, despite the leaden weight on his heart.

'I will do for what, ma'am?'

'Church, Adam. We are going to church.'

'I do not think—'

'You will come,' she said decisively.

He glared at Giles.

'Do you know what this is about?'

His mother answered for him.

'No, he does not, but it is time he learned the truth.' There was a heightened colour in her cheeks and a challenge in her eyes as she continued. 'I have something to tell you. Last night I might have been able to do so here, but this morning I need a little more...spiritual support.'

Amber awoke in a strange room. For a while she could not remember where she was, and as her memory returned so did the dull, aching misery. She had dragged herself back into the bed when the first grey fingers of dawn crept into the room, knowing it would distress Mrs Jeffries to find her on the floor. Such was her exhaustion that she had then fallen into a deep, blissfully peaceful sleep. She wished now she could return to that oblivion, but the housekeeper was bustling into the room carrying a tray.

'Good morning, madam. I hope you are feeling better today? I have brought you a cup of hot chocolate and a little bread and butter. Miss Lily thought you would prefer to break your fast here.'

She pottered about, ostensibly tidying the room but Amber suspected Miss Lily had ordered her to make sure she took some nourishment. When she had eaten everything, the housekeeper picked up the tray, beaming.

'Now, your clothes are all here for you, Mrs Hall, everything clean and dry. And when you are dressed, Reverend Seagrove would like you to join him in the parlour.'

It was kindly said, but Amber took it as a summons, nevertheless, and a short while later she made her way downstairs. The vicar was waiting for her. He put down his reading book as she entered, and got up to escort her to a chair.

'Did you sleep, my dear?'

'Yes, very well.' The lie came easily. 'I must thank you for your kindness to me.'

'Not at all, my dear Mrs Hall. You were clearly unfit to return to your house and the weather was so bad I did not hesitate to send a note to tell your maid where you were.'

'Yes, thank you.' She hesitated. 'Reverend Seagrove, have you been abroad this morning? Is... is my situation generally known?'

He would not meet her eyes.

'I am afraid so, my dear. Mr Parwich was... vociferous in the lock-up overnight. But you are highly regarded in Castonbury.' He smiled. 'Mrs Crutchley tells me that the villagers are inclined to be sympathetic, and she is generally well informed on these matters.'

She tried to drag up a smile for his gentle attempt at humour, but it was impossible. Reverend Seagrove was watching her anxiously.

'My dear, is there anything else you want to tell me?'

She shook her head.

'No, not yet,' she whispered.

Confession about her relationship with Adam might help at some point, but for now she could not share that hurt and anguish with anyone else. She sat for a long time, pulling her handkerchief between her fingers. So much had changed. Helping to prove that Adam was innocent and finding the real culprits had raised her spirits so much she had thought, for a while, that she would be able to build her business again, that perhaps there was even some way that she and Adam could— She tore her thoughts away. She must never think of Adam again. A sob was wrenched from her. She dropped her head into her hands and wept. After last night she had thought her tears were all spent, but it seemed she was wrong.

Such desperate anguish could not go on for ever and the reverend sat patiently until the storm of tears subsided. Amber raised her head, wiping her eyes.

'I beg your pardon,' she sniffed. 'I never meant—'

'It is better to express your sorrow, my child. You can have no peace while you hold such sadness within you.'

'I do not think I shall ever find peace again.'

'I sincerely hope you will.' He offered her his own handkerchief. 'If I may make a suggestion? Wipe your eyes, my dear. It is a fine morning. Let us go to the church to pray. You may find it helps.'

Amber doubted it, but she dutifully dried her face and accompanied the vicar the short distance to St Mary's. The morning was well advanced, and the sun shone brightly as they walked across the road to the church. Inside, light flooded through the windows, casting golden bars across their path. At any other time Amber would have been enchanted, but her spirit was too bruised, too raw, to feel anything. Obediently she knelt and closed her eyes. The vicar's murmured prayers washed over her, calm and soothing. She allowed her mind to drift.

The same questions returned to torment her. Why had no one told her? Why had her mother taken this secret with her to the grave? She went back over her childhood, trying to find some clue, something to tell her that her parents were not the loving, happy couple she had always thought them. There was nothing. Reverend Seagrove was right, they had always been loyal to each other, and devoted to her. How could she regret that?

If only they had told her the truth!

The lifting of the heavy door latch distracted her. Raising her head she looked around. Lord Giles entered, followed by Mrs Stratton and Adam. Her heart lurched. He was very pale, his jaw clamped tight, as if he, too, was doing his best not to break down.

'Oh.' Mrs Stratton stopped by the door. 'I beg your pardon, Reverend, I did not know—'

'God's house is open to everyone, Mrs Stratton,' he replied quietly.

Amber struggled to her feet and made for the door, keeping her head bent. Tears were welling up again, choking her. She must get away before they saw her grief.

'Please.' Mrs Stratton stepped in front of her, catching her arms. Her voice was low and urgent. 'Amber, please stay. You need to hear this.' Defeated, Amber's shoulders slumped. Hannah pulled her close and wrapped her arms about her as she addressed the vicar. 'Reverend Seagrove, thirty-two years ago I took a solemn oath upon the Holy Bible. I am going to break that vow.' Amber felt Hannah's body straighten, as if she was preparing herself for some ordeal. She continued, 'I intend to tell the full story, with or without your permission, but I should like to have it.'

Silence followed, then the vicar gave a long sigh.

'Yes,' he said at last. 'I think it is time, Mrs Stratton. I fear there have been too many secrets in Castonbury.'

Hannah put her hand up and gently stroked Amber's hair.

'Hush now, there is no need to cry.'

'I am a—a—' Amber could not say the word, she could only shudder. She raised her head. 'Why did they not tell me? Why was I not to know? If I had done so I would never— It is unforgivable!'

'I know, my dear. Just as it was unforgivable of me not to tell my son about his real father.'

Amber pushed herself away and hunted for her handkerchief.

'But he always knew. The rumours—'

'The rumours are untrue.' Hannah's soft words fell into the silence.

Amber looked up, frowning, and Hannah nodded.

'Yes, you heard aright. Adam is *not* the duke's son. He is no relation to you at all.' She walked across to the south wall of the church and pointed to the white marble memorial. 'This man was Adam's father.'

Hannah looked at the faces before her. The vicar, his wise old eyes benevolent and encouraging her to continue, Lord Giles, anxious, intrigued, and Amber and Adam, both pale, both with the same stricken look. How she wished she could have spared them this, but perhaps she could do something now to put things right.

Adam gently guided Amber to a bench and sat her down, then he walked over to the plaque.

'"Captain Richard Abraham Soames,"' he read. '"A man who excelled in virtue and integrity, Who was lost at sea off Cape Finisterre in January 1785, aged twenty-six years. His loss is universally regretted by his family and friends. This monument is erected by his afflicted father."' He paused before reading the final line. '"Not eschewing the world but passing through it unspotted."'

'Unspotted.' Hannah repeated the word. 'His

father would not countenance anything less than perfection.'

Then, clasping her hands before her, she quietly began her story.

'The Strattons are not known in Castonbury, my parents lived on the far side of Buxton. I was their only daughter, and they expected great things of me. I was to marry well and my marriage settlements would add to their already comfortable income. Then I met Richard.' Her face softened as she looked back into the past. 'He was from an old Castonbury family, the only son of Sir Abraham Soames. Richard was a captain in the king's navy and we met when he was home on leave. You will think me fanciful, perhaps, but just one look was enough for us to know we loved each other.'

'Not fanciful at all, ma'am,' murmured Adam, gazing at Amber with just such a glow as Hannah had seen in his father's eyes all those years ago. She smiled.

'We would have married then, but our parents were against it. Richard was a young man with little fortune. We were to wait until he had progressed in his career. He went back to his ship in the autumn of '84.' She sighed. 'It was some weeks later that I knew I was carrying his child.

I wrote to tell him, and he replied, promising that as soon as he returned we would be wed. But he never came home.' She paused, blinking rapidly to clear a sudden mistiness in her eyes. 'When it was confirmed that Richard's ship had gone down and he had been drowned, his father paid for this memorial to be put in the church. Richard was a local hero, his name could not be sullied by anything as sordid as a child born out of wedlock. Sir Abraham refused to acknowledge that the child I was carrying was his grandson. He and my parents arranged everything very neatly between them. I was sent away to have the baby, which was to be given up. Only then would I be allowed to return to the family home.

'I went to stay with an aunt near Bath. Everyone assumed that the child would be put in the local foundling hospital.' She looked up at Adam. 'When you were born you were so small, so *perfect*, I knew I could never part with you.' She reached out and he took her hand, squeezing her fingers.

'What happened then?' he asked. 'Did your parents relent?'

Hannah shook her head.

'No. They wrote to my aunt, telling her I was

ungrateful and she must cast me out. She had little enough to live on, so there was no possibility of my remaining there unless I could pay for my keep, and that of my new son. It was then that His Grace came to find me, only of course, he was not the duke then, but Marquis of Hatherton.

'He and Richard had been great friends, and Richard had asked him to look out for me until his return. The marquis visited both families, but there was nothing he could do, they would not be moved. So he came to see me, with a plan to take the child into his own care. I begged him not to take Adam away from me, and in the end he relented, but he insisted Adam was to go to sea when he was old enough. Richard had often told him that he would want any son of his to follow him into the navy. I agreed. What else could I do? I was penniless, I had no home, no way to provide for myself, let alone my child.

'The old duke was persuaded to take me in at Castonbury Park, where I could work and still have Adam with me. His Grace gave me the courtesy title of Mrs Stratton, and no one ever challenged it. Strangely, I felt closer to Richard here. He had lived in Castonbury as a boy, he had walked the village streets, prayed in the church. And I could see his memorial every Sunday.'

'That is why we brought the flowers each winter.' Adam ran his hand along the bare marble ledge. 'I thought we left them here because the vicar would not want such a petty offering cluttering up his altar.'

'No gift is too small for God, my son. If it is offered with love and reverence.'

Adam looked at the old man.

'You knew the secret?'

'I did. His Grace told me of it years ago.' He glanced from Amber to Adam. 'I did not realise that the two of you...if I had known—' He sighed and shook his head. 'Forgive me.'

Adam's hand came up in a defensive gesture. He was not ready to consider how he felt about all this. Enough that his worst fears had not been realised. He looked up.

'Continue, Mother, if you please.'

'My presence at Castonbury Park caused talk, of course, but I had sworn a solemn vow that no one should know the identity of Adam's father. The idea that he was the then-marquis's son was encouraged by Sir Abraham, but living at the Park shielded us from any real harm.' She smiled at

Adam. 'You had advantages I could never have given you alone, and you did not seem affected by the rumours.'

He shrugged.

'By the time I understood them I was about to go to the naval college. It made me more determined to be my own man, to prove myself.'

'When you were little you asked me about your father and I never told you,' said Hannah. 'I fobbed you off then, and later, ten years ago, when you challenged me...' Hannah raised her handkerchief to dab away a surreptitious tear. 'I resolved then, if you ever came back, I would break my vow and tell you.'

'And when you mentioned it to me I would not let you.'

She shook her head at him.

'I was glad it did not seem important to you, but you have a right to know, and with all your grandparents now dead, all those who might object have gone, except one.' Her head came up a little. 'I spoke to His Grace's valet.' Hannah glanced at the vicar. 'You know how jealous Smithins can be of his master's health, but he agreed to let me know when it would be a suitable time to see him. I visited His Grace yesterday and told him what I was about to do. He gave me his blessing. He also gave me this.' She reached into her reticule. 'It is Richard's last letter to him. He acknowledges here that he is your father, Adam.'

Adam took the folded paper and opened it carefully. It was stiff and yellow with age, but the writing on the page was strong and bold, very much like his own.

'I have often wondered,' said Hannah slowly, 'if I had told you who your father was, perhaps you would not have been so eager to leave the navy....'

Adam considered for a moment.

'No, Mother. I am glad I acquitted myself well for my country, but as I told you, after Trafalgar I had had enough of war. I wanted to build something for the future, which I have done. And now I want a family of my own.' He looked across at Amber, sitting alone, pale and silent.

Lord Giles cleared his throat. 'Mrs Stratton, Reverend, there are a couple of points I wanted to discuss with you both, about, erm, the Sunday services...shall we go to the vestry?'

It was a clumsy excuse to leave them alone but Amber barely noticed. Adam came across to sit beside her.

'So many shocks and surprises I can scarce take

it in.' He reached out and took her hand. His grasp was warm and comforting. 'You look quite worn out.'

'It is difficult to make sense of it all,' she said at last. 'To find that all I had believed in was false— so much was kept hidden. From both of us.'

'I know, but I believe it was done with the best of intentions. Out of love rather than malice.'

'Perhaps that was why my father was so anxious for me to marry, to see me established. Even though he was sadly mistaken in the man...' A shudder ran through her.

'Was it so very bad?' he asked gently.

She drew a breath.

'My father wanted to expand the business. Bernard was a gentleman and he had money that he was willing to invest. He became a partner, and then my husband. To my father it seemed a natural progression.'

'And to you? What did it seem to you?'

She sighed.

'I had grown up in the business and wanted to continue in it. If my mother had survived perhaps things would have been different, but I was eighteen, with no one to advise me, and marriage to Bernard seemed to be the solution. As my father's partner he had always been very obliging. Only later did I realise that his polished manners and honeyed words concealed a vicious nature.

'He promised that once we were married I would take a more active part in the business. In fact, it was quite the opposite. He did not keep a single one of the promises he made me before we were wed. I was allowed no say in the running of the business. Bernard had already persuaded my father to hand over almost total control. When I saw him taking money out, money that we could ill afford, I tried to argue, but that did not help. That was when he became violent.' The words were pouring out, so much that she had told no one before. 'Oh, he made sure the bruises never showed. Outwardly he was a devoted husband. And I dared not go to my father. He had taken refuge in drink, Bernard had encouraged him in that and he had so worn him down that he was a mere shadow of the man he had been. My un-happiness distressed him, but he was powerless to help, so I chose not to inflict more pain.'

'And this...this beast was your husband!'

She nodded. 'I think he derived pleasure from inflicting pain. Punishing me seemed to...arouse him, he would take his pleasure then, while all the time making sure I understood that he infinitely preferred the attentions of his mistress, a slattern that he kept in luxury in Hatherton.'

'By heaven, he might have spared you that!'

'It was not his way to spare me anything,' she replied in a low voice. 'When Bernard died I went to Hatherton and paid her off—'

'You did *what*?'

Amber shrugged. 'I owed her something. She gave Bernard the infection that killed him. I nursed him, of course, but I cannot tell you the relief it was to know that he could not inflict any more pain upon me or my father.' She looked down at her hand. The knuckles were gleaming white where she was gripping on to Adam so tightly. 'Oh, I am hurting you.'

She began to release him but he put his other hand over her fingers, holding her firm.

'No, it is all right. Go on.'

She took a breath. She had told him the worst. This next part would be easier.

'The business was in a parlous state. There were huge debts. Father was too weak to be much more than a figurehead so I took over. I had no one to help me, but I worked hard, persuaded the sup-pliers that there was more to be gained by supporting me than calling in their debts. Gradually I paid them off, built up my order book and even began to make a little money. The name of Ripley and Hall became respected again in Castonbury.'

'No wonder it means so much to you.'

'It does, or rather it did. Now, everything has changed.'

'Not everything. I love you, Amber Hall, and I still want to marry you, if you will have me.'

Her eyes, still raw from weeping, filled with tears again.

'I do not deserve that you should want me, after all that has happened.'

He turned towards her, putting a hand under her chin and gently forcing her to look up at him.

'You are still the beautiful, fearless woman I fell in love with. There is no reason why we should not marry. All you have to do is say yes.'

'Then, yes,' she said, smiling through her tears.

Adam's heart soared at her words. He wanted to drag her into his arms but instead he lowered his head and kissed her, very gently.

'I want you to be sure,' he said. 'I have letters at the lodge from Rossendale, and I suspect that amongst them is the contract I had my man draw up, assigning the business of Ripley and Hall back to you, upon our marriage. I had planned to give it to you before our wedding—'

She put her fingers to his lips.

'I have discovered that my business means nothing to me if I cannot have you, Adam,' she said softly. 'I shall put my trust in you, since you already hold my heart.'

He kissed her again and pulled her into his arms.

'I will make you a rich woman in your own right. My wedding gift to you will be shares in my own mills.'

She gave a watery chuckle.

'Is that wise, sir? When you know I have my own opinions on so many subjects.'

'Then we will argue the matter out, as even business partners will do, sometimes.' He held her away, looking deep into her eyes. 'I want to marry you for what you are, Amber, a woman with a mind of your own. We will have our differences and we shall air them,' he said earnestly. 'But neither one of us shall have dominance over the other.' His eyes narrowed and he continued in quite a different tone. 'Save when you look up at me as you are doing now, with *just* such a look in your eyes. Then I know myself beaten. You may ask anything you want of me!'

'Then make an honest woman of me, Adam Stratton. All these business matters can wait. First and foremost I want to be your wife....' Her voice trailed off and a look of wonder came over her face. 'I thought I would never want such a thing again, but knowing you, loving you, I find it is the dearest wish of my heart to call you husband.'

Adam lifted her hands and kissed first one, then the other.

'You do not know how happy that makes me,' he told her, his voice not quite steady.

'I hope it will always be so,' she murmured, putting her arms about him.

Adam sighed. Just holding her was like finding a safe harbour from the stormy seas.

A movement caught his eye. He looked up to see his mother, Giles and the vicar emerging from the vestry. Hannah read the happiness in his eyes and clasped her hands to her chest.

'Well?'

Adam stood up, gently pulling Amber to her feet beside him.

'I am to be married, Mother. She has agreed.'

'Then I am very happy for you, my son.'

'A moment.' Lord Giles stepped up. 'Forgive me, Adam, but I must say this.' He turned to Amber. 'I know Adam's feelings on this, but you, madam—Amber—please do not feel under any obligation to marry to protect yourself. The truth about your birth has spread quickly in the village, but I have made it known that my father acknowledges you. You will have the protection of the Montagues, whatever you decide to do.'

'Th-thank you, Lord Giles.' Amber pushed herself away and reluctantly Adam released her. She retained hold of his hand and he waited anxiously for her to continue. 'Your acknowledgement is very welcome, but it does not affect my desire to marry Adam.' She looked up into his face and Adam's heart leapt again at what he read there. 'A lot has happened, we both have a great deal to come to terms with, but I hope we can help each other. I would marry him this minute,' she murmured. 'If it were possible.'

With an exclamation Giles clapped his hand to his pocket.

'By Jove, it may well be possible! I had almost forgotten this.' He pulled out a paper and handed it to Adam. 'Your special licence arrived this morning. The combination of a first-class lawyer and your enormous wealth must have had an effect on the good bishop to turn it round so quickly.'

'Indeed.' Adam looked down at the paper in his hand.

Giles grinned. 'You have the licence, the parson and the church. You do not need to wait any longer. I wish to heaven Lily and I could be wed as easily.'

Adam looked across at the vicar.

'Well, Reverend, how soon can you marry us?'

The old man blinked at him and said, as if surprised at himself, 'Today—now, if you wish it.'

'So there you are.' Giles slapped him on the back. 'The lady is willing—go to it, man.'

'Then it is decided,' Adam declared. 'We would like to be married here, now. Mother, Lord Giles, are you willing to be our witnesses?'

'Of course,' declared Hannah.

'I am only surprised it has taken the two of you so long to decide,' growled Giles.

Adam was smiling so much it was almost painful. He looked at Amber, who nodded.

'Very well,' he said. 'Reverend Seagrove, marry us, if you please!'

'It will be my pleasure. Let us approach the altar.'

As they followed the vicar Amber took off her

glove and slid Bernard's wedding ring from her finger. Adam groaned.

'I had intended to go to Buxton to buy a ring… We are not quite so prepared as I thought.'

'It need not be a problem.' Hannah pulled the plain gold band from her finger. 'Use this. His Grace bought it for me when I moved to Castonbury Park. It has never been blessed with a marriage ceremony.'

'Oh, no,' cried Amber, 'I could not take your ring!'

'It would please me very much if you would.' Hannah held up her right hand. The emerald on her little finger flashed green fire as it caught the light. 'Richard gave this to me before he went away that last time. It was his pledge that we would marry upon his return. I have no need of anything else.'

Adam looked at Amber.

'Well? It must be your decision. We can delay the marriage a day or two if you would rather wait until I can buy you a ring of your own…'

He held his breath. She stood before him, all he wanted in life. Without Amber all his success, all his achievements, would mean nothing. When it came, her smile rivalled the sun in lighting up the little church.

'I would be honoured to wear your mother's ring.'

It seemed to Amber the most magical of weddings. The little church glowed with sunlight, and Hannah's ring slipped so snugly onto her finger it might have been made for it. They took their vows with only Hannah and Lord Giles as their witnesses, but it was enough.

'May I be the first to congratulate you, Mrs Stratton?' The vicar beamed at her and Amber smiled back. Hannah kissed her and wished her well. Amber clung to her for a moment.

'I will do my utmost to make him happy,' she whispered.

Hannah blinked, trying to hold back her tears.

'Bless you, child, I know you will. I hope you will be very happy running his house in Rossendale.'

'But you will be there too.'

Hannah shook her head.

'A house cannot have two mistresses.'

'Mine will,' declared Adam firmly. 'At least for a while, until I have built the new house for my wife and children. I always intended the present building to be yours, Mother, you know that.'

Hannah looked at them, shaking her head.

'But—'

'There will be no arguments,' said Amber firmly. 'When we return for Lord Giles's wedding we will take you back with us, to make your home in Rossendale.'

'If you are sure.'

'Very sure, *Mama*!' said Amber, her eyes twinkling. She sobered. 'Shall we take Billy with us? After rescuing him from Mr Parwich I cannot bear to think of him being left to fend for himself.'

Hannah laughed.

'You need not worry about that young man! He expressed a liking for horses so I sent him over to the stables where Tom Anderson has taken him under his wing. When I called in there this morning they were getting along famously!'

Amber was relieved, but concern for one other person was playing on her mind, and she looked around for Lord Giles.

He was congratulating Adam, but when she caught his eye he turned to her and she smiled shyly at him.

'I need to speak to you, my lord, about Lady

Hatherton.' Immediately his face hardened. Undeterred, Amber carried on. 'Whatever else you may think of her, she had the courage to come forward and speak up for Adam yesterday. I hope you will take that into account, when you consider her situation.'

'It is certainly a point in her favour,' Giles said slowly. He nodded. 'You may be sure I will remember it, whether she proves to be Jamie's wife or not.' He shook his head and reached for her hand. 'But this is not the time for such talk. I wish to congratulate you, sister.'

'Oh, no.' She blushed furiously. 'No, you do not have to call me that.'

'I do not have to, but I will!' His rather hard grey eyes softened slightly when he smiled. 'We never spoke of it, but until today I thought of Adam as my half-brother. By marrying you he continues to be just that.'

'But what will the rest of the Montagues think of it? What will they think of *me*?'

He grinned.

'Very little, I suspect, they are all so tied up in their own concerns. You need not worry, I have already given you my assurance that Father and I will support you. Not financially, perhaps, you have no need of that now you are Mrs Adam Stratton, but our acknowledgement will ensure you are not ostracized by anyone here. I will explain everything to the rest of them, and by the time you return for my wedding it will be as if you have always been part of the family.'

'Oh, no, it won't!' retorted Adam. 'We will not be coming to your wedding if it means we have to do the pretty with all your relatives up at the great house. I intend to join in the celebrations with my mother, below stairs.'

'Very well, if that is what you wish,' said Giles, his eyes glinting. 'But since you are as rich as Croesus I shall expect a magnificent wedding gift from you.'

Chapter Fourteen

'What did Lord Giles mean,' asked Amber, 'about you being so very rich?'

They were walking along the high street, having left Giles to escort Hannah back to Castonbury Park.

'I told you I had my own business,' Adam replied.

'Yes, but I thought you had—' she sought for the right words '—a comfortable independence. Not that you were—what was the phrase he used? As rich as Croesus.'

'Does it make a difference?'

'Yes. Especially now, when I have so little to bring you. The warehouse was totally destroyed. Everything that was rescued from the shop is now in the stables, but it is pitifully little, compared to what we need to satisfy all our orders. Fred has been going through it all, checking what we can use.'

'You trust him, after what he did?'

'I do,' said Amber firmly. 'He is so eager to make amends.' She glanced up at him. 'He betrayed you, too, Adam, but I hope you can forgive him. He—' She bit her lip. 'I think he is—was—a little bit in love with me, and it made him jealous.'

He put his hand over hers, where it nestled in the crook of his arm. 'That at least I can understand. If he has learned his lesson, then yes, I will not hold it against him. His knowledge of the business will be very useful.'

She shook her head.

'It would have been, but now it is all too late.'

'Why?' said Adam. 'You will have the insurance money. We can rebuild. I will help you—'

'No, Adam, it will not work. Now everyone knows what I am they will not want to buy their cloth here, whatever Lord Giles might say.'

'You cannot be sure of that.'

'Yes, I can. This is a small place. Word will have spread by now that I am—that I am not John Ripley's child. They will shun me. I will pay off old Jacob and Fred and have done with Castonbury.' She tucked her hand in his arm. 'But do not let that make us sad. It means I can go with you into Lancashire and throw myself into life there.'

'I admit there is plenty to be done,' said Adam. 'I want to build a new schoolhouse for my apprentices, and as my mills grow bigger so the need for good housing increases. And of course there is our own house to build. I will need your help to design it.' He stopped and pulled her into his arms. 'The world is changing so fast, Amber. It is a new and exciting place for us.'

'And I cannot wait to be a part of your world, Adam.'

She turned her face up for his kiss, and afterwards they walked on arm in arm. Presently she said, 'I have been going over it in my mind, wondering how different things would have been if His Grace had acknowledged me when I was a child. I might not have been allowed to take on the business. I might have been married off to some rich gentleman. I would not have liked that half so well.'

'And I would not have liked it at all,' he declared. 'I think you were destined to be my wife, from that very first time I rescued you, when you were a child, and the Montague children were teasing you.'

'And now I find I am related to them.' She sighed. 'You do not mind,' she said shyly, 'that I was born out of wedlock?'

His smile was a caress.

'You have never objected to my birth.'

'That was different.'

'Because you thought me the son of a duke?' he teased her. 'Now you know me to be the son of a humble sea captain.'

'You know that makes no odds to me,' she said fiercely. 'You are still the man you always were. The man I love.'

He pulled her into his arms again.

'Then apply that logic to yourself, my darling.'

He kissed her, and Amber responded. The aching sadness in her heart eased. She would make a new life with him.

The burnt-out ruin that had been her warehouse was in sight, open to the sky, the walls blackened and windowless. Only the shop and the living quarters above it were undamaged.

'Good God,' exclaimed Adam, who was seeing it for the first time since the night of the fire. 'You are living here?'

'Yes, my rooms are undamaged. There was a lot of smoke and ash, but once we had cleared it away most of my possessions were found to be safe.' She took his hand. 'Come in and see.'

She pushed at the hastily repaired door and led him through the empty shop. They had not gone far before they heard footsteps clattering on the stairs, and Maizie appeared.

'Oh, Mrs Hall!' She dropped a quick curtsey and looked closely at her mistress. 'Are you well, now, ma'am? I had the message yesterday, sayin' as how you was staying at the vicarage...'

'Yes, I am very well, thank you, Maizie.' She added, after a moment's hesitation, 'And it is Mrs Stratton now.'

'Oh, Lord, bless us an' save us!' declared Maizie, her eyes as round as saucers. 'But, I heard last night—that villain Parwich said...'

'Whatever Mr Parwich said, Maizie, Mr Seagrove knows the true story,' Adam told her. 'He married us not two hours ago.'

The maid's face cleared. 'Oh, well, that's all right, then.' She remembered herself and dropped a deeper curtsey. 'May I be permitted to congratulate you, madam, and you, sir?'

'You may,' laughed Amber. 'I have brought Mr Stratton here to show him what has survived.'

'Aye, well, 'tis all clean an' tidy upstairs now,

madam. I was frettin' that much when I thought of you stayin' at the vicarage that I couldn't settle, so I swept it all out o' doors, and save for the smell of the smoke, which I can't get rid of no matter how I try, your rooms upstairs is as good as new. An' I was just off to the butchers to see what we might have for our dinner. But I suppose you won't be stopping here now.'

Amber twinkled up at Adam.

'Well, sir, will you take dinner here with me tonight?'

'Anxious as I am to carry you back to Lancashire, we cannot leave for a day or two,' he replied solemnly. 'By all means let us dine here. We will ask Fred and old Jacob to join us too. And you, Maizie. It shall be our wedding breakfast!'

Maizie's eyes grew even more round at this, and she went off, determined to provide a fitting feast for the occasion while Amber, laughing, led the way upstairs to inspect her living quarters.

'She is right,' she said, wrinkling her nose. 'The smell of burning pervades the air.'

'But it is very faint,' said Adam. He opened the bedroom door. 'And Maizie has excelled herself in here! Flowers in the fireplace, the bowl of herbs by the window—' He glanced at Amber. 'She might almost have guessed we were coming.'

Amber blushed.

'No, I assure you. How could she, when we did not know ourselves? And I had not given any thought to where we would sleep tonight.'

Adam pulled her into the room and shut the door.

'Nor had I, but as I remember, this is much more comfortable than my narrow bed at the lodge.' She heard the click of the lock. 'Shall we see just how good my memory is?'

She turned her face up for his kiss, her lips parting instinctively as he lowered his head. The first touch was gentle as thistledown and she found herself reaching up towards him, eager for more. He nibbled at her lower lip and she trembled, an ache of desire curling low in her belly. Her body liquefied at his touch, she leaned into him, driving her hands through his hair, revelling in its silky softness. She deepened the kiss, eager to move on, but he pulled away. His breathing was ragged.

'Gently, Mrs Stratton,' he murmured. 'We do not need to hurry.' He ran his thumb over her lower lip. 'I thought we would never be together again.'

'I, too, thought that, but now we *are* together, and will be, for ever.' She smiled up at him, her eyes misty with tears. 'My husband.'

'My wife.' His eyes burned into her. 'I want to savour every moment with you.'

Between lingering kisses, they undressed each other. Amber wanted to pounce, to rip and tear Adam's clothes away, to uncover the smooth hard body that lay beneath and press her own against it, but he held her away, determined to go slowly. She shivered as he unhurriedly opened her gown, pressing warm, butterfly kisses on the back of her neck as he pushed the soft muslin away. It was the sweetest torture to hold back while she returned the favour, easing his coat and waistcoat from the broad shoulders, taking her time to pull his neck cloth free before removing his shirt and trailing kisses across his chest, running her fingers through the dark cloud of hair that covered his skin. She forced herself to keep still while he drew the laces from her stays, his fingers brushing but not dwelling on the soft swell of her breasts. They tightened, pushing towards him of their own accord as the ache inside her grew. Only when he had freed her from the restraint of cotton and whalebone did he cup her breasts in his hands, circling his thumbs gently over her nipples. They grew hard and pert. He replaced one hand with his mouth, his tongue circling the hard nub, teasing and sucking so that she gasped, throwing back her head and almost swooning as a wave of exquisite pleasure washed over her.

Amber closed her eyes and sank her teeth into her bottom lip. Her nerves were screaming. She wanted to beg him to be done with this sweet agony. Adam gathered her in his arms and carried her to the bed, where between kisses they discarded the last of their clothes. Amber felt the tension in him, but he continued with the languorous caresses. She admired his restraint; her own body quivered under his slow, deliberate onslaught, his hands moving lightly over her skin. Sparks of desire coursed through her blood until she was burning up.

Suddenly it was important he should feel it, too, that she should give him the same edge-of-control pleasure that was consuming her. With a soft moan she moved away. She pushed him down on the bed, suspending her own desires as she caressed him, sweeping her hands reverently over him, covering his hard, aroused body with hot kisses, licking, sucking, teasing, until he was groaning beneath her. She straddled him, bending to capture his mouth with her own. As her breasts brushed across his chest he arched beneath her. Desire pounded between them. He pulled her close and rolled her beneath him, preparing for the final union. She felt herself softening, opening to him like a flower. She put her arms around him and clung on tightly as he entered her. Still he held back, taking the time to kiss her again, a warm, intimate embrace that made her sigh with satisfaction. His lips found her ear. She heard his soft murmur.

'With my body, I thee worship.'

It was too much. She thought she would explode with happiness. The ache deep within would no longer wait. It must be satisfied. Amber tightened her hold and tilted her hips, pushing against him, every nerve-end singing. His iron control shattered. Amber clung to him, their bodies moving in perfect time. She heard her own voice crying out, but it came from such a distance, as if she had left her body somewhere far below her. They were flying, soaring, higher, ever more out of control. She embraced him, clinging tight as he plunged into her again, one final time, and her body tightened. Outside she was rigid as iron, while inside wave after wave of intense pleasure pounded her. Rainbow colours filled her head. Adam held her close, his body momentarily as unyielding as her own. Then as he cried out, her rigidity shattered and they collapsed, exhausted and trembling onto the bed.

The thud of a door somewhere below roused them. Adam was curled around Amber. He pulled her closer and nibbled her ear.

'That is your maid returned. I suppose we should get dressed.'

Amber sighed. She wanted to remain here, safe in Adam's arms, untroubled by the world, but it would not do.

'We should indeed.' She sighed. 'Heaven knows what she will think when she sees us!'

Whatever Maizie's thoughts when they came downstairs she kept them to herself. She was bustling around the kitchen and barely looked up as Amber led Adam past the open door and back to the shop.

'You know, it would not take a great deal to get this shipshape,' mused Adam. 'New doors, glass in the windows—'

Amber raised her hand.

'No, Adam, let it be. I would rather close now due to the fire than have Ripley and Hall die from lack of business.'

She thought he would argue with her and was relieved when he merely suggested they should look outside. The yard had been cleared, all the debris was piled against the warehouse walls. They found Fred there, talking to Mr Elliot. The surveyor lifted his hat when he saw them.

'I believe I am to congratulate you, Mr and Mrs Stratton.' His tone was as calm and measured as ever. He might as easily have been talking of a disaster as a marriage.

'Thank you,' she said coolly. 'Is there anything else you need from me?'

'I think not, madam. Mr Aston has provided me with a list of what you have lost and we have the real culprit locked up and awaiting trial.' His cold eyes flickered over Adam. 'I shall return to Buxton today to make my report. I see no reason to delay paying out what you are due, Mrs, er, Stratton.'

With another stiff bow he turned and walked away.

'Well, that is some good news,' said Amber.

'But I thought he might offer you an apology for all the trouble this has caused you, Adam.'

'Not he.' Adam grinned. 'Tight as a barnacle, that one!'

Fred cleared his throat.

'Maizie told me you were married,' he said, shifting uncomfortably from foot to foot. 'She didn't know the whole until she went to see the butcher. Mrs Crutchley said Reverend Seagrove had been to see her.'

'Ah.' Adam sent a laughing glance towards his wife. 'Then everyone in Castonbury will know our history by now.'

Fred flushed to the tips of his ears.

'Yes, well. Please accept my congratulations.'

Amber smiled at him. 'Thank you, Fred.'

He turned his pale, troubled eyes towards Adam.

'Mr Stratton, I…that is—' He broke off, then said in a rush, 'I did you a grave disservice, sir. I—'

'That will do,' said Adam. 'No lasting harm has been done. Let us hope we fare better in the future.'

'I cannot tell you how sorry I am—'

'Then do not. Tell me instead what has been salvaged from the wreckage of the fire.'

The young man looked grave.

'Not a great deal, I'm afraid. We can fulfil only one or two of the outstanding commissions, and I have ordered more supplies for the rest.'

'We may not need them,' said Amber sadly. 'I doubt all our customers will wait. Have you had any cancellations?'

'One or two, but—'

'I expect there will be more over the next few days.' She drew herself up. 'That is why I have de-cided—' She broke off as a familiar voice called to her from the gateway. It was Mrs Crutchley.

'So there you are, Mrs Hall—Mrs Stratton, I *should* say!' The butcher's wife bustled up, beam-ing. 'I was never more pleased than when the vicar dropped by to tell me the news, in confidence, of course. We couldn't be happier for you! But that ain't why I'm here. After Maizie came into the shop earlier, Mr Crutchley said I should come and tell you that you are not to worry about the drapes we ordered to match the bed-hangings.'

Amber nodded.

'Thank you, I quite understand that you will want to order them elsewhere—'

'Elsewhere? Whatever are you thinking of, dear ma'am? And where else *could* we go, now that Mr

Parwich has proved himself to be such a villain? I believe you will find yourself with even more business now there is no other cloth merchant this side of Buxton. No, Mrs Stratton, my dear Crutchley wanted to make sure you understood that we will wait until you can get the material in for us.'

'Th-thank you, Mrs Crutchley,' Amber stammered in surprise.

'And I saw Mr Leitman on my way here. He has had to buy a couple of lengths of blue superfine from Buxton but says to tell you that he will be calling on you shortly, to let you know his requirements for the winter.'

'I...I see. Thank you.'

She watched in silence as Mrs Crutchley hurried away. Beside her, Adam chuckled.

'It seems there is still a place here for Ripley and Hall.'

'A couple of orders. We will, of course, honour them, but—'

She broke off again as a horse trotted into the yard, the messenger dismounting only long enough to hand her a note.

'This is from Castonbury Park,' she said, breaking the seal. 'Heavens, it is another order! Two dozen Holland sheets, ditto pillowcases, pat-

terned linen union for tablecloths and napkins…
Damask…huckaback towels—all to be delivered
within the month.' She looked up, a sudden frown
in her eyes. 'This must be your mother's work.'

'And what of it? It is business.'

'But—'

'Can you not fulfil it?'

'Of course I can, but—' She shook her head at
him. 'Do you not see, Adam? This is mere sympathy, a few orders from friends—'

'No, it's not,' Fred broke in. 'That's what I was
trying to tell you, mistress. Mrs Finch called in
with another order, and she is not the only one.
I have had a stream of people here all morning,
some confirming their orders, others with new
commissions. Even the carrier came to say he
would be honoured—honoured!—to have your
business again. And some just called to wish us
well and to say that as soon as we are open for
business they will support us.' He stopped, his
face flushing at his own impertinence. 'That is,
support *you*, Mrs Stratton.'

'No, you were correct, Fred,' said Adam. 'Mrs
Stratton will be returning to Rossendale with me
next week and she will need you to run the business here.'

The flush died from Fred's face. He stared at them.

'Y-you mean you would let me—' He made a valiant attempt to swallow. 'After what I did...'

'I think you have learnt your lesson, and if Mrs Stratton trusts you, then I do too.' Adam held out his hand, then drew it back. 'But I forget myself. This is to remain Mrs Stratton's business. It is for her to seal the agreement.' Amber started and he smiled. 'My expertise is manufacturing. I am content to leave Ripley and Hall in your hands, my dearest love.' He touched her cheek. 'I know how important your independence is to you, and I want us to be equal partners in our marriage. What say you, madam?'

Amber's heart swelled. She straightened her back and looked him boldly in the eye.

'I would settle for nothing less, Mr Stratton.'

* * * * *

Mills & Boon® Online

Discover more romance at
www.millsandboon.co.uk

- 🌹 **FREE** online reads
- 🌹 **Books** up to one month before shops
- 🌹 **Browse our books** before you buy

...and much more!

For exclusive competitions and instant updates:

 Like us on **facebook.com/millsandboon**

 Follow us on **twitter.com/millsandboon**

 Join us on **community.millsandboon.co.uk**

Visit us Online   Sign up for our FREE eNewsletter at
www.millsandboon.co.uk

WEB/M&B/RTL5/LP